HEREDITARY CURSE

THE GATEKEEPER'S CURSE SERIES: BOOK TWO

EMMA L. ADAMS

To be notified when Emma L. Adams's next novel is released, sign up to her author newsletter.

1

The ghost wailed, his hands buried in my neck. It was seriously beginning to creep me out.

"Look, I'm sorry you're dead," I told the man. "If you want to know what happens next, you'll have to ask a necromancer. I'm not one."

Thankfully. I was Ilsa Lynn, Gatekeeper-in-training, and an unfortunate side effect of my new role was the ability to see and speak to the dead. Now the local ghosts had picked up on the fact that I could see and hear them, I couldn't go more than a minute without one of them tagging along after me. They complained, howled, refused to believe they were dead, and this guy was in desperate denial that I wasn't the one who'd shuffled off this mortal coil.

"Can you stop doing that?" I didn't exactly feel pain when the ghost pawed at my insides, just an uncomfortable sort of cold like stepping into the shower fully-clothed.

"Are you *sure* you're not dead?" said the ghost. "I can't be. I was alive."

"That's usually the way," I responded. "Is there any particular reason you stuck around?"

1

There didn't have to be a reason for a ghost to get trapped here after death. Since the faeries attacked the mortal realm, the lines between human and spirit realms had been screwed up, too, and ghost appearances were more frequent than they used to be. Often they didn't remember their own names, and they had the attention span of a hyped-up toddler hand in hand with a desperate need for attention. Which was kind of unfortunate, considering most people couldn't even see them.

I was starting to think that maintaining a quiet existence in a city full of ghosts like Edinburgh was a futile prospect.

"I need to find Becka and tell her I'm going to be home late tonight."

"Pretty sure she already knows," I said. "You've been here a day." I'd seen the ghost floating around the same spot on the road several times over the last twenty-four hours, long since they'd removed his body after he'd been hit by a car. Ghosts usually haunted either the place where they'd died, or somewhere important to them.

"Oh," he said faintly. "I'm really dead, aren't I?"

"Unfortunately, yes," I said.

"Then you're... you don't look like a necromancer. Those clothes are wrong."

"That's because I'm not a necromancer." Why did everyone have an issue with my fashion sense? I wore ragged jeans and my favourite hoody, aka my 'leave me alone' outfit. Most necromancers wore black cloaks, probably for the same reason, but I didn't need to take tips from the dead, thanks. Unlike my sister, I didn't pay particular attention to my appearance, but in fairness, I wasn't generally under scrutiny by the impossibly beautiful Sidhe. I had brown eyes which hadn't turned green with the faerie magic of our family, and kept my curly dark hair loose to hide the invisible mark on my forehead designating my status as Gatekeeper.

As I wore a witch charm twenty-four seven, it was only visible within the spirit world, but I liked to keep my close brushes with death to a minimum.

Being Gatekeeper hadn't exactly been a smooth ride so far. Thanks to my distant aunt's quest to pursue immortality by screwing up the veil between life and death, I'd been claimed by a hereditary talisman and now had a type of necromancy unlike any other: the ability to banish faerie ghosts and control the gates of Death. But there was no point in using my ability on this spirit.

As the truth dawned on him, he became more transparent, and floated away, hopefully to pass Beyond and stop drifting around being miserable. Not that I was one to talk. Since I'd moved back here, I didn't quite know what to do with myself. I'd left my old job a few weeks ago after a rogue poltergeist had stripped naked on the counter and knocked a bunch of beer glasses over. My boss hadn't appreciated my attempts to explain how I'd banished it using necromancy, so I'd resigned to keep my dignity intact. Since none of my other interviews had panned out and I had yet to submit my PhD application, I'd taken to wandering around the streets, switching my spirit sight on and off to fine-tune my ability to distinguish dead people from living ones. Because that was a sane, normal thing to do.

Maybe I shouldn't have come back, but after five years, Edinburgh felt more like home than the Lynn house did. Since I literally had a sign on my head telling all the dead to come and hound me, my best bet was likely to find a job running ghost tours, but the sort of monsters who came after me were probably too hard-core for most tourist crowds.

A whisper of air stroked the back of my neck. *Not again.*

Behind me, a man without a soul shambled along with the uncoordinated steps of the recently dead. If seeing dead people in the streets wasn't creepy enough on its own, my spirit sight showed me that the body was an empty vessel, propelled by necromantic energy with no will of its own.

I reached into my pocket for the salt shaker I kept on me all the time. Salt dissolved undead and deterred ghosts, without exception. The most undead could do was flail around and claw at you, but if someone had raised it from the grave, trouble would undoubtedly follow.

I followed close behind the undead, which walked so clumsily that it made me look positively coordinated in comparison. I grabbed a handful of salt, rolled it into a ball, and lobbed it at the back of its head.

The undead went down, hard. I ran after it to check there weren't any others, and a second undead collided with me from the side.

Should have seen that one coming. The undead's hand grasped my arm, coldness radiating from its body. *Oh hell.*

A current of icy magic blasted me off my feet. I hit the ground, landing hard on my shoulder. Grimacing, I scrambled to my feet, tossing salt at the zombie. It kept going even when its arm decayed and fell off, and its skeletal face sank in on itself as the magic sustaining it withered away. This time when my spirit sight switched on, it showed not a blank space, but a shadowy mass shaped vaguely like a person. A faint grey glow kicked up around its edges. Not good. The wraith directing the zombie still had magic.

The undead fell as its decaying legs gave way, but the wraith continued, bodiless, hovering above the road.

"Hey there." I raised a hand, my heart thumping, and willed the book's magic to rise to my fingertips. A thrill coursed through me when a familiar white glow enveloped my hand, binding words replaying in my head. For a stronger wraith, I'd need to trap it in a spell circle first, but just a whisper of my power sent the wraith flailing backwards. Reciting the banishing words, I gathered the magic in the palm of my hand and hurled it at the wraith, which exploded into shadowy pieces.

The grey haze faded, revealing streets slick with fallen rain, shop windows shuttered and closed. I'd unintentionally followed the wraith into a non-human area of the city, which had suffered damage in the invasion. After the faeries came, humans and supernaturals alike had to allocate their shattered resources towards rebuilding civilisation, with the result that huge swathes of land and whole areas of cities ravaged by the invasion had been left in ruins. Broken-down houses, overgrown roads, shadows where dark fae lurked and fed on anything that moved. Most humans avoided those areas, except thrill-seeking mercenaries looking for an easy kill. I was the opposite of thrill-seeking, but as far as wraiths were concerned, I was the only person I knew in this city who could kill them.

Up until a few weeks ago, I'd never seen one at all. Wraiths were dead faeries trapped in the magic-free Grey Vale until they became a terrifying concentration of necromantic energy held together by pure rage. At their worst, they could even use the faerie magic they'd had while they'd been alive, which wasn't supposed to last beyond death. My distant cousin Holly had worked with rogue necromancers to summon them, but had disappeared in the Highlands three months ago. I fervently hoped she wasn't behind the latest batch of wraith attacks, because she was the last living Winter Gatekeeper. My sister and I had until the winter solstice to find her and return her to her rightful position, but considering it was only September and there was little hope of finding a Lynn who didn't want to be found, we had no leads on her whereabouts.

It'd been three months since I'd banished my distant aunt through the gates of Death—and three months since I'd last seen River, the half-faerie necromancer who'd promised to help me learn how to use my abilities. Since Faerie operated on a different time scheme to our realm, counting on him to help me figure out my new powers wasn't an option. I stepped away from the zombie and extended my spirit sight to cover the general area, morbidly curious about what showed up in faerie-only areas of the city. Faeries didn't have souls, the necromancers said. I didn't think that was true, but I sure as hell couldn't sense anything living—*oh, crap.*

Another undead lunged, icy energy blasting me in the chest. I shuddered, my immunity to faerie magic not extending to the necromantic energy wraiths used. The bigger their attacks, the more powerful they were. This one hadn't reached high levels, but the guy it'd possessed was a brute. Recently dead, from the fresh blood staining his broad chest. Not good.

Once more, I called the book's power. My pocket glowed as my hands lit up white, grey filming my vision. A wrathful being appeared beyond the zombie, propelling it forwards. Nothing survived of the faerie it'd been before aside from the drive to destroy everything in its path. My breath stuttered, cold fogging my vision, and I kicked the zombie in the leg. He didn't go down. Cold air whirled around me, and my hands began to numb. I gritted my teeth, pushing against the invisible force with all the energy I could conjure from the book, but this one was stronger than the first. I'd need to use a binding spell. Problem: I didn't have any necromantic candles on me.

I spoke the binding words anyway, letting the strange yet familiar language flow over my tongue. The wraith blasted me in the face with necromantic energy. My back hit the wall, and I gasped, winded, my shoulders aching. *Ow.* If I let it go, it'd escape the area and go after the living.

"Don't you dare." I kicked out, tangling my legs with the undead's. It finally went down, but grabbed my ankle, pulling me after it. Deep coldness tugged at my bones as the wraith possessing it latched onto my spirit, onto my very essence. It wanted me to join it in cold, empty death.

The vision of the gates swam before my eyes. I gripped the pavement with one hand, focused on the present, and shouted the banishing words in the zombie's face.

The wraith burst apart, leaving the zombie. Its body went limp, collapsing onto me. Ugh. I pushed at it with shaking hands. Then its weight disappeared as someone lifted the dead man away. I sat up, shuddering—and froze. Two hooded, cloaked humans looked down at me. Necromancers.

One spoke in a female voice. "Untrained rogue," she said. "C'mon, Lloyd. We have to bring her in."

2

Being arrested wasn't how I'd planned to spend my afternoon. My captors were Lloyd, a tall guy with medium brown skin and dreadlocks, and Jas, a pale-skinned twenty-something woman with jet-black hair and a lip piercing. It turned out they only wore their hoods up when it was raining, and the rain had stopped by the time we'd reached Princes Street. I was kind of surprised at the piercing, but then again, as far as I knew, the necromancer dress code consisted solely of black cloaks. For all I knew, they all wore pyjamas underneath. That's what I'd have done if I had to go to one of their infamous gatherings in the middle of the night, anyway.

"I didn't know the necromancers had a jail," I commented.

"Oh, yes," said Lloyd, nodding seriously. "There are a hundred and fifty laws and you've broken seven of them."

I raised an eyebrow. "You know them all by heart?"

"Just in case we run into a dangerous rogue like you? Yes."

I suppressed a snort. I'd never been called dangerous before. I'd also never been arrested, despite almost ending up a wanted criminal back in the village I'd once called home.

We crossed the bridge above the disused rail tracks—down for maintenance, since the faerie invasion had effectively shut down the train lines across the country—and continued into Edinburgh's historic Old Town. I was kind of surprised the necromancers would have their headquarters within the fairly busy tourist district, but we walked past bars and restaurants, down side streets, and finally stopped at a large, old building with spired towers on its roof that surely hadn't existed in its current form before the faerie invasion. Its faded brown brick facade fit right in, until you looked up close. The bricks were laced with grey streaks, indicating that iron had been built into the building's very foundations, and the door was solid metal, too. On the surface, witch runes shimmered with green light, indicating other protective spells were at work. These guys didn't mess around.

"Nice," I said. "I thought your HQ would have been in a graveyard, or one of the haunted tourist spots." I waved vaguely in the direction of St Giles Cathedral, besides the Mercat Cross which had been the site of various historical executions. Admittedly, the ghosts created since the faerie invasion probably made most of the local spirits look tame by comparison.

Neither of the necromancers reacted to my comment. Instead, Jas approached the heavy oak doors and pulled on the gold handle. My heart drummed against my ribcage and my hands curled into fists. I hadn't broken any supernatural laws, technically, but the comment about rogues made me wonder what they did to necromancers who didn't want to join the guild.

We walked into the building, through a wide lobby which branched off into various corridors. Though it had windows, the drapes were down, and an aura of gloom permeated the whole place. I shivered, burying my hands in my pockets.

Should have figured the necromancers wouldn't install heating. In fairness, the presence of the dead sucked all warmth and joy away. Okay, so the necromancers standing and chatting in groups looked fairly animated, which came as a surprise, but there seemed no real reason for them to dress like the Grim Reaper other than encouraging people to play up to stereotypes.

"Where are we going?" I asked to fill the silence.

"To the interrogation room," said Lloyd.

Ah. I couldn't exactly kick things off by saying, "Hi, I'm the Gatekeeper. I'm a more powerful necromancer than you are despite never having studied a book on the subject, and I can banish dark faeries most people in this world don't even know about. Oh yeah, and the Vale outcasts want me dead."

I also couldn't say I carried a faerie talisman with necromantic magic even if I wanted to, because the book was under a spell to keep its contents hidden unless it specifically wanted the person to know. It might be an inanimate object, but the book definitely possessed a disturbing sense of awareness, possible due to the spell my ancestors had used to store their magic inside it.

But maybe Great-Aunt Enid had known the local necromancers. If she had—and her abilities, like mine, were close enough to necromancy that she'd have had reason to interact with them if she'd ever come to Edinburgh—I might be able to talk my way out of this. At this point, it was the last hope I had to maintain my freedom.

We halted beside a small room not unlike a university seminar room. It did not contain handcuffs or torture instruments, just an old-fashioned projector and a bunch of tables.

"Is this a classroom?" I asked.

A pause. Lloyd said, "Technically."

"So you don't actually have an interrogation room."

"We don't typically arrest people," said Jas. "Most rogues we run into are too far gone to help."

I read between the lines. "You mean, you kill them."

"Generally they've caused enough damage to justify self-defence, yes," she said. "So you're a necromancer."

"I guess I am."

"You're not with the guild," said Lloyd.

"No, I'm not," I said. "I'm independent. I'm a PhD student." Independent necromancers were usually trouble-makers who summoned undead for fun, but how else was I supposed to explain my abilities?

"That's not how we do things here," he said. "Particularly skill of that level. Where'd you learn to do that?"

"At home, in Foxwood. It's a village in the Highlands."

"You're part of their guild?" asked Jas.

"No. I only came into my powers recently, and as I said, I'm a student—"

"You're to speak with our leader, Lady Montgomery."

My brows shot up. *Lady?* She must be a hell of a lot more important than old Greaves had been. "I will if you promise not to lock me up. I didn't hurt anyone. If anything, I stopped that undead from attacking people."

"There's a procedure," said Lloyd. "If it turns out you've committed no crimes, you'll have to register."

"Since when? I thought necromancers were allowed to be independent." River didn't belong to the guild—at least, I didn't think he did. Then again, he was half-faerie, so the Sidhe had more of a claim on him than the necromancers did. But who knew how things worked around here? I didn't want to spend the next week in a cell, but fighting back would put me at the mercy of several hundred highly trained necromancers. *Goddamn you,* I thought at the book. Rare and dangerous talisman or not, if the damn thing got me arrested, I'd throw it into the river.

"In a city of the dead, we find it best to take precautions," said a severe female voice from behind me.

I turned around, my heart sinking. A woman with steel-grey hair to match her voice entered silently. She was taller than me—and I wasn't exactly short at five foot nine—and her black coat was embossed with several badges and silver cuffs.

"I am Lady Montgomery, leader of the city's necromancers," she said. "Name?"

"Ilsa."

"Full name."

That's what I got for not using an alias. "Ilsa Lynn."

"Lynn. The Gatekeeper?"

"That's my sister. We have necromancer ancestry and it apparently skipped a few generations. I only discovered the ability recently." Best to tell as much of the truth as possible. It'd be easier that way.

"I see. Have you ever used necromancy before today?"

"Yes." I spoke in the sort of tone Mum used when dealing with nosy clients. It usually meant *that's all the information you're getting, unless you'd like to spend the next month as a tree.*

She didn't press further, to my surprise. "Have you ever raised the dead?"

I shook my head. "I've only banished things."

"I see," she said again. "If you're really a necromancer, then you won't object to me putting you through a few tests."

"I guess not. Look, I don't see why—"

"You need to learn how things work here. No common necromancer could have banished the force possessing that undead, which either means you possess high level power you can't control, or you're lying about the extent of your knowledge."

Damn. She knew about the wraith, if not its name. But

how could I explain anything without the book's cooperation?

She slammed a stack of papers down on the desk. "Fill out these. Then I'll assess you verbally. Then we'll run some controlled tests. Watch her, both of you."

In one sweep, she was out of the room. She'd had maybe ten minutes' warning that I was coming and she'd managed to devise a whole testing process. I looked down at the papers. It resembled a job application, with sections on my own pertinent details as well as the basics of necromancy. Seemed straightforward enough—I could have answered most of it without the need for the book, since my sister and I had had a thorough education in all things supernatural. I looked at the door. The other two moved to cover the way out. Damn. Causing a public disturbance wasn't my thing, so I took a seat at the table, picked up the pen she'd left with the papers, and got to work. The two necromancers raised their eyebrows when I put the pen down.

"You seriously finished that fast?" asked Jas.

"You're welcome to check." There was no point in hiding that I'd been educated by the Summer Gatekeeper herself— hell, it worked as an ironclad cover for the real source of my knowledge. If they hadn't met Mum in person, the necromancers knew her by reputation. Every major supernatural in Scotland did. There was no point in playing stupid, and I had the suspicion that Lady Montgomery would see through any deception.

Jas took the papers and skimmed through. "Wow. She really did. Haven't seen anyone fill out a paper that fast since Lady Montgomery's son."

I leaned back in my chair. "She has a son? She doesn't look like the motherly type."

"I thought the same," she said, putting the papers back into order.

"I heard he resurrected a T-Rex once," said Lloyd.

"Don't talk crap, Lloyd. You can't reanimate something that's been dead *that* long."

"Can't you?" I said. "I always wondered about that."

"See, there is something she doesn't know," Lloyd said in a self-satisfied manner. "Good. I can't be outclassed by a rogue we ran into wrestling an undead on the streets, right, Jas?"

"How'd you kill that thing anyway?" asked Jas.

I shrugged. "Got lucky."

"Lady Montgomery will question you," he said. "Surprised she hasn't already. They say she has a magical lie detector…"

Jas rolled her eyes. "She doesn't."

"Along with the interrogation room, right?" I said wryly. It might not be a good idea to poke the necromancers, but I slotted these two into the category of 'harmless' and the grey-haired leader into the same category I put Mum in. The 'do not mess with this person unless you want to get turned into a tree' category. Or whatever the necromancer equivalent was.

Jas's lips quirked in a smile. "I hope we don't have to lock you up. I think you're going to give Lady Montgomery a run for her money."

"You *do* have a jail?" I checked my last paragraph and laid the paper aside. "Or do I get buried alive?"

"In an iron coffin," Lloyd said. "Nah, there's an underground dungeon we use occasionally… you're handling this weirdly calmly, by the way. No wonder she's suspicious."

"Yeah, do you have other necromancers in the family?" asked Jas.

"Kind of," I said. "My family's involved in all things supernatural. It's sort of complicated."

"You're a hybrid?" she asked, with an expression of great interest. "Witch? Or… no, you're not hairy enough to be a wolf shifter."

I snorted. "Nope. Heard the name 'Lynn'?"

"Are you quite done gossiping?" said Lady Montgomery, walking into the room and picking up the papers. Her keen eyes scanned them, then she tossed them into the nearest bin.

My mouth fell open. "What was the point in all that?"

"To see what you were capable of."

"So I get to skip the verbal interrogation?"

Her eyes narrowed. "Certainly not. Tell me what's easier—banishing an undead or a spirit."

"Banishing undead is easier," I said. "Because the spirit isn't there. When the body is destroyed, that's it. Spirits are more stubborn—they usually stick around for a reason—but they can't cause any physical harm. Except poltergeists, who can use kinetic energy to affect the physical world."

She ran through a few more basic questions, while Jas and Lloyd looked on with fascinated expressions.

"You've had a thorough education. Who trained you?"

"Nobody did. I'm an academic," I said. "I also had an education in all the supernatural types before I knew I was magical. I've been living here for over five years. My records—"

"Will be searched, of course," she said. "So you could answer the same level of questions about witches, or mages?"

"Yeah, I could." I wouldn't normally flaunt my knowledge—where I came from, it was hardly notable at all, and the Sidhe didn't care. "I guess I'm part necromancer, but they don't do DNA tests for these things."

"And you can't use any other type of magic?"

"No, I can't. I'm not—our family's tied to Faerie, but I don't have faerie blood."

"Good. Faeries often find it difficult to use our tools when they're sensitive to the presence of iron."

"Wait, there *are* faerie-necromancers here?" Might one of those be summoning the wraiths? I'd got the impression the two Holly had hired hadn't been alone, but the village was miles away from here. Then again, she could use the Ley Line to travel anywhere she liked.

Instead of answering, Lady Montgomery said, "Now we'll move onto the practical component."

Ah. Crap. I could explain away my knowledge, but I'd have to be careful what I let them see if I wanted to avoid further interrogation. Not to mention if any of them looked directly at me in the spirit realm, they'd see my spirit mark blaring like a beacon on my forehead. Even if it was likely none of them actually knew what it meant.

She beckoned to me to follow her down the corridor, leaving the others behind. The other necromancers we ran into stepped sharply out of the way as she passed by. Lady Montgomery inspired respect and terror in equal measure, apparently. I couldn't believe I'd never heard of her before today. Then again, it wasn't like I'd hung out with a ton of supernaturals while I'd been studying at the university. Every time I thought of making a break for it, she was at my side. I'd lost track of the way out several corridors back, so I kept walking.

She stopped in a corridor filled with closed metal doors and opened one of them. A cold breeze swept out, but the pitch black room didn't appear to have any windows. Not that I could see much, light switches included. She looked expectantly at me.

"I have to go in there alone?"

"You're not afraid of the dark, are you?"

"No." More like afraid of what might be lurking in there. My mind conjured up images of wraiths and dark fae, but the iron door was something of a reassurance. Warily, I stepped forwards, hoping I didn't trip over in the darkness. The floor was cold, stone, maybe, and lights came on after a few steps. Twelve lights. The necromancers' electric candles, arranged in a circle.

A summoning circle.

"What do I have to do?" My voice echoed back at me.

"Use your spirit sight."

Okay... I blinked, and grey filtered over my vision. And then I jumped, my heart leaping into my throat.

A man appeared inches from my face, so close I couldn't believe I hadn't seen him in the waking world. He screamed in my ear, shoving at me with outstretched hands. Coldness filled my bones and I stumbled backwards, catching myself before I tripped over. *They wouldn't. Not here.* I'd been ripped out of my body before and I had no desire to repeat the performance. What was I supposed to do—bind the spirit into the circle?

I sidestepped as the man hit out at me, relieved when his hands sailed straight through me. I'd had the impression yanking people out of their bodies was *not* an entry-level skill. Neither was binding, considering you needed to learn the necromancers' language to do it. She wouldn't expect me to know it, so he must be low-level enough for me to persuade to get into the circle without the need for a strong binding.

Breath. He might have scared the shit out of me, but if I'd been trapped in a room as a ghost and forced to terrify new recruits to see what they were made of, I'd be a little annoyed, too.

"This'll go easier if you get in the circle," I told him. "Just get in. It's right there."

The ghost stuck his hands in my chest. I stumbled, fetching up at the circle's edge. "Hey! Stop that."

He whirled around, screaming loud enough that surely people would come running—but the door had closed, and even Lady Montgomery had gone.

"Hey—you can't shut me in the dark." Even the luminous candles provided no light outside the circle.

Fine. If persuading him didn't work, then tricking him was the next available option.

I stepped back in the direction of the candles. "Come on, then," I taunted. "Show me what you're made of."

The ghost flew directly at me, hands outstretched, but avoided the circle by a hair's breadth. I swore quietly. He knew it was there. He'd probably done the same test a thousand times.

I stepped over the candle, carefully, drawing the ghost in that direction. He lunged and again, he avoided the circle. I kept walking backwards, knowing it was a bad idea. I wasn't coordinated enough to pull this off even if it hadn't been pitch black in here. I couldn't even see the walls. Just the circle.

The spirit let out a bone-rattling roar that raised the small hairs on the back of my neck, and dived at me. I willed myself to keep still, not unlike what I did whenever a small faerie threw magic at me, but the blast of icy air stirred the candles. I stepped backwards, and the spirit plunged through my chest, at the circle. The candle wobbled. *Poltergeist. Crap.* I lunged for it, and the spirit dived through my back.

The candle went out.

"Hey!" I tripped over my own feet, cursing the dark room. I felt the book's presence, its magic creeping up my hands, but damn, I'd sworn not to cheat. Wasn't setting a poltergeist on me with no warning technically cheating anyway, though? *I can't believe I let myself get talked into this.*

I gripped the candle, feeling for the switch. It lit up again, and the ghost appeared, laughing. The light connecting the candles had shifted when the ghost had unleashed its spiritual attack on the circle—right in front of me. I stepped forwards and fetched up against the circle's edge.

"Really funny," I said through chattering teeth. "Do you cheat against all your opponents or did I just get lucky?"

At this point, I was ninety percent sure this was an advanced test not used on all novices. Most people would have curled up whimpering in the corner by now. My feet were numb, and I now the bastard had trapped *me* in the circle. Great one there, Ilsa. At least I'd unintentionally cemented my reputation as a clueless newbie who'd wandered into this by accident.

The lights looked brighter from this angle, showing me the room's boundaries, and the ghost floating around. I halted, watching carefully. Now the lights were closer, it was clear to see that for all its flailing around, the ghost seemed to be stuck on a certain pattern. It couldn't diverge from its route. And every third sweep of the room brought it right up to the circle's edge.

I kept still, waiting. Then when the ghost swooped around the edge, I tapped the candle's switch with the toe of my boot and jumped through the ghost, throwing in the tiniest bit of kinetic power.

The ghost shrieked, unbalanced, floating over the candle. Swiftly, I dropped to the floor, switching on the candle again. Lights converged, trapping the screaming ghost in a circle of whiteness.

Thank god for that. Breathing heavily, I stepped in the direction of the door. "Can you let me out now?"

Silence followed. She hadn't locked me in here, had she?

Coldness gripped me, and my body left the ground. I let out a startled cry, looking down at my body standing there as my spirit—the very essence of me—drifted into the air, pulled by an invisible force. Pain tore through my very being, my body frozen, helpless. *It's not the ghost!* The creature couldn't move.

The door flew open behind me and Lady Montgomery stalked in. "What manner of necromancer are you?"

"Hey" I gasped. "Stop that. *Ow.*"

"Stop," said a quiet, commanding voice. One I'd never expected to hear in the necromancers' headquarters.

River.

3

Lady Montgomery turned on him with a frown. "I'm in the middle of an interrogation, River."

"Looks more like torture to me," he said, his voice rough and furious. "Put her down. She's no threat to us."

"And you'd know?"

"I would," he said. "Ilsa isn't a rogue necromancer. She's untrained, but a natural."

"You've met?"

"She saved my life."

I'd have stared at him in surprise if I could move. A moment later, the spell broke and I crashed back into my body with such force that I dropped to the stone floor, wincing as it scraped my knees. Shivering, I climbed to my feet, and Lady Montgomery gave me a look that made me want to jump into the circle again.

"You passed the test," she said, "but your power is off the charts for a new necromancer. You're a liability to leave untrained. I'll assign someone to you immediately."

I opened my mouth to speak, but River stepped in first.

"That won't be necessary. I'll take charge of her training myself."

She gave him a disapproving look. "Son, as an inactive member of the guild, you're not qualified to train anyone."

"My qualifications didn't go anywhere while I was away," he said, while I gaped at both of them. "But if you have a better candidate with enough free time, given the state of things, then I'd be glad to give up the position."

What? She was River's mother? He'd said he had necromancer relatives who lived here in Edinburgh. Not that his mother was leader of the guild. And it was plain to see where his stubbornness had come from. But he'd taken after his faerie parent in his appearance, apparently, because she was severe-looking with steel-grey hair, while he had light blond hair cut short for a half-faerie, pointed ears, and bright green eyes. He must have come here from the Court—but how had he known I'd be here?

"Given the state of things," said Lady Montgomery, "most of the senior necromancers are busy. I trust you won't allow your bias to cloud your judgement. The girl has yet to prove herself trustworthy in my eyes."

"What do you mean by 'the state of things'?" I asked.

As though I hadn't spoken, she said, "You know the procedure. Take her with you, induct her, and if either of you compromise the rules, the consequences will be on you."

"Of course," he said. "She's a natural. I expect to see her make master level within a few weeks."

"Few do. You're an exception."

"So is she."

My face heated. *Play it cool...*

"If you're right, she'll be an asset. Otherwise, see to it that she's under watch, all the time. There's something not quite right about how she handled that test."

And to think I'd been on my best behaviour. "I won't

cause trouble, but I'd like to know what I'm being volunteered for before I sign anything."

Her frosty expression thawed—just a little. "River will explain. If you have any questions, ask him, or any of the senior staff. They wear the grey badges."

She locked the door to the testing room and walked away, leaving us alone in the corridor.

"So that's why you don't think it's a big deal to answer to the Sidhe," I said.

River grimaced. "I hoped they hadn't found you yet. When I heard they'd brought in someone with unusual magic, I suspected it was you."

"They caught me killing an undead. I didn't know everyone in the city with necromancer blood had to undertake training."

"They don't," he said. "That is—they didn't. I'll ask her. It might be due to the nature of your skill. It's up to you how much to reveal, but I'd play it carefully around Lady Montgomery. She's suspicious by nature."

Yet for him to exist, she'd been captured or put under a spell by a Sidhe. Or fallen in love with one. I couldn't decide which was least likely, but I didn't want to pry, especially where she might overhear.

"I don't want anyone to know yet," I whispered. "I can keep my powers hidden to a point, but if I'm put in a position like I was in that test..."

"You weren't prepared," he said. "We'll cover everything in training. There are several levels, but I suspect you can skip over the basics. Not too many, however... it won't do to rouse suspicion."

"I thought not," I said. "They don't know. I mean, they know I'm a Lynn, but I don't think they're informed on Faerie, at least, or the Lynn curse. Just the name."

"No, my mother doesn't know," he said. "I don't doubt she's researching it as we speak, however."

"That figures. Are you supposed to be training me now?"

"I'll give you the tour. It'll give me an excuse to fill you in."

River took off down the corridor. Even when playing human, he couldn't disguise the fact that he moved quicker than most people, with a kind of careless grace that came entirely naturally. I was still shaky from the test, but marching after him returned some of the sensation to my frozen limbs. No wonder the necromancers wore those thick coats.

Between pointing out the various rooms at a speed that made my head spin, he finally paused long enough for me to ask him what he'd been doing for the last three months.

"The Seelie Court kept you a while," I said.

"Yes, they're unusually busy." He spoke lightly, but his voice retained that rough edge. Last I'd heard, he'd had trouble convincing them that the wraiths were a threat to the faerie Courts as well as the mortal realm. The Sidhe weren't given to trusting the words of mortals—partly because like humans, half-faeries could lie, and mostly because the Sidhe were complete pricks who only looked out for their own self-interest.

"They didn't blame you for what my aunt did, right?"

He shook his head. "I'll tell you more when we're not here, but they believe the fault rests with Winter."

That might cause problems later, especially if they still don't believe the Vale's a threat. But I needed to deal with the present problem before I began thinking about the Courts.

"You said you were a high-ranked necromancer," I said. "I didn't know you still worked here."

"I'm still an official member, yes. Where's your sister?"

"At home, getting on with her life," I said. "Like I was getting on with mine, until I got dragged here and locked up by your mother. Why didn't you mention she was leader of the guild of necromancers?"

"It wasn't relevant to our mission."

Our mission. Like we'd both been hired on a job, not that I'd been 'volunteered' for it by my dead relatives because nobody else was around. I'd have preferred to have the magic without the part where both the human and faerie realms had almost come to an untimely end, but the one perk that had come out of the whole thing was River's apparent interest in being friends. Or more than friends. From his tone, we might as well have been strangers.

"I'd say her wanting to lock me up is fairly relevant," I said.

"I didn't know you planned to move back here," he responded.

"I'm fairly sure I mentioned it at some point. Between all the death and destruction." I folded my arms, still shivering. "And you said you wanted to train me. Did you plan this?"

He'd implied a lot more when he'd left… not long after we'd kissed. Okay, so we'd both been ghosts, but considering how long it'd been since I last had any action, that counted. Which was depressing as hell, but being a target for destructive faeries had wreaked havoc on my social life, and when you added in the dead, my chances were shot. After three months apart, it'd have been nice to see some warmth, a sign of interest. For him, it'd have only been a few days since we'd last seen one another.

"I did intend to come back to the guild, but I didn't expect you to be dragged here against your will," he answered. "I apologise for that."

I shook my head. "It's not your fault. But I wouldn't have held it against you if you'd told me Lady Montgomery was your mother upfront."

"You might change your mind when you reach the final

level of training," he said mildly. "I'll show you the weapons room."

And he took off again. *That was hardly an answer.* Maybe he thought Lady Montgomery was listening in. I hurried after him, catching up beside a half-open door to a room containing several rows of shelves.

"Our props are in here," he said. "You won't be allowed to carry them yet, but I'll give you some pointers."

He showed me the types of candles for different purposes, witch-made iron spells to keep faeries out of the way while setting up a summoning circle, various forms of dispensing salt, and odd devices shaped like remote controls.

"Spirit sensor," he explained. "Your spirit sight is strong enough that you probably don't need one, but there's also this..." He pulled the back cover off, revealing the spring-like mechanism inside. "It contains concentrated salt. It'll work on almost all poltergeists, and undead... just don't waste it on smaller enemies, because they contain a limited amount of shots." He put it back on the shelf. There were also a number of knives, daggers and other weapons.

"I didn't know necromancers were combat trained," I said.

"Some of them are, at least here," he said. "This place was a stronghold in the faerie invasion, and we lost more members than most cities."

"Your mother went up against the Sidhe?" My voice rose in surprise.

"Yes, she did. She also converted this place into a temporary shelter and those who couldn't fight focused on rescuing as many people as possible. The iron kept the Sidhe out."

"Damn," I said. "I don't remember the invasion that well. I didn't know the necromancers were involved in the resistance."

"The mages led the assault. That's how so many of them were killed. Necromancers and witches were more for defence... except here. They say *that—*" He indicated a long curved knife mounted on the wall—"killed a Sidhe. Its owner is dead."

"Wow." I couldn't picture a necromancer facing off against a Sidhe and walking away in one piece. The same went for most humans, admittedly. River's mother, though? Maybe I could see it.

"In any case, Edinburgh's necromancer division is large enough that we can afford to specialise. I moved between three different departments when I reached master level."

"I didn't know any of that."

"We don't broadcast it. Also, in that small village, the necromancers didn't have anywhere near the resources we do."

That's how they'd nearly been destroyed. And we still didn't know where those faerie-necromancers had come from, and if there'd been any more of them. Considering the two wraiths I'd encountered today, it wasn't a phenomenon unique to Foxwood. And knowing the true purpose behind River's last mission, I'd bet they were the real reason he'd come back here.

"Speaking of resources," I said in a low voice. "Does this place have a library, or somewhere you keep records of... I don't know, past necromancers?"

"We do have a reference room and a library." His tone was neutral, without a hint that he'd guessed the direction of my thoughts. "Lady Montgomery has her own private library, but it's restricted to the master necromancers."

Well, crap. I'd better be able to pass this training as quickly as I'd hoped if I wanted to get my hands on classified information which might point to a link between the necromancers and the Gatekeeper's talisman. If I was willing to risk my secret getting out.

"For now…" He handed me a book. "Basic guide. You probably know it all, but you'll need to sit some written tests. You'll also have another practical element, but it'll be in front of a panel of judges, so nothing bad can happen."

I wasn't convinced. "What if I say no? She can't legally force me to join. I have other obligations."

"So do all of us," he said. "The guild pays well enough, when you reach the right level. They'll also offer you accommodation should you need it."

"I don't," I said. Possibly, I was being petty, but being forced into a decision by nature of my magic—or lack thereof—was something I had entirely too much experience of already.

He finally looked directly at me with those pale emerald eyes. "It'll be okay," he said.

He'd said the same when redcaps had stabbed my sister, when the world had been falling apart. And it had, in the end. But whatever skills I might have, I was way out of my depth when it came to non-faerie-related supernatural business. The Sidhe might not give a shit about my existence, but I'd spent a lifetime studying how they operated. The Edinburgh necromancers were an unknown element.

"I'll think about it," I said. "I'm not promising anything. I've had bloody enough of invisible contracts, let alone ghosts. You know one of them followed me around playing the bagpipes for three hours yesterday?"

His mouth twitched. Finally, something resembling a smile. "There are ways to discourage them from following you. I can teach you. It won't do any harm for you to learn how it all works here."

He must know I'd been going by guesswork when I used my powers, self-teaching the best I could, but the necromancers limited the amount of information they allowed to get outside their doors. I wouldn't have a better shot at finding out what being Gatekeeper actually meant than by joining the guild, and both of us knew it.

River walked me to the doors. "Can I get your number? I'll call you tomorrow."

"Sure." He offered me his phone. Hey, it wasn't all bad—at least I'd got River's number out of this.

I left the oppressively cold building with relief, finding it was growing dark outside. And raining. Pulling my hood up, I began the long walk home. Only when I'd reached the road's end did I remember that I hadn't pushed River for information on his experiences in Faerie—including what'd happened to my mother. If he knew, he'd have told me right away... unless the Sidhe said otherwise.

Why was he really here? He'd told me he believed there was a conspiracy in the Grey Vale to act against the Courts, and while the threat seemed to have been eliminated after I'd banished the Winter Gatekeeper, the fact that there were still wraith attacks suggested that she hadn't been the only person working against the Courts. If there was a wraith epidemic, I could do worse than team up with the people who had all the ghost-eradicating weaponry. Not to mention knowledge.

I ducked into a takeout place to shelter from the rain, figuring that if I was apparently going to luck into a properly paying job within a few weeks, I deserved to grab something to eat that wasn't instant noodles. I'd been low on cash since I'd left my job, since my only steady work lately came through tutoring and proofreading students' essays. I charged a pittance, but it was easy money. Being with the necromancers, though, would give me some semblance of structure, and more to the point, a job where the dead hounding me would actually be an advantage. Two ghosts even followed me into the takeout, wailing about not being able to taste anything. I tuned them out, bought some food and ducked out into the rain again, wishing I had one of the necromancers' hooded cloaks.

I'd been at the guild less than three hours and now I was fantasising about wearing a cape. Next I'd be dreaming of spending my nights hanging out in graveyards. *Really, Ilsa.* Admittedly, despite the near-death experience, our clash with the Winter Gatekeeper had been like waking up after a long sleep, and now I had magic, I didn't want to shut it away. I wanted to explore it, and the necromancers could help me do that. I could behave and play by the rules for now —I just hoped the book did, too.

A bird-shaped shadow passed overhead. I looked up into the face of a raven with a white stripe on his forehead. Arden, the Lynn family's messenger. Or ex-messenger. He cackled and swiped a fry from my takeout container.

"Hey!" I snapped. "You little shit. Where have you been for the last few months?"

"Caw." I wouldn't have thought it was possible for a bird to leer at me, but he certainly managed it.

"Why show up now?" I grabbed a handful of fries before Arden stole them. "Come to laugh at me for getting arrested?"

"Be careful with that book."

"Little late for that." I sidestepped a puddle, feeling rain sliding down the back of my neck where my hood had fallen down. "You can't mess with the dead in this city and *not* draw the necromancers' attention sooner or later."

"Caw. Watch your step."

My foot sank into another puddle, deep enough to drench my entire right ankle. Cackling, the raven disappeared.

"Thanks for nothing." I shook water out of my shoe, scowling. In fairness, 'watch your step' was possibly the most useful piece of advice Arden had given me in the last twenty-odd years, which didn't say much for his usual record. Considering he'd walked—or flown—alongside at least one Gatekeeper and had been in my family for longer than I'd been alive, he was annoyingly stingy with helpful advice.

I slowed down as I reached the right row of terraced houses. Someone stood outside the door to my house, seemingly oblivious to the pouring rain. I prepared to throw my salt-covered fries on his head, but there was no way an undead could know where I lived, nor have the patience to wait for me. I switched on my spirit sight. He was alive. Human.

I knew him.

My older brother stood on the doorstep.

4

"Hey, Ilsa," he said. "Can I come in?"

"Morgan," I said, stunned. "You—what are you doing here?"

He sneezed. "Can I come in and explain? I think your housemates think I'm a vagrant."

I didn't blame them for having that impression, given the ragged state of him. His overlong hair was plastered to his unshaven face, while he wore tattered jeans and a jacket, not waterproof. I briefly switched my spirit sight on to check he wasn't an impostor, but the spirit sight didn't lie. It was really him.

I let my brother into the hall, where he shook water all over the rug. I beckoned him to follow me upstairs, hoping I wasn't making a huge mistake. If I'd been Hazel, I'd have left him outside in the rain until he apologised for not keeping in touch for the last eight years. Really, I had more cause to do so than she did. But curiosity outweighed anger, and some stupid part of me hoped he'd come up with a reasonable explanation for vanishing off the face of the earth. When we were teenagers, if he wasn't out on drinking binges, he was making impulse purchases using Mum's bank account. The final straw was when he'd stolen several family heirlooms to sell behind Mum's back in order to buy a fancy car, at which point she'd kicked him out. None of us had thought he'd actually leave forever, but that was the last time we'd seen him.

"How in the world did you know where I lived?" I asked quietly. "I haven't been here long."

"I asked around." Morgan staggered into my room, dropping a rucksack on the floor. "Knew you'd be here. You were always the smart one." He spoke in that slurred way of someone drunk trying to pretend they weren't, and not doing a particularly convincing job of it. He smelled of cheap booze, and leaned on the door at an angle that suggested he was using it for balance. No wonder I'd mistaken him for a lurking undead.

I closed the door behind me, and a sudden rush of emotion welled in my eyes. I wanted to punch him and hug him at the same time. We'd always been closer than I'd been to Hazel, which had made his departure that much more painful. Eight years was a third of my life, not something you could just brush aside.

"How's the car?" I asked to fill the silence.

"I wrecked it seven years ago."

Figures. I kept my tone cold. "Last time you texted me, you said you had a job."

He cast his gaze around the room, lingering for a moment on the desk where I'd left my laptop. "Which job?"

I sighed. "If you think you can sponge off me, I barely make enough to cover rent payment."

"I wasn't gonna…"

"You were eyeing up my laptop, you complete tool. I need that for work. If you're desperate for cash, ask Mum."

He winced. "No thanks."

"So you haven't been in touch with Hazel?" I doubted so. If he was in trouble, I was the one he went to. But that last time, he hadn't even given me a chance. I wouldn't have told on him to Mum even when we'd been kids, and I'd thought he knew it.

"No," he muttered, scratching his chin. "You look different. Older."

Anger spiked. "I *am* older," I said, through gritted teeth. "Last time you saw me I was fifteen. It's not like I'm a faerie."

"Definitely not. Faeries are—"

"Morgan, I really wouldn't finish that sentence."

"I was going to say, 'faeries are psychotic'. You weren't this grumpy last time I saw you, either."

"I can't imagine why." I folded my arms. "So where in hell have you been the last eight years?"

"Around."

I narrowed my eyes. Generally, members of the Lynn family suffered side effects if they moved too far from the Ley Line running through the middle of the country, so I'd always assumed he hadn't left Scotland at least. But while Hazel had tried to run away from her responsibilities on occasion when we were younger, she'd never actually gone through with it.

"Get out," I said.

He straightened upright. "What?"

"If you can't conjure up a smidgeon of remorse for what you put us through, then I don't have to deal with your bullshit."

Bleary eyes fixated on me. "You're really mad at me."

"What gives you that impression?" I said, my voice brittle. *Don't even think about crying.* "Eight years, Morgan, and not even an apology."

"Jesus, I'm sorry, okay? I thought that was a given."

"Not with you, it isn't," I said. "You can't stay here forever either."

"I'm gonna go," he slurred. "I just need somewhere to crash tonight."

That sounded familiar. "Only if you promise I won't wake up to find the police on the doorstep or the house on fire. How are you this drunk at five in the evening?"

"I won't stay long, I swear. I'll sleep on the sofa. I just needed… somewhere…" He stared at the wall as though the blank grimy plaster contained the secrets of the universe.

I frowned. "Are you on drugs?"

He jumped. "No. I'm not. Why?"

"Just checking. You're kind of… twitchy."

He grimaced. "Don't make fun, but I think I'm being haunted."

I stared at him a moment. "Seriously?"

Normally I'd have said he was talking crap… if I hadn't spent most of the afternoon around necromancers.

"Seriously," he repeated. "It's been following me for days."

"A ghost?" I asked. "What does it look like?"

He shrugged. "I can't exactly describe it."

Okay…

"So when did this ghost appear?"

"Few days ago, in Oban."

"But… that's miles away." Ghosts were usually tethered to one place. It took a particularly strong-willed spirit to leave and follow someone around, and only necromancers could walk back and forth between the veil and the waking world. But I'd never heard of one travelling across the country before.

"Yeah, s'pose it is."

Right. Once his back was turned, I'd switch my spirit sight on and see if it was true. I didn't want him guessing what I could do, not until I knew for sure he hadn't run into Holly or anyone with unsavoury connections.

My phone buzzed. Hazel. "I need to answer this. Can you try not to touch anything?"

I didn't wait for an answer. I slipped out of the room and downstairs, into the hall, where I could hear the muted noise of several people watching a football game from behind the living room door. I switched on the hall light before accepting the call.

"Hey, Ilsa," Hazel said. "How's it going?"

"Hey. You won't believe the day I'm having."

I briefly ran through my forced induction to the necromancers, ending with River's return, and steamrollering through her attempts to ask questions right up to Morgan's arrival.

"Morgan," she said. "Tell me you're joking."

"You think I'd joke about that?"

"No. That scrounging little shit actually had the nerve to show up on your doorstep?"

I let her blow off steam in a torrent of insults, and when she paused to catch her breath, I said, "Yeah. I know. I'm still trying to figure out where he's been. God knows. He claims to want somewhere to crash tonight and I couldn't exactly say no."

"Don't," she said. "He's—you know what he's like. He can't show up after no calls for years and expect us to welcome him back with open arms. Mum would tell you to throw him out."

"Didn't you think she was kinda harsh on him sometimes?"

"Sometimes, I guess, but are you forgetting when he melted my Barbie's face? Or when he stole her family heirlooms?"

"I know, I know, but it's been eight years. He also claims he's being haunted."

She snorted. "Yeah, right."

"I'm gonna check if it's true, but something tells me he's in trouble. Can't say whether it's supernatural or not, but he *is* related to us."

"Isn't that a good enough reason to toss him out?"

"Probably," I said. "If he's not gone by tomorrow, I will. I just need to check. Wait, I can do it now."

"Go ahead."

I pulled the phone back from my ear and tapped into my spirit sight. Greyness fogged my sight, creeping through the house, and I sensed the blazing brightness of the others' spirits. I extended my awareness upstairs to my room, where my brother's spirit glowed equally bright. I'd started being able to distinguish humans from necromancers or faeries, but other supernaturals looked the same as ordinary humans through this view, even Lynns. But there was an odd flicker upstairs, which disappeared almost instantly.

"Ilsa? You still there?"

"There's something off about him," I said to Hazel. "Maybe not a ghost, but it's in the spirit world, whatever it is. I'm signed up as a necromancer anyway—might as well put it to good use."

"It's up to you," she said dubiously. "Personally I'd kick him out."

"He gets one chance. Besides, if he is being haunted… you know our family's track record with that, since we all have necromancer ancestry. He might even know something I don't."

"About the book, or Great-Aunt Enid? I suppose he's old enough to remember more about her than we are. If you want to tell him—"

"I *can't* tell him, that's the problem. The book… oh hell,

maybe he *can* know about it, since he's a relation." But I didn't want my deadbeat brother getting an inkling of its rarity. Knowing him, he'd try to sell it. "I will ask him. And I'll tell the necromancers if it turns out he really was followed here by a ghost."

"You know best, Ilsa. Just check in with me, okay? I didn't know those wraiths were around where you are."

"They were low level," I said. "Like the ones in the cemetery the first time around. But I'm not sure what they're doing here. The necromancers are so much more organised here than in Foxwood, if it's any consolation."

"I guess it is, but be careful."

"Will do."

I hung up, then tried my spirit sight again. A slight flicker where Morgan's spirit was… that was my only clue. I'd never personally experienced a ghost haunting a non-necromancer, but it was the sort of thing they dealt with on a weekly basis. If he was wrong, it was better to be certain. After all, he carried the Gatekeeper's bloodline, too.

I went back upstairs to find Morgan sitting on the bed with one of my sci-fi paperbacks in hand… upside-down. He'd also stolen what was left of my food, but considering the takeout container was soaked in rainwater and he looked half-starved, I let it slide. What the hell had he been doing, sleeping in ditches and living on scraps for the last eight years?

Morgan lowered the book. "Did you tell her?" he asked.

"I had to. She'd have tossed you outside, so be glad you came here."

He put the book down. "No more than I deserve, I 'spose."

"See? A little self-awareness never hurt anyone," I said. "Come and meet the housemates. If you're crashing on the sofa, you'll have to wait until they finish watching the football match."

Since the faeries had destroyed my last house, I'd found new accommodation and now lived with nice, normal people who couldn't hear the dead wailing and beating at the windows. This time I'd specifically asked for supernatural housemates in the ad, figuring they had a higher tolerance for weird crap. In the living room, Al the half-troll had commandeered the sofa, while Corwin the witch stood in the corner surrounded by broken chalk and herbs, signs of a failed witch spell. Torrance, the shifter, sat in a chair, beer bottle in hand.

"Hey, Ilsa." Corwin waved. "Who's that?"

"My brother, Morgan," I said. "Don't offer him a beer—he's had quite enough already. Is it okay if he crashes here tonight?"

"Sure." Affirmative grunts followed from the others, all eyes on the football sailing across the screen.

"What's that?" said Morgan, making right for the witch circle in the corner.

"It *was* a tracking spell," said Torrance from the armchair. "See, there's this girl I have a crush on, and Corwin volunteered—"

"He decided that using a stalking spell was more effective than actually talking to her," put in Al from the sofa.

"Shut up," muttered Torrance.

"You like it?" Corwin asked Morgan. "You a witch?"

"Yes, I am," he said.

This was going to end well. "No, he isn't," I said. "He's non-magical. Morgan, behave yourself." He'd picked up the nearest witch spell, because of course he had.

"Just looking," he said. "So you put this on, and—"

A snapping noise came from the spell, and smoke momentarily filled the room, earning a disgruntled shout from the people in front of the TV.

When the smoke cleared, Morgan had turned green. You

had to love witch spells for their sheer versatility. There were two types of witches—those who'd worked to keep magic hidden in the old world, who wanted to make use of their skills to help people... and people like Corwin, who specialised in flashy explosions and charms that turned people green.

"Oops," said Corwin. "I don't have a reversal charm. The good news is that no witch spells are permanent."

I pressed my hand to my forehead. "You know what, I think I'm going to hang out upstairs tonight."

"You should know, I'm being haunted," Morgan announced.

Oh boy.

5

The sound of my phone buzzing woke me from sleep. I fumbled around and knocked it off the table. "Shit." I dived and grabbed it, rubbing my eyes with the back of my hand. Seven a.m.? What in the world had I agreed to do at this hour in the morning?

"Hey, Ilsa."

"River." I rubbed sleep from my eyes. I'd stayed up until midnight to make sure Morgan didn't do anything too outrageous, with the result that I'd forgotten to set an alarm.

"I wondered if you wanted to meet me, before going to the guild," River said. "There's a cafe down the road from headquarters."

"Er, sure. Give me twenty minutes."

"No problem."

I clicked off the phone then swore under my breath. Morgan had said he'd leave today, but given the state he'd been in last night, I had my doubts.

Frankly, I had no idea at all what the necromancers expected me to wear, but they hadn't complained about my fashion sense yesterday. I put on jeans and a plain T-shirt with my grey hoody on top, and put the necromancy guide-book River had given me into my shoulder bag. Checking the talisman was thoroughly hidden deep in my inside pocket, I left the room. Downstairs, I found Morgan sprawled on the sofa in a nest of empty beer bottles and the remnants of destroyed spells. And he was still green.

He looked blearily at me as I passed. "Where're you going?"

"I'll be out until this afternoon," I told him. "If you're not in a decent state when I come back, you're sleeping out on the streets tonight."

I left before he could respond, wishing I'd never agreed to let him stay. Knowing him, he'd sleep the day away, then he'd be too drunk by the time I came back for me to kick him out. Repeat for a week until someone snapped and tossed him into the garden.

At least no ghosts trailed me to the necromancers' place—or Arden, for that matter—but my thoughts were too scattered even to dwell on the fact that River had asked me to meet him alone. The coffee shop he'd chosen was a place run by witches, where the pancakes were good enough that I'd occasionally broken my rule not to go near supernaturally inclined places when I'd been at the university. I'd been on several unsuccessful dates there, too. I wished I'd paid attention to River's tone when he'd asked me. If it actually was a date, I wasn't exactly dressed for the occasion, and my head was several miles away.

River waited for me inside the coffee shop. He'd already got us a table and ordered me hot chocolate.

I sat down opposite him. "How did you know this is what I like?"

"I've been at your house," he reminded me. "I can't promise it's up to the same standards as your house's magic, but this place is run by witches."

"Thank you," I said, scanning the menu. "I've actually been here before." Some conversationalist I was. I'd finally got River alone in a date-style environment, and what was on my mind? My idiot of an older brother.

"So… I have to go to the necromancers again later?" I asked, jabbing a fork into the witch-made blueberry pancake and taking a bite.

"Yes, but it's not a formal assessment this time," he said, turning over his own plastic fork in his elegant faerie hands. Like few supernatural-catering places, this café provided alternatives to metal cutlery for the sake of its faerie clientele. "I'm training you. That means I can set the schedule and also assign you to missions if you're at the right level. Which I think you are. It's probably best to downplay things at first if you don't want to give away how much you know, but we'll start off at the lowest level and go from there."

"Seems pretty informal."

"Most necromancers have to fit in training around study or other jobs until they're qualified, so there aren't set hours. But if you're on the clock for missions, they can call you out at any time."

"And are you?"

He nodded. "Since I got back. There's always a shortage of highly qualified necromancers for serious missions, and considering you saw those wraiths yesterday…"

"They weren't hunting me," I said. "Hell if I know what they were doing, but is there a way to find out who summoned them?"

"Two other necromancers took on that case. The ones who brought you in, actually. They'll be patrolling later, and I asked if you'd like to join them. I figured you'd prefer to start off by working with people you know."

"Thanks. If you forget the part where they arrested me, they were pretty nice." I took another bite. What with the stress of last night, I'd forgotten that the person who'd summoned the possessed undead was still out there, probably plotting revenge on me. As I'd spent half my life trying to avoid the Gatekeeper's enemies, I'd certainly done a spectacular job of acquiring my own collection of adversaries lately.

"Something's bothering you," River commented. His sharp faerie's eyes didn't miss much, and whenever he looked at me, he gave me his full attention, in a way few other people did. It made me feel pretty crappy about having my head in the clouds, enough not to blame it all on the wraiths.

"My estranged brother showed up out of nowhere yesterday," I admitted.

He raised an eyebrow. "I thought what you said about twelve siblings hidden in the attic was a joke…"

"Very funny. No, he ran away eight years ago—well, technically, Mum threw him out. Long story short, he makes me look like I have my shit entirely together. And he doesn't know about any of this. It's kind of throwing a wrench in my plans to keep all this quiet, let's put it that way."

River took a sip of coffee. "I wouldn't say the guild would mind, but part of your agreement with the necromancers is that you aren't to speak a word of our secrets to humans, and that includes him. Unless he has magic…"

"Nope, but I haven't told him about the book, either. Also, he claims he's being haunted, but I think he's having me on. I didn't sense anything when I checked, anyway."

He put down the coffee cup. "I'll come and talk to him, if you like."

I shook my head quickly. "You don't want to meet him, trust me. He didn't even ask about Mum until I prompted him. He's… just not a particularly likable person."

"You forget I've been dealing with the Sidhe for the last week," he said.

"A week? Is that how long it was? It's been three months here."

"They tend to take a while to get round to the point."

"No kidding. So what did they want to talk about? Or can't you tell me?" The Sidhe's version of a confidentiality agreement generally came in the form of a vow, which prevented the person from speaking a word on literal pain of death. If you made a promise to a faerie, you were bound to keep it by any means necessary. River's task to guard me from harm had almost cost him his life, and now he was sticking his neck out for me again. Sure, he might not have mentioned our kiss, but there was little doubt he had my back. I was grateful for that, if nothing else.

River paused before saying, "They wanted to discuss the assignment. I did tell them about the wraiths, but they're a rare sight outside the Vale, and the Court doesn't believe they're a direct threat."

The reason he'd ended up on the mission to protect our family was because he'd stumbled across what he believed was evidence of a conspiracy against the Courts, involving the wraiths. It clearly bothered him that the Sidhe weren't taking the threat seriously.

"And now they're coming here," I said. "How many people actually know how to banish them? I *can't* be the only one. It's not possible."

"Smaller wraiths like the ones you dealt with earlier can be banished by anyone with necromantic abilities," River said. "What concerns me is who's summoning them."

"Holly," I said. "Maybe she's in the Vale herself."

"Only Sidhe can cross realms as they please," he said. "Those with the magic of a Sidhe can travel with an invitation or if a Sidhe takes them along for the ride. I've long suspected there's a full-blooded outcast Sidhe behind this, but the Vale is hard to traverse and easy to hide in. In any case, it's highly unlikely your cousin is there. She wouldn't survive it."

"Guess not. I'm supposed to find her by the solstice, but... it's that missing heir crap all over again. Did you get to speak to the Seelie King? Is he still alive?"

"Last I heard, yes," River said. "As for heirs, I've heard nothing, so I assume it was a false trail sent to lead you astray. The Court didn't give me a specific mission, so I was able to return here as soon as I reported in."

He wasn't telling me everything. Questions brewed, but if River was tied into a vow, he wouldn't be able to spill his master's secrets. Like it or not, that's how Faerie operated.

"And—my mother?" I asked.

His gaze dropped. "Not a word from her, unfortunately."

"Like the messenger Sidhe said." I hardly believed that I'd come face to face with both Summer and Winter Sidhe and walked away unscathed and without anyone declaring war on one another. And they'd listened to *my* account of the events. Whenever they'd come to speak to Mum or Hazel, the Sidhe had treated me like less than dirt. And Morgan too, come to that. We had common ground in our experiences, but the gaping rift of the last eight years made it difficult to figure out if it was possible to bridge the gap. Some wounds didn't heal. Hazel probably wouldn't forgive him, and as for Mum...

River picked up his phone. "It's time we went to the guild. You're listed as patrolling with Jas and Lloyd today, and then I can help you with training. Lady Montgomery won't be around, but she'll be asking me for periodic updates on your progress."

He stood, and I did the same. So it was all business, then.

As we left the coffee shop, a group of teenagers wearing necromancer cloaks walked past.

"New trainees," he explained. "We usually get permission

to take them out of school. The talent tends to manifest around the age of twelve, same as mages and witches."

"So I have the skill level of a twelve-year-old. Awesome."

He shot me a smile, the first he had since he'd got back, which pretty much short-circuited my brain cells. Faeries were disturbingly attractive, and if anything, his rougher human edges only made him more handsome. "Your skill level is beyond most of the fully qualified necromancers," he said in a low voice. "It's up to you when you want to let them know that."

Hmm. I'd never particularly liked drawing attention, but personal hang-ups aside, if the wraiths got wind of my presence here, they might target the necromancers on purpose. Look what'd happened in Foxwood. On the other hand, it wouldn't hurt to have other people on my team.

River opened the doors to the lobby and approached a group in the corner. I recognised the two necromancers who'd hauled me in for questioning yesterday, wearing their usual black cloaks.

"Hey," said Lloyd. "Er, sorry about yesterday."

"Likewise," added Jas. "Sorry we got suspicious."

"No worries," I said, as though being arrested was an everyday occurrence for me. "Worth it to see your interrogation room."

"We don't have an interrogation room," said River.

"Am I ever going to be allowed to forget that?" said Lloyd.

"Nope," said Jas, nudging him in the arm. "C'mon. We're patrolling the High Street again. You're coming with us, right… Ilsa? Lady Montgomery said."

"I'll see you later," River said.

"Sure," I said. "What exactly is this patrol about? Looking for rogue undead, or ghosts?"

"Either," said Lloyd. "More likely to be ghosts. This place attracts them like the plague. You'll need a uniform first."

"I get to wear one of your Batman capes?"

Jas snorted. "Yeah, they do look a bit stupid. But you can wear whatever you like underneath. Even nothing."

"Mental images, Jas," said Lloyd.

"I did wonder if everyone was wearing pyjamas and dressing gowns," I admitted.

"You never know," said Lloyd. "There was that time Lady Montgomery sent someone home for wearing fluffy tiger slippers…"

I cracked a grin. Maybe I could get on with the necromancers after all. They weren't all gloomy like old Mr Greaves from Foxwood. Or Lady Montgomery. I couldn't help wondering how in the world River had turned out so different to her. It wasn't like Faerie was a particularly nice place either. And from my brief scan of the lobby, most of the other people here looked human. I didn't see any other pointed ears… wait, there were one or two, but the majority of people here would be fully necromancers or half-ordinary human, because necromantic magic tended to come second to other types, like mage and faerie magic.

Uneasily, I remembered that faerie-necromancers might be the ones summoning wraiths. Surely if the possibility had occurred to River, he'd be keeping an eye out for trouble.

Ten minutes later, I left the guild with the others, holding my new cloak off the ground to avoid tripping over the end. It seemed to have been designed for someone a few inches taller than me, but at least it had a hood to keep the rain off. The skies were bruised grey above the old buildings, but the drizzle hadn't turned into a full-on downpour yet. While patrolling, we stopped at each corner to tap into our spirit sight, reaching out for any hints of spiritual activity.

You'd think the supernaturals being exposed would have put off most tourists, but there were even a few ghost tours running, groups of humans huddled under umbrellas on the cobbled High Street. Their eyes followed us with interest. *Really. It's not like necromancers are a rarity.* Jas and Lloyd seemed cheerful enough, pointing out spots where particularly famous ghosts had appeared.

"So there was this ghost with bleeding eyes who took *four days* for us to exorcise," Lloyd said.

"Ghosts don't bleed," Jas said.

"He did. All over my clothes."

"That was ectoplasm." She rolled her eyes. "Tell Ilsa about the time we accidentally solved a murder instead."

"This guy claimed to have a ghost haunting his apartment. We got there, and figured out pretty quickly that the spirit was out for revenge. Being a poltergeist, he could only levitate the crockery, not do any real damage. We traced the body, and handed the guy over to the police."

"Wow," I said. "Sounds like you had a narrow escape."

"We would have done if Jas hadn't wrestled him into a summoning circle beforehand," said Lloyd. "You can do that to the living if you bind their spirit. Tricky high-level magic, though."

She cleared her throat. "Yeah, well. We got lucky. Definitely one of our most exciting missions."

"We can't always have mass zombie swarms," Lloyd said.

"Why do they do that, anyway?" I asked. "Whenever I hear about zombies, it's always a swarm. Never just one."

"Because the culprit's usually a rogue necromancer without enough training to apply moderation," explained Lloyd. "They use all the power they have, which raises a dozen undead at once, and then they're burned out. So the undead go rampant without anyone controlling them."

"Ah." I nodded. "Makes sense."

"I'm surprised you didn't know," said Jas. "I was told you were some kind of prodigy."

I shrugged. "I'm supposedly a natural, but I don't know all

the theory." And now I sounded like I was bragging. How else was I supposed to explain it? Surely it wasn't unheard of for someone to wake up one morning with the ability to control the dead. Okay, they were usually twelve years old, apparently, but still.

Lloyd pulled a device from his pocket which I recognised as the spirit sensor, and swore. "Speak of the devil. Undead, and no other necromancers in the area."

"Must be our lucky day," Jas commented.

No kidding. The book shifted in my pocket and if not for the cloak, its glow would be incredibly difficult to ignore. Instinctively, I switched on my spirit sight, reaching out to detect where the activity came from. My mind was pulled in the right direction without conscious thought, past the glow of the living bodies and towards the odd colourless light that indicated a spiritless body... on the bridge.

My brother stood right next to an undead.

6

I changed direction down a side road, so suddenly that the others exclaimed.

"Where are you going?" Lloyd asked.

"This way." Dammit, Morgan. Why had he decided to wander outside with undead around? Okay, he probably didn't know... but he'd said he was being haunted. And instead of bringing him to the necromancers' place with me, I'd left him alone at the house.

"How do you know?" Jas hurried alongside me. I might be walking at top speed but I wasn't particularly athletic, so they easily kept pace with me. "You don't have a spirit sensor."

I shook my head. "My spirit sight goes pretty far."

"That's like—master level," said Lloyd in disbelief. "The undead are that way. I can't let you run off—"

I stopped dead. The air above the alley began to swirl in a horribly familiar way. *Oh hell.* My spirit sight couldn't detect wraiths until they were too close to hide from. And the other two likely couldn't even see it. But there were innocent humans in the streets behind us, with no idea what was coming.

Cold air blasted the three of us full in the face. I staggered backwards but managed to keep my balance.

"Holy *shit*," exclaimed Lloyd. "What the hell did that?"

Bye, bye, normality. "Guys," I said out of the corner of my mouth. "I'll take it. If it doesn't work, get some candles down, asap. It works better if we all speak the banishing words at once."

Worst case scenario: I had to use the book. Publicly.

Cold energy flooded my veins, and banishing words rose to my tongue. The current of air continued to swirl, and with my spirit sight on, the glowing white light that indicated the spirit's presence burned like a dark, furious star.

"What *is* it, a poltergeist?" demanded Jas, coming in behind me.

"I said, stay back. Please." I stepped closer, and spoke in the necromancers' language, words which would send the beast beyond the veil forever.

Another blast of air struck the nearby houses, and roof tiles slid free, getting caught in the whirlwind. I'd never faced a wraith in a confined space before, but when the first one I'd met had attacked our house, it'd managed to shatter the magically enhanced windows. Even the book didn't protect me from being struck by falling roof tiles. I stepped out of reach, my words faltering. The banishing spell hadn't worked.

"Lloyd, the candles!" I shouted. "I can't banish it without—"

Lloyd and Jas yelled as roof tiles rained down, bouncing off the cobbled alley floor only to be sucked into the whirlwind again. Drain coverings and other debris joined it, a deadly trap completely blocking the alley. Jas backed up with an expression of terror while Lloyd stumbled over his own feet.

"Retreat!" he yelled, and they ran.

Damn. I pelted after them, cursing with every step. My magic-proof shield only blocked faerie magic, and this wraith was using kinetic energy, poltergeist-style. If the debris hit me at speed, I'd die. My lungs burned, my legs protesting, and the whirlwind grew louder behind me. Someone was going to get seriously hurt if I didn't think of something, fast.

I grabbed Lloyd's arm and dragged him into another alley adjacent to the one we'd come from. "Throw down those candles, *now.*"

He fumbled his pockets, rightly looking terrified, and tossed the candles onto the ground without a word. I dove to the ground and threw them into the main alley as fast as I could, my thumping heart drowned out by the growing roar of wind as it sucked more debris inside it. *It can't go on forever.* The circle was wonky as hell but I didn't have time to worry about aesthetic appeal. I threw the last candle into place, and the tornado exploded. I raised my arms over my head as broken glass and shattered roof tiles roared through the air, smashing more windows and dragging more debris along with them. At the last second, I lunged behind the circle and snapped my fingers, shouting the command. The lights came on at once, as another roar of wind sent me flat on my back. Raising my head, fingers digging into the cobbled ground, I half crawled to the alley opening and flung myself behind it.

Windows shattered above the circle. Shards of glass stung my hands but the candles remained standing. "Speak the words when I do," I gasped out. "Now."

Two voices rose to join mine. From the stunned tones of the others, they were in shock. I should be, too, but something—perhaps the book—held me icily calm. Wild power flowed in my veins, and some unrestrained part of me wanted to walk right out into that tornado and tell it to do its worst.

Jas's back straightened and her hands splayed, necromantic energy pushing back at the wraith. Lloyd did the same, more hesitantly. They could see it now. The wraith appeared on ground level as a human-shaped shadow, sucked towards the candles. As our chanting finished, their light flashed, and the beast exploded into fragments, blown away on the breeze. The wind died down in a series of shattering crashes. I winced at the sound, hoping nobody was hurt. The sound of sirens cut through, and I wobbled to my feet. "Get the candles," I said to the others. "There might be more of them."

"Excuse me, what in hell was that?" Lloyd asked. "You're not supposed to know how to do a banishing on that level."

"It's a long story," I said. "Trust me, though—if it didn't come alone, we're in a world of trouble. It takes more than one person to banish them."

If the wraiths were bold enough to make an overt attack in a crowded city, the necromancers needed to know. But… it wasn't the spirit I'd sensed. *Morgan?*

I reached out with my spirit sight, but didn't detect him on the bridge anymore. Panic spiked my already-racing heart. *Where is he?* I reached out, my sight spanning the city. And I sensed him near the train station, no undead or ghosts in sight. He was safe. I breathed out, hands shaking, knees threatening to give way.

"You're gonna have to talk to Lady Montgomery about this," said Lloyd. "If you won't tell us… she has to know. That thing nearly killed us."

"I know." *Damned book.* "Believe me, I want to explain it, but it's complicated. River knows, and he might already have told her." I hoped he had. Because I'd been framed for summoning a wraith once already, and looked more guilty than the majority of the necromancers at the guild.

Lloyd picked the candles up. "Don't leave blood on the candles. It's the number one rule. I heard if you get blood in a summoning circle, it summons the angel of death."

"Bullshit," said Jas.

"Is it true?" I hadn't heard that rule before, beyond the vague knowledge that anything to do with blood magic was bad news.

"It is. I heard one guy set up a summoning circle and accidentally dripped blood into it. The circle sucked him inside, never to be seen again."

Jas shook her head. "You're talking crap, Lloyd. Don't scare Ilsa."

"Nothing scares Ilsa," said Lloyd. "The madwoman nearly walked out into a kinetic tornado."

Yeah. I did. Just how much control did the book have over my decisions? Maybe it was for the best that I was trying to impose some level of control over my abilities.

No more wraiths materialised on the walk back. People stared on the way into the guild, but that might have been because we all bore cuts on our hands and faces from the broken glass. But it could have been far worse. Jas got a call saying another team had taken down the undead we'd been sent to deal with. If we'd gone that way instead, I dreaded to think what the wraith would have done.

Lady Montgomery waited for me in the lobby, an expectant look on her face. "Come with me, Ms Lynn." She led the way down a corridor to a strong oak door bearing her name on a gold plaque. Her office was better than a cell, but I wished I'd been allowed to discuss my cover story with River first so we didn't accidentally contradict one another. And if there were more wraiths out there, it was plain to see the necromancers were under-prepared to say the least.

Her office was as severe as I expected. Oak wood desk and chair, bookshelves, and little else.

Lady Montgomery faced me across the desk. "What exactly happened back there?"

"I banished a wraith. I'm guessing River told you what they are?"

"Faerie ghosts." Scepticism tinged her voice. "As the witnesses said its actions resembled a poltergeist, we're treating it as such. You spoke our binding words. Where did you learn those?"

"River," I said. "I copied him when I saw him banish a wraith the same way. Guess it's lucky I remembered right."

She looked at me with narrowed eyes. "You remembered the exact words correctly? What are you studying, languages?"

Sarcasm now? "Folklore. I told you I've studied all types of supernaturals, and I lived here for five years. I've also spoken to necromancers in Foxwood."

"Yes, you said," said Lady Montgomery. "I spoke to a representative and I heard that their leader died recently. Rumour suggests you were involved."

My heart sank. *Who told tales on us?*

"You don't deny it?" She took a step closer to me, and power hummed in the air as the book jumped to attention. I remembered some of the things River had done—shown Holly the veil to terrify her, used necromantic power to blast our door open—and I had no doubt that this woman could do me some serious damage. Her necromantic abilities were off the charts. Doubtless she could banish a wraith, too... if she could see it.

"I didn't kill him," I said. "I don't know what they told you, but there was an incident with a horribly powerful spirit attempting to break through the veil. He died defending us against it."

"A spirit like the one you faced today?"

I nodded. "Yeah. The ghost used some kind of advanced necromancy to preserve her own spirit beyond death. We managed to banish her—River and I did."

"The Winter Gatekeeper."

My breath caught.

"None of these words will leave this room," she said. "I know the Sidhe, and how they love their cruel games. They will not pry any secrets from me."

Right... because she'd either been to Faerie itself or been visited here, in some capacity or other. Some part of me wanted to toss caution aside and ask her outright about her presumably short-lived fling with a Sidhe lord, which had resulted in River's birth.

"Yeah," I said. "But those wraiths—River said they'd rarely been seen outside of the faerie realm before. I don't know what they're doing here in Edinburgh, but someone must be summoning them. I guess you guys keep tabs on that sort of thing?"

She gave me an appraising look. "I'm intending to inform the other local supernatural leaders of this threat, and to be on the lookout. It's not good timing, with the upcoming summit, but it can't be helped. But it leaves the question of your training and your position here."

My body tensed. *Please don't lock me up... or worse, punish River for what I did.*

"Unfortunately, we can't have a novice going around using advanced spells," she said. "You'll skip over the first test, and now we'll add you to the records as a junior necromancer."

I stared for a moment in disbelief. "Er... thanks." Damn. Not that I'd usually complain about getting to skip over exams, but the more scrutiny I was under, the more likely it was that the book would be exposed. And if Holly was behind this, whatever her motives, she'd been willing to kill to get hold of the book once. With her mother gone, logically she didn't need it anymore… unless she still hadn't given up on using it to raise her mother's ghost from the grave.

One thing was clear—I needed to find the person behind this before the next attack ended with fatalities. And I couldn't do it on my own power. I needed the necromancers' resources.

"So you have records of everyone who's ever worked here?" I asked. "Including non-registered necromancers, right?"

"Yes. Why?"

"Because I wanted to know if anyone else named Lynn has ever worked for you," I said. "I know there have been necromancers in my family, but the only records at my house are of the Gatekeepers. There's one per generation, but there have definitely been necromancers. I don't know if any of them came here, but I thought it was worth asking."

"If you want to look for the records, you'll have to ask one of the people who works in our archives, like Jas," she said. "Information on current necromancers is confidential, of course."

"Right." I nodded. "Just wondered."

I probably shouldn't push my luck further, so I took her clear indication of dismissal and left. To my surprise, I found Jas and Lloyd waiting outside.

"There you are," Lloyd said. "She didn't skin you alive, did she?"

"Surprisingly not."

"I knew she wouldn't," he said. "It'd look bad, considering everyone knows you saved our lives."

Ah crap. "Seriously?"

"Of course," Jas said. "You didn't think that would stay quiet, did you? That, and you're a prodigy."

I'd literally never been a prodigy at anything in my life. I'd left school with top grades through sheer persistence, and earned every single one of them. I didn't feel like I'd earned this, at all. Not that I'd ever in a million years tell Lady Montgomery that.

"I guess."

Lloyd smiled. "Thanks, by the way. You saved our necks out there."

I blinked. "What, you don't think I'm a freak?"

"We raise the dead for a living," Jas said.

"Put the dead to rest, technically," said Lloyd. "But it's cool. Just wondering… are you a faerie?"

"No. What gave you that idea?"

"You saw that thing when neither of us did," said Jas. Despite her profession of gratitude, suspicion lurked in her gaze. Lloyd seemed easy-going enough to accept any explanation I gave. Jas might require more convincing.

I shook my head. "I didn't see it. That's the problem. You can't see them until they're right on top of you."

"You've seen them before?" asked Lloyd.

"A couple of times, yeah. But I don't know where it came from, or who summoned it." I paused. "Don't tell anyone this, but there's a chance a faerie might have been behind it. Possibly. Not necessarily a guild member. Unless… have any guild members disappeared recently?"

"Disappeared how?" asked Jas. Again, her expression betrayed suspicion.

"Just… left. I don't know." If they'd been in Faerie, months or years might have passed since they'd gone, but for all I knew, the two I'd run into had never set foot in the faerie realm *or* Edinburgh. Except to summon beasts from the Vale, they must have been in contact with someone from the other side. But they'd also been fully trained necromancers. I didn't even know their names, so I wasn't like I could look them up, but I could ask River if he knew.

"Not that I know of," said Lloyd. "I've been away from the guild for a couple of years, studying, so I don't know all the newbies. That's why I've only just been promoted to junior level."

"So that's common?"

"Sure," said Jas. "Not everyone wants to work here for a living. They need a certain number of staff, and when shit really goes down, they ask for volunteers. But generally, we're allowed to come and go as we please if we give Lady Montgomery enough notice. There are quite a few newbies at the moment... there was a rise in undead activity last year."

If anyone can get their resources, maybe that's how the faerie-necromancers found out how to summon wraiths. I paused as we reached the entrance hall and everyone openly stared at me. I'd always wanted to be admired, to be noticed for any reason other than my sister or mother. Especially when Hazel and I had looked more alike and everyone got us confused. Now I was being assessed for something only I could do—excelled at, even—and I couldn't shut off the stupid voice in my head telling me the book was entirely responsible for it all. And telling me that if I hadn't used that power, we'd all be dead.

No. It wasn't cold feet, it was fear. I didn't know *who* had sent the wraith after us, but I could still hear the awful noises when shattered glass had struck the ground next to where I'd been standing. If an undefended human had been there... I couldn't finish the thought. But I felt more like vomiting on the polished floor than celebrating.

"Hey," said River, spotting me. "Ilsa, after the morning you've had, I don't blame you if you want to go home. I've persuaded Lady Montgomery to move your next written assessment until tomorrow, since you're moving up a level."

"Oh—thanks," I said, grateful for the excuse to look away from the crowd. Lloyd and Jas stepped back, giving us space. My nausea subsided a little as River fell into step alongside me, skirting the crowd until we reached the doors.

"You had me worried for a moment there," River said in a low voice. "I've asked Lady Montgomery to equip all future patrollers with spirit sensors. It's entirely too dangerous that nobody can sense those wraiths until it's too late to avoid them."

"No kidding," I said. "Your mother seems to be surprisingly okay with me being an untested prodigy. Was it you who told her the Winter Gatekeeper went rogue?"

"No, but she's persistent enough to go digging. She most likely would have asked everyone in the village she could contact until she found someone with answers."

"Figures." I groaned. "The only person with the full story is Hazel… and I guess Agnes and Everett at least knew we weren't guilty."

"Don't worry," he said. "My vow to keep you safe hasn't disappeared now I've completed my task as bodyguard. She won't have you arrested."

"I can take care of myself, River." Though I had to admit it was nice not to feel like the whole burden was resting entirely on me. "Anyway, it's not me I'm worried about. Those two —they couldn't even see the wraith. Even I couldn't at first. We're in over our heads if there are more of them. Are you telling the other necromancers so they can prepare if another one attacks?"

"The necromancers have called a summit to discuss this situation. Ordinarily novices wouldn't be invited, but considering the circumstances, you're allowed to attend. It's at seven tonight."

"Okay," I said. "I don't know if Lady Montgomery mentioned it, but I had to tell her that I got the banishing words from you. I said I copied you when you banished the first wraith."

"Right." He nodded. "That was a good idea."

"I think someone here might be after the book," I said. "Or at least connected with those two faerie-necromancers. They had formal training. They were also Scottish, and this is the biggest necromancer branch in the country. Plus they wore glamour, so they might not have looked the same if they were members here."

"Faerie glamour isn't forbidden in the guild, but it tends to fade while close to iron, and the guild's headquarters is made out of it," River said. "Someone would have noticed. I'll ask around, but I'm needed on patrol in ten minutes."

"If another wraith appears—"

"I'll handle it." He moved in closer, and I smelled the earthy scent of his faerie magic, a contrast to the coldness of necromantic power. Both fit him like a glove, and he looked as at home here as he had in the garden of the Summer Gate-keeper. I envied him that, I wouldn't lie. If I knew for sure I belonged here… but if anything, taking out that wraith had only made me feel more of an outsider. "Will you be okay walking home alone?"

"Pretty sure my odds are better than most people's." Warmth filled my chest at his concern on my behalf, and the smell of his magic grew stronger in the inches separating us. God, I wanted to kiss him again, if just to know what it felt like for real. *Dangerous thoughts, Ilsa.* He was my mentor, and his mother held my freedom in her hands.

River smiled at me. "I'll see you later, Ilsa."

"See you."

There was no backing out. No running away. It'd be a dick move to leave the guild now, and I somehow doubted Lady Montgomery would tolerate a vigilante necromancer swooping around like a superhero and saving people from wraiths. I grinned at the mental image, mostly because I couldn't fly, and I'd look damned stupid in a cape. The necromancer cloak was bad enough.

I ducked into an alley to take the coat off so my brother wouldn't ask questions when I came home dressed as a necromancer, and shoved it into my bag. Spotting movement out of the corner of my eye, I instinctively tapped into my spirit sight. Nothing appeared. I shifted it in the direction of my house, surprised at how easily my sight extended. It didn't show me the surrounding areas, but zeroed in on my brother. Maybe I could easier track people I knew…

And he wasn't at home. He was walking down the road where the wraith had attacked. The faint pinprick on my sight told me all I needed to know—my brother was about to run into another zombie.

I broke into a run for the second time that day. Who needed a gym membership when the restless dead wouldn't give you a moment's peace.

7

I skidded to a halt at the road's end, clutching a stitch in my side and glad I carried the necromancer coat. Grabbing my salt shaker from the pocket, I reached the mouth of the cobbled alley where the wraith had attacked. A hunched figure lumbered forward, and the smell coming from him was foul enough to make me gag. And in front of him, Morgan stood staring blankly into space, completely oblivious to the undead sneaking up on him.

"Hey!" I shouted, not that the dead could hear me. Morgan turned slowly, his expression blank, and I tackled the undead from the side, flinging salt into its face. Its skin—or what was left of it—melted, and I shuddered at the sensation of flesh giving way to bone as I kicked it solidly in the leg, causing the undead to fall to the ground.

Morgan's expression cleared. "Ilsa?"

"What in hell are you doing here?" I demanded. "That undead was right behind you and you were just staring at thin air."

I switched on my spirit sight again, but saw nothing

within reach. The undead hadn't been possessed by a wraith this time. Thank the Sidhe for that.

"I dunno," he said. "I went for a walk."

"Why?" I asked him. "Why did you think wandering around here was a good idea, especially after—" I caught myself before I admitted I'd sensed him using my spirit sight before I'd actually seen him.

"After what?" he asked.

"Didn't you hear about the ghost attack? And the undead?" My voice was steady, but my throat closed up at the thought of him being hurt.

"No."

I sighed. "Just be careful. C'mon. Let's head back to the house."

He followed me out of the alley. I was fairly sure he was wearing the same outfit as yesterday, and hadn't even sobered up yet. Like I needed to handle babysitting my older brother on top of keeping the city safe from more wraith attacks. Especially when he seemed determined to make himself into a target.

"Thought you were going to kick me out," Morgan said as we reached my road.

"I am kicking you out. Tell me you at least have somewhere to go?"

A ghost chose that moment to float in our direction. *Nope. Not interested.*

"Hellooooo?" the ghost said. "Can anyone see me?"

Nope. Ignore. Do not engage.

"Hey!" The ghost flew directly in front of my face. Despite myself, my steps faltered as my body automatically responded to the ghost's nearness.

"You can see me?" he said. "Where's Maurice? And Claire? Hellllp…"

"Go away," I muttered under my breath, walking after Morgan. He hadn't stopped, so hopefully he hadn't seen.

"Ilsa?" asked Morgan. "I thought I heard…" He trailed off, looking just to the left of the ghost. "I dunno."

"Nothing," I said. Now he'd think *I* was losing my marbles. Unless he'd seen it, too. His expression was unfocused enough that I couldn't tell. "I'm just jumpy, because you were standing on top of an undead."

"Undead," he said. "Since when could you destroy them?"

"I've lived here for five years. You get more undead here than back at the Lynn house, trust me. If you leave the house, carry salt. I have some spare. They seem to be everywhere at the moment."

"I figured," he muttered. "I—I don't suppose you've told Mum?"

Ah. He didn't know she was missing. If I told him, he'd go and start hassling Hazel instead, and she'd had enough of ghosts in the family home already.

"No idea. I'm not really in contact, except with Hazel. I did tell her, but I think she's mad at you."

He frowned, but not like he was surprised. "She's good at holding grudges."

"That she is." I walked to the house and unlocked the door, relieved to see no more ghosts around. "Please, spare my sanity and stay indoors tonight. Apparently you're a zombie magnet."

"I'm supposed to let my kid sister order me around now?" He folded his arms.

"I don't think it's unreasonable to expect my brother *not* to dye himself green or walk around unarmed and inebriated with a zombie outbreak every other day."

He slouched off through the open door into the living room, grumbling to himself.

Siblings. How Hazel, Morgan and I had survived fifteen

years in the same house without one of us suffering a similar fate to Hazel's melted Barbie dolls, I'd probably never know.

———

At six in the evening, the doorbell rang. I checked my necromancer coat was in my bag—I'd change later, so Morgan wouldn't realise where I was going—and went downstairs.

River stood on the doorstep wearing his necromancer coat, his pale hair gleaming in the light of the street lamps.

"Hey. How is it everyone knows my address?" I asked.

"You put it on the necromancer signup form when you joined the guild."

Right, of course I did.

"Who're you?" asked Morgan from behind him.

"My name is River. I'm a friend of Ilsa's."

"You're a faerie."

River looked at him. "Half-faerie, technically. You must be Morgan. It's nice to meet you."

"Anyway, River and I are going out," I said quickly, before Morgan made another unwise comment. "If you need me, send me a message."

"Where're you going?"

"The Mortar and Pestle." I named a popular student pub amongst supernaturals.

"You a student?" he asked River.

"I already graduated, but I have friends who are," he said, not missing a beat.

"See you later," I said pointedly, and closed the door behind me. "Was that true?" I asked River, when I'd made sure Morgan wasn't going to follow us out of the house. "Did you ever study there?"

"I didn't, no. Why?"

"It just occurred to me that I never asked if you had a degree as well as being a professional bodyguard and necromancer at the same time."

"They don't tend to offer degree courses in either of those subjects. I've never had much patience for studying, besides."

No, I couldn't imagine him in a stuffy classroom. He seemed a more hands-on type, not that I knew for definite. I hadn't begun to get to know the real him. Every time I thought I did, he came out with a new surprise.

"Did you read the book?" he asked.

He meant the handbook, but another book came to mind. "Yeah, I read it cover to cover."

His gaze dropped to my pocket like he'd guessed my thoughts. "And the other one?"

"That too," I said, "but I'm sure it's hiding more information. There's almost nothing on the Vale, for one thing. And it hasn't tried to communicate with me again lately. Not sure why. I could technically have used it to send that wraith through the gate, but last time..."

The image of spirits being sucked into a whirlpool stole across my vision. The gate's power was raw and terrifying, and for all I knew, if I'd used it against the wraith, Jas and Lloyd might have been dragged into it, too. I couldn't risk it. Not here. Already, carrying the book felt as normal as breathing, but no matter how accomplished I became at necromancy, I'd never think of the gates as safe, normal, and easy to control. I was supposed to be Gatekeeper, but I'd nearly met my own demise at the hands of the book's magic.

"You haven't told your brother about the book, you said."

I shook my head. "I'm not mentioning it to him. There's no point, since he doesn't have the spirit sight. But I'm not sure our alibi for tonight will hold up. He probably thinks we're dating." I stole a glance at him. "Is that an issue?" It seemed childish to ask *are we dating,* but I never had been particularly good at reading cues.

There was a pause before he said, "I'm not technically allowed, as you're my apprentice, but if it's easier for your brother to believe we're involved, then I suppose it can't hurt."

His words stung more than I expected. Had he forgotten what'd passed between us that easily? Or had he never been interested in the first place? A bitter taste rose on my tongue. "We don't have to if it's easier for you."

Some of the hurt had apparently crept into my tone, because he stopped walking, catching my gaze. "Ilsa."

I flinched. "Can you please not? If you're not interested, it's fine, but this isn't the best day to play head games, River. I'm really not in the mood."

"I apologise," he said softly. "I meant to say we should play it safe. Certainly around the necromancers. It won't help their suspicions that I'm giving you outside help."

"You mean Lady Montgomery, right?"

He nodded. "Unfortunately, she has the power to make things particularly unpleasant for you, and hasn't entirely let go of the possibility that you might be working with Holly. I shouldn't have put the idea into her head by bringing up the Gatekeepers, but she's already done enough research of her own."

"She thinks I'm in league with Holly?" I gaped at him. "Okay… this is getting way out of hand. A few hours ago she was totally fine with me coming to the summit."

"I made it clear you had nothing to do with what Holly did. And at this rate, you'll pass training quickly, then we'll be colleagues. There's no rule against colleagues dating."

I tilted my head. "I'll hold you to that. But don't forget my brother thinks it's for real."

"Pity, that," he said, a smile ghosting his lips. "One would think I might have to walk you home in order to cement that impression and stop him from suspecting where you really were tonight."

Oh. I liked River in flirtation mode. A lot. I'd be more than happy to play up the so-called ruse, once we were out of the cold night and somewhere warm. I just had to pass training. How hard could it be?

"Where are we actually going, anyway?" I asked.

"The necromancers traditionally hold their summits in their own private churchyard."

"A graveyard. At night. Have they lost their minds?"

"It's protected," he said. "The summits occur at least every month, sometimes every couple of weeks. They're rarely targeted by attacks."

I gave him a sceptical look. "That's a cue for a fae beast to jump out of the shadows at us."

"I'll keep you safe from monsters, Ilsa."

"Ha ha. I have no problem with the dark. With my spirit sight, it's not so dark anyway. I've been meaning to ask—can you sense people a mile away?"

"A mile? No. Can you?"

"I didn't measure the exact distance, but I picked up on my brother at home when I was near the guild."

"That's a part of your gift, I'd guess. Later, we'll see how far you can go."

I can think of a few places. Mind out of the gutter, Ilsa. He'd eliminated my bad mood, at least, though the idea of standing out in the dark and cold wasn't particularly appealing. At least I wouldn't be alone.

We stopped at the graveyard, where a number of cloaked figures grouped around the low stone wall surrounding the place. The sunset gilded the church in molten shades of golden light, accentuating the shadows. Even knowing that everyone here had the spirit sight didn't quell my growing uneasiness, especially seeing the candles arranged in a circle between the headstones.

"Are they summoning someone?" I whispered to River, who joined the other necromancers. Everyone had pulled their hoods up so I did likewise, relieved to be able to hide my face. The mark might be hidden, but spirits could still see it.

"Their ancestors, yes. The summit is for the dead as much as the living, and it's tradition to consult necromancers past about current events."

Like the wraiths. Old Mr Greaves had said that most of the necromancer Guardians were at least partially aware of the Grey Vale and the monsters on the Ley Line. Presumably this graveyard didn't directly overlap with the Line, otherwise it'd be too volatile to use necromancy nearby without side effects.

As the cloaked figures gathered in line, two of them stepped towards the circle. I recognised Lady Montgomery's purposeful stride even with her face hidden. The candles lit up with a snap and several ghostly figures appeared within the circle. Lady Montgomery spoke to them, too quietly to hear. I trod from one foot to the other, growing cold from standing still, and hoped they'd get to the point soon.

"They have to go through the formalities," River said. "I think she's telling them about the wraith."

"River?" Her voice rang out. "Come here and speak to Lord Simeon."

River stepped towards the circle, subtly hiding me from view. I stood tense, unable to rid myself of the suspicion that more than the ghosts watched me. Was it paranoia, or like when I'd sensed the wraith the first time? My mark wasn't invisible in the spirit world, and it was a damn good job nobody had thought to give me a second glance.

Calm down, Ilsa. The people who are haunting you are right there.

The circle shimmered with white light, and the murmur of voices passed over my head. My skin prickled all over, and I reached out with my spirit sight.

There was a shout from outside the graveyard. Morgan.

8

Heart sinking, I climbed over the wall, running in his direction. My spirit sight snapped on and I sensed him behind the wall, cowering away from a transparent figure. Not one of the necromancers.

"Shove off," I snapped at the ghost.

It turned on me, its body shimmering all over, reforming into that of a shaggy creature the size of a cow. Oh crap. Not a hellhound, but I couldn't tell if the beast was solid or transparent. Reaching for a weapon, I backed away as teeth snapped inches away from me. Ghosts couldn't be solid, which left one option—a faerie creature like a sluagh. Partly physical, partly spirit, and a shapeshifter. No magic, so no use relying on my defence mechanism—but one major weakness.

I dug in my pocket for my iron shards and flung them at the sluagh, sending it scrabbling backwards out of range. Its dog-like form flipped through several other dog breeds and settled on a small basset hound. I ignored its pitiful whine and grabbed my knife, glad I'd armed myself to face worse than ghosts.

The sluagh's whine turned to a growl, and it grew again, teeth lengthening, shoulders hunching, its face a grotesque mix of human and dog like an illustration of a werewolf. It leaped at me and I swiped my knife sideways, but the blade passed through its body like it wasn't there. Being part spirit, part corporeal, it could deflect some physical attacks. I stabbed again, and the knife passed through the sluagh's horrifically mangled face. With my free hand, I grabbed the salt canister in my sleeve. The shapeshifter lunged forwards, and I flung the salt into its face. Hissing in fury, the creature reeled back. *So salt does hurt it, huh.* Tapping into the book's power, I let its cold light wash over my hands.

The sluagh reeled back, a strangled cry ripping from its throat. *Oh, now you know who I am?*

Necromantic power sprang to my fingertips, rushing towards the creature. It flew through the air and landed flat on its back, where it changed forms again, flipping between a ghoulish over-sized doll and a giant dog, and finishing on a human child-sized beast.

Green light collided with the necromantic power pouring from my hands, and the sluagh exploded into fragments. River stepped up beside Morgan, lowering his hood. "Are you okay?"

"Yeah," I said. "Bloody creature kept turning transparent."

"They do that. Faerie magic does work on them. What…" He looked quizzically at Morgan, who'd pushed himself up against the wall, his jaw slack.

Of course, Lady Montgomery chose that moment to march up to us.

"What is the meaning of this?"

"Faerie beasts," River interjected before I could speak. "They attacked Ilsa, and…"

"Morgan's my brother," I said quickly.

Her gaze snapped onto me. "You invited a non-necromancer to our summit?"

"No, I guess he followed me." He stared off into space, apparently not hearing a word we said. "Or a ghost. He thinks he's being haunted."

"Is that so?" She sounded so much like River when she used that tone.

"I didn't see anything when I checked," I admitted, "but we're related, so it's possible he picked up on what was going on here. I should make sure he gets home safely."

Please, don't draw attention in front of the others. The sluagh was a nasty piece of work, but I dreaded to think how Morgan would react to the attention of the other necromancers. I needed to shoot her suspicions in the foot before both of us wound up deep in crap.

Lady Montgomery looked at him, her nostrils flaring. "Is he a necromancer?"

"No, he has no magic," I told her. "He's also drunk and probably won't remember this later. I need to get him home before he makes a public fool of himself."

"Is that likely to happen?"

"Yeah," I said, and instantly felt bad. Even though it was true, I didn't need strangers to cast judgement on my family members' terrible life choices.

Lady Montgomery said, "I need to ensure nothing else is present near the graveyard. Come and talk to me tomorrow morning. River, I want you to assess whether it's necessary for us to bring Ilsa's... family members in." She gave Morgan a distasteful look.

River nodded and walked up to join me. "It's late now, but I think you should bring your brother to the guild tomorrow," he said in a low voice as his mother returned to the others in the cemetery.

"If he's up for it, I will. But I need to get him home for now. I'll let you know later, okay?

He gave me a look, then nodded. "Let me know if anything comes up."

"Sure. I'll see you tomorrow."

I hope so.

I looked for Morgan, only to find he was already walking away.

"Hey." I ran after him and caught up. "You know, by 'don't do anything stupid', I meant, 'don't follow me to the graveyard at night and get jumped by a faerie monster'."

"That's where your date took you? A necromancer summit?"

"You followed me. Are you *trying* to get yourself killed?"

"You're the one who didn't tell me you were a necromancer."

"I'm new to the guild and I didn't want you screwing everything up for me. So you're going to stay *in* the house tonight, and first thing tomorrow, we're off to the guild so we can get this sorted out once and for all. Got it?"

"Whatever," he muttered. His shoulders were hunched, his face pale and drawn.

I swallowed down my anger, knowing how it felt to be slammed in the face by unwelcome revelations. "You scared the shit out of me twice today, Morgan. I've been a necromancer less than a week and I didn't expect to have to rescue my own family from certain death before I was even qualified."

"No way you're not qualified," he said. "You have to be, to kill one of those things."

"I can explain—"

"No, you're right," he said. "I'm not to be trusted. Like the necromancer lady said. Keep your secrets."

We walked the rest of the way to the house in silence.

———

I woke hourly that night, tossed between nightmares of undead attacking my family, and when I finally dozed off for real, I jerked awake moments later to the sound of the door closing. I was on my feet in seconds. Grabbing my hoody and shoving my feet into my shoes, I ran downstairs and caught up to Morgan halfway across the road.

"Dammit, Morgan."

He didn't respond. Didn't even look at me. I sidestepped around him and waved a hand in front of his face, then tapped into the spirit world. A female figure hovered alongside him.

"Hey!" I said. "Get away from my brother."

"You'll do." She glided over to me. Her transparent form shimmered against the grey. "Nobody can see me. Help me."

"You're dead," I told her. "Go away and leave us alone." Bloody ghosts. My head pounded, and it hit me too late that I'd left the book in my room. No wonder I felt out of sorts, aside from the obvious.

Morgan kept walking. I moved in front of him, thinking fast. Either he was possessed or someone was controlling him, neither of which I knew how to deal with when the person was living. I hadn't brought any weapons, and while I could probably overpower him in the state he was in now, every step drew us further away from the book. Necromantic power sprang to my palm and I gave him a firm shove. He tripped backwards over his own feet, and the ghost appeared again.

"Go away," I said in a low, warning voice, my hands glowing with kinetic power. The ghost took one look at me and faded into greyness.

Morgan staggered forwards, his eyes opening. "Ilsa?" He frowned at me. "What are you doing?"

"Stopping you sleepwalking." I let the power die down. "Maybe I should have locked you in."

"I thought you did."

I cast my mind back, remembering putting the bolt on the door. "Apparently you can unlatch the door when sleepwalking."

"Huh." He frowned. "I thought I was awake."

"You were following a ghost," I told him.

He stared at me. "What?"

"How can you not remember?" I didn't think ghosts could mess with people's minds, and she'd been human. So either he'd been half asleep, or something even weirder was going on. Given my track record lately, I wouldn't go with the easy option. "Was it the same with the graveyard? When you followed me?"

He paused for a moment. "I heard a voice."

"The ghost?"

"No. But it was creepy as hell."

He walked back into the house, and I followed. "Are you sure you aren't on drugs?" I asked him. "I don't think the necromancers will check, but I want to rule out any other explanations for you hearing creepy voices."

"I get what it sounds like." He took up a position on the vacant couch in front of the TV. "That's why I didn't tell anyone. But I think the ghosts want me dead."

"I'm beginning to get that impression, too."

I ran up to my room to retrieve the Gatekeeper's book, having had about enough of the sensation of tapping on the back of my skull. "Stop that," I muttered to it. As an afterthought, I stuck it inside the necromancer guidebook and went back downstairs. I brushed shifter fur off the remaining armchair that wasn't covered in witch props, and put my feet up on the coffee table, balancing both books on my knees.

"What's that?" asked Morgan.

I held up the cover of the necromancer handbook in answer, glimpsing the headline on the page underneath. *The Sacred Oath of Necromancy.* The necromancers' Sacred Oath was to protect the veil. If I was properly inducted, I'd have to swear it, too—except I'd broken almost all their rules when I'd banished the Winter Gatekeeper's spirit, so I'd be implicitly lying at best. I'd deal with that one later.

Skipping back to the Gatekeeper's book, I searched for the section on faerie spirits for the word *sluagh*. I couldn't help noticing that there were no instructions on how to actually summon any of them.

The book shifted in my hands as though in reproach. *I don't actually want to summon one. I want to know how the person who did managed to do so without being detected.*

I didn't think the book could read my thoughts, but the pages flipped by themselves, taking me to the back section— dark magic, blood magic and evil necromancy. That was it. The title stood alone, with no other words on the page. I got the message. Either it was beyond my skill level or I wasn't allowed to learn even the theory.

Okay... then I need to look up if it's possible for a ghost to influence someone from far away.

The pages flipped approvingly. Wait, since when did books have feelings? Even faerie talisman ones? I was definitely reading too much into its rustling pages. At least it wasn't calling me an amateur any longer.

According to the book, ghosts could temporarily possess someone if the force used to summon them was particularly strong, or if there was another powerful source of necromantic energy nearby. Same with attacking people in spirit form. What those two faerie-necromancers had done was no common skill. Most necromancers couldn't leave their bodies behind without using a circle on themselves as a tether.

But my brother hadn't seen any spirits. He'd heard them, if I believed him, but had been completely oblivious to that ghost following him. I flipped through the book again, but it only covered the Gatekeeper's talents, not other supernaturals or even general necromancy. I'd heard of telepathy... but that was a mage talent, and a rare one. And there weren't any mages in our family.

I looked up to see Morgan watching me oddly. "What?"

He shook his head. "Nothing. You always used to do that at home. I could drop something on your head while you were reading and you probably wouldn't notice."

"Hmm." I didn't particularly want to stride down memory lane, not with our present dilemma swamping everything else.

"Uh... I was gonna ask what you've been up to since I left, but... I guess you answered that."

Where to even start? He'd left the summer before I turned sixteen, and not long after, I'd gone slightly off the rails in my own way. Rather than drunk and disorderly behaviour, my own teenage rebellion had involved hooking up with a local half-Sidhe. Actually, I didn't mind too much that Morgan had missed that part, considering the trouble I'd had keeping Mum from finding out. But he'd missed Hazel taking up her position as Gatekeeper when she'd turned eighteen. He'd missed all our exam results and leaving school and my university graduation... okay, only Hazel had shown up for that, since Mum had been in Faerie.

I put the book down and said, "Does that mean you'll enlighten me on what led you to turn up here looking like death warmed over?"

"Maybe."

I grimaced. "There's not a whole lot to say. You know I've

been at university. Hazel's more or less Mum's full time assistant, but I think she hoped I'd stick around and help, too."

He snorted. "Obviously."

"You left me," I said, annoyed at his flippant tone. "You know why I'm mad at you, right? You left me to deal with the faeries' bullshit on my own. If this necromancer ability of mine hadn't shown up when it did, I'd be dead."

"How in hell is that *my* fault?" he wanted to know.

"Look, even if you discount the fact that I've had to save you from certain death since you came here, our family's being targeted by more than Hazel can deal with." I swallowed. "You—I get that you didn't know any of that. But you used to have my back, Morgan, and you left me alone for eight sodding years. You can't expect me to forget that."

"Guess not." He paused. "I really don't have anything to report. You know what I've been doing. Running into trouble. Running away. Same old."

"When did the voices start?" I asked him.

"When did I ever say they stopped?"

I lowered the book. "You said you were being haunted for a few weeks. Are you telling me this isn't the first time you've heard voices?"

He shrugged. "Mum wouldn't listen and said I was talking crap. Hazel didn't give two shits and you spent all your time tailing the two of them around. So…"

"You've seriously been hearing ghosts your whole life?"

He shrugged again. "Yeah. What I said."

"I would have believed you. We lived in the Sidhe's property next to a village full of supernaturals. *Not* having magic is unusual."

"It's done now."

"No, it isn't," I said. "Not if you're hearing murderous ghosts."

"They're not murderous, just creepy," he said. "I can't always hear what they're saying. It's more... odd words, occasionally, and flashes of images."

"I'm gonna ask the necromancers," I said. "This is way out of my area, but you really should have told someone."

"Mum thought I was just trying to get attention," he muttered.

I winced. He might well be telling the truth. Considering all the other stunts he'd pulled to draw her away from Hazel and her Gatekeeping responsibilities, though, no wonder she hadn't listened.

"Do you actually have any spare clothes with you?" I asked. "Because if you want to make a good impression on the necromancers, you might want to try not dressing like a vagrant."

He looked down at his ragged clothes with an expression of vague confusion, and climbed to his feet. At least he'd sobered up, but how'd he gone for years hearing ghostly voices and never thought to consult a necromancer? Telepathy might not be an option, but it didn't sound like he was reading minds. Not of the living, anyway.

What in hell is wrong with our family?

9

At nine, Morgan and I left for the guild. While I wore my cloak, he'd pulled out a spare outfit identical to the one he'd already been wearing, only cleaner. Hardly worse than what I'd been wearing when I'd first been to the guild myself, so I didn't nag him. River messaged me saying he'd speak with Morgan while I took the exam I'd almost forgotten about. I also needed to speak to Lady Montgomery about last night's incident, but I'd deal with one crisis at a time.

"Last chance to change your mind," I told Morgan as we reached the high street. "I'll be in the shit if you refuse, but I'm fairly sure I am anyway."

He eyed the black-cloaked figures approaching the guild. "Nah, I'll go ahead with it. Not like I had other plans today."

"Sure." I hadn't really expected an apology, but it'd have been nice to have some acknowledgement of how much of a shit show he'd managed to turn my life into in the space of two days. Between him and Hazel, it was no wonder I'd had trouble making and keeping friends when we'd been kids. I spotted River speaking to two other necromancers I didn't know, and walked over to him.

"Hey," River said, nodding to Morgan. "Ilsa, Lady Montgomery is busy, so she'll speak to you after you're done with the test. The council have offered to take your circumstances into account and postpone it, if you'd prefer."

I shook my head. "I'll get it over with. What about Morgan?"

"These two have generously offered to do some introductory tests to determine if he has necromantic powers or not."

Okay. I took a deep breath and nodded. "Sure. Talk to you later, Morgan."

He merely grunted in response, looking around the entrance hall as though suddenly regretting his decision. No ghosts or undead could follow him in here, so any trouble he got into was entirely his own fault.

It was a wonder I managed to focus enough to answer all the questions on the test, but I'd read enough of the handbook to easily be able to write detailed answers. The moderator was nice enough to let me leave early, but Lady Montgomery put a wrench in my plans to sneak off and check on Morgan by waylaying me outside the testing room door.

"Er—hi," I said. "Is my brother around?"

"He's still undergoing testing, but he shows clear signs of being a psychic sensitive."

I stared at her. "A… psychic?" I asked. "You mean, like a telepath or something similar?"

"Similar, but rare," she said. "He seems to be able to pick up on any ghosts in the vicinity and hear their thoughts. If he's psychically sensitive, it might be that the voice he heard wasn't anywhere near him."

"Oh." That made a lot of sense. "But—where was it? I guess he doesn't have the spirit sight."

"Not so far, but he can definitely sense spirits."

"He picked up on the creature at the cemetery yesterday," I said. "I think he did, anyway. And he says he's been hearing one ghost fairly consistently all the way from Oban. I didn't know ghosts could travel long distances, but if it's been in the same place the whole time…"

"Very few ghosts would be able to project their thoughts over such a long distance," she said. "I'd be inclined to say he was mistaken, but he definitely has potential. I think the spirit sight might come naturally to him with a little encouragement."

"What—you want to train him as a necromancer?"

"Personally? No. Some of the others feel differently."

They do? Wow. I hadn't given him enough credit, apparently. "I didn't know you could encourage necromantic talent if it isn't already there."

"Oh, it's there, all right," she said, sounding less than thrilled at the idea. I didn't blame her in the slightest. But who knew, maybe being a necromancer-in-training would encourage Morgan to get his life back on track. "Considering he's already been targeted, this might be the safest place for him."

I couldn't argue there. "Sure. Is there anything else you need me to do today?"

"River will come and find you later for training, but you're free until the exam period finishes."

I'd finished half an hour early, so I went in search of the archives. There, I found Jas sitting at a table filling out a form. "Hey," she said. "I'm working on a report. Are you looking for anything in particular in here?"

"I'm looking for someone who might have worked for this guild," I said. "Several someones. Is there anyone on record with the surname Lynn?"

She frowned. "Not that I'm aware of. I was asked to look into the name after you signed up."

Lady Montgomery really covered the bases, huh. So Jas hadn't been assigned to me by accident—Lady Montgomery had probably asked her to report everything I said and did, on the off-chance that my actions threatened the guild or the safety of the city.

"Take it you didn't find anything incriminating?" I asked.

"No," she said, tapping her pen on the table. "You're off the charts for a hybrid, but that's not so unusual."

"It isn't?" I'd thought River was an exception.

"Very few of us have two necromancer parents," she said. "The spirit sight can stay dormant for generations. Tons of humans in the old world had the ability with no clue about it, since the veil wasn't always this screwed up. So most of us are hybrids in that sense."

"Are you?" I asked.

"Sure I am. I'm more witch than necromancer, but I was a magical dud." Her mouth turned down at the corners again. "So no coven would take me. I'm like, an *eighth* necromancer, but my spirit sight registers higher than my ability to use magic. So here I am, volunteering in the archives to stay on Lady Montgomery's good side."

"You're her assistant?"

"On a temporary basis. I've been at the same level for a while." She put down the pen. "I didn't meant to offload on you… is there anything else you're looking for?"

"On the subject of hybrids," I said, "are there any necromancers with faerie ancestry on record? Aside from current guild members."

"That's not something we keep track of, since as I said, it doesn't really mean anything," she said. "Is this about that creature?"

I nodded. "There were two necromancers I ran into lately

who broke the law in a major way. They're dead, but they had the same abilities as the person who summoned that creature which attacked us. Only faeries have that ability, but I assumed they had formal training from somewhere. But they might have used aliases. They could use glamour, too."

"We don't track our member's secondary talents. Generally half-mages or half-witches favour their other magical side over ours. And half-faeries, too."

I'd suspected as much. Maybe this wasn't where I should be looking, but there were hundreds of half-faeries in the city, and surely a portion of them had necromantic talents. River wasn't *that* unusual.

Looked like I needed to start somewhere else if I wanted to track the culprit. Part of the issue with ghosts was that usual tracking methods didn't work on them. And since the book refused to tell me *how* people summoned wraiths, except that it involved evil magic, I didn't have a clue where to start looking.

"Is there anything else I can do for you?" she asked.

"I don't suppose you have any books on the faerie ghosts? River can't be the only person who knows about them. Sluaghs, wraiths... that type of thing."

"That'll be confidential. I believe Lady Montgomery keeps those in her office."

Typical. "Thanks anyway," I said, resigned, and left the archive room. Maybe I was better off using the book and hoping the gates of death didn't swallow up everyone around me...

"Hey," said River, stepping out in front of me. "Lady Montgomery sent me to find you. I have a free hour for training. Is there anything you'd like to work on?"

"For a start, is there anything on my current skill level which might help me find out which ghost is screwing with my brother?"

"Not if the ghost isn't close by. Thanks to the iron within these walls, it can't bother him here. I've been talking to Lady Montgomery about the situation and it might be best for him to stay here for the time being. You said he tried to walk outside last night…"

"Yeah, he unlatched the door while sleepwalking on the orders of a deranged ghost," I said, smothering a sigh. "I can't watch him twenty-four seven, but I don't see how I'm supposed to track this thing when it might be hidden. I guess I'm never going to develop a similar ability?"

He shook his head. "If you were, it would already have happened."

"I just don't see who would try and target my brother. They don't need to torment him to get at me either, considering I'm just as easy to find."

A thoughtful look came over his face. "Did Morgan tell you whether he chose to unlock the door of his own accord or not?"

"What—you think he's possessed?"

"No, he wouldn't have been able to get in here if he was. Also, no spirit can possess a person for longer than few seconds without requiring a major energy surge. If I had to guess, the spirit influencing him has some sort of psychic element of its own."

"It," I said. "You mean, not human. Don't tell me there are evil psychic Vale faeries on top of everything else."

"Psychic abilities are even rarer amongst faeries than humans, if they exist at all. But it's possible someone, or something, has picked up on his talent and is exploiting it. I'll have to look into the matter further."

"It'd help if he could remember what it actually said to him," I said. "All he said is that it's been bugging him for a week."

"We can ask him later," he said. "For now—I'm supposed

to be training you in necromancer skills. Is there anything in particular you want to cover, or do you feel like you have all the basics down? If you'd prefer, I could teach you how to fight with a sword. We have a training room here."

"No thanks." I said. "I think I'll stick with the necromancy. I have binding and banishing spirits down... what about summoning them? We haven't covered that yet."

"It's fairly straightforward. I'm afraid we're going to have to go to one of the testing rooms again."

"It's cool." *It's also quiet.* Not that the freezing, haunted room was a particularly appropriate place for romantic trysts, but I'd take what alone time with River I could get. And if I could summon ghosts, maybe I could do the same for the creature haunting my brother.

We left the room and walked down the corridor, thankfully going into a different room to the one with the ghost of the old man inside it. This one was actually lit with artificial lighting, with a circle of candles in the centre. Still bloody cold, though. I found myself moving closer to River for warmth.

"So I can summon anyone here? Any necromancer or ghost?" I asked.

"No, just Guardians. Otherwise the spirit must be present within the city. I don't know the precise range, but it's only a few miles. And they must be recently dead. Even then, they usually don't appear for long. The necromancers who specialise in helping to solve murder cases or summon deceased relatives to resolve family disputes generally find it easier to take their own props closer to the scene of death."

"Makes sense. Wait, can I summon old Greaves from here?"

"Yes, you can. You know his name, that's enough. I think you should read the actual text this time rather than copying the book."

"Knew I wouldn't be able to get away with cheating forever." I opened the necromancy handbook, and felt the talisman move slightly in my pocket, perhaps in protest at my ignoring it.

"I wouldn't say it counts as cheating considering your position as Gatekeeper," he said. "But I think it's wise to learn the text as backup."

In case I lose the book? At the thought, coldness trailed down my spine. Okay, that thing had way too much influence over me even when I wasn't touching it. I ignored the book and read over the text in the necromancy guide instead.

"The necromancer language isn't an actual language, is it?" I said. "It sort of reads like Latin crossed with Scots Gaelic, but it's pronounced like modern English. Did someone make it up?"

"You caught us," River said, with a slight smile. "It's not the words so much as the intention. Some of our older Guardians insist on using actual Latin with the proper pronunciation, but considering none of them actually spoke the language while they were still alive, I'm convinced they were just trying to mess with the new recruits."

"Because it makes you look sophisticated and cultured, until you meet someone who's actually fluent in Latin. I haven't learnt Gaelic since I was in school, but I'm pretty sure this isn't it either."

"No. You can try switching the words out, but you have to learn it the proper way to pass your exams."

"Figures." I faced the circle, feeling oddly self-conscious with River watching me. The talisman's persistent tapping sensation in my head didn't help. I read from the page, River occasionally correcting my pronunciation. He was a patient teacher, more so than I'd expected. When the older Mr Greaves actually appeared, I jumped.

"You," he said. "This place looks familiar."

"Edinburgh Necromancer Guild," I said. "Sorry I uprooted you."

"The guild? So you're making use of your talents after all. I sensed so little disturbance back in the spirit world in Foxwood, I thought you'd retired from your troublemaking ways."

"So nothing's happened back there?" I asked. Hazel hadn't mentioned any new incidents, suggesting Holly was keeping her distance.

"Nothing you'd find reason to return for. It's been dull, if anything. Is there any reason you called me here?"

"Just to check up on the village," I said. "And see who I could summon from here. I wondered—is there a way to track one particular spirit? Like a tracking spell, but for the dead?"

"Normally? No. As Gatekeeper… perhaps there is."

"The book won't tell me," I said. "I think it's fixed so it only shows me skills of my own level, and it's reverted me back to the basics. Better than blank pages, but not particularly helpful right now."

"Careful, Gatekeeper. The power you hold is beyond most people. If misapplied, it could destroy you."

"I know." I wouldn't forget holding the gates of Death open, seconds from being sucked into the void. "But if I don't use this power, people get hurt. Most people can't even see wraiths, much less kill them. And even I can't detect them until they're on top of me."

"I may be able to assist with that," he said. "Do you have a spirit sensor?"

"We do," I said.

"They're usually about ten percent accurate," River said.

"I didn't know that," I said. "That's… not helpful."

"Spirits aren't easy to track," said old Mr Greaves. "But I see no reason why the sensor wouldn't pick up on wraiths as well. As an added bonus, it works as an exterminator on ghosts."

"Okay," I said. "I suppose it's better than—"

A shout came from outside. Alarmed, I stepped away from the circle, and the lights went out, plunging us into darkness.

River swore. "We're under attack. Something slipped through the defences."

"How?" *Please say Morgan wasn't involved.*

Feeling my way to the door with my hand, I pushed it open. In the corridor, lights flickered on and off and a bitterly cold breeze raised the hair on my arms. I tapped into my spirit sight, but the glowing tangle of necromancers' spirits coupled with paler lights that presumably belonged to resident ghosts made it all but impossible to pinpoint anything out of place in the spirit world.

River took off down the corridor, stopping at the weapons room, where I took my chance to grab a spirit sensor as well as an iron knife.

"I'm not the only faerie here," he said. "And I think one of them might just have been unmasked."

"What—how?"

I tapped into the spirit sight again as we ran, scanning for anyone familiar. My senses honed in one particular spirit, which kept flickering from bright to pale, from living to dead.

Jas… she was dying.

What the hell attacked her?

Gripping the spirit sensor, I ran after River into the lobby. There, necromancers ran around in a panic, while Jas lay in a pool of blood, a horrified-looking Lloyd crouched over her.

"It's my fault," said Lloyd, faintly. "Jas told me what you said, Ilsa—about faeries being able to use glamour, and we caught someone stealing from the archives. When we chased them, they transformed…"

Morgan ran up to me, looking panicked. "What's going on?"

"Rogue faerie, loose in here," I said. "It shouldn't be able to hide with so much iron around. How'd it even get in?"

"Faeries can bypass iron wards as long as it's possible to walk past without touching them." River looked down at Jas with a horrified expression. "I should have foreseen this."

"It's not your fault. I put the idea into their heads and now she's—" My breath choked. "I have to fix this."

I switched on my spirit sense, drawing on all the book's power, searching for any intruder.

Morgan yelled and dropped to his knees. "Stop that!" he yelped.

I switched off my spirit sight. "What is it?"

"You're fucking *loud*, Ilsa."

I stared at him. "Did you just read my thoughts?"

"It sure sounded like you." He blinked. "Wait. That noise I heard before…" He stared into space for a moment.

"Wait—can you read the thoughts of the intruder?" I asked. "A faerie, hiding… looking for a way to sneak out without being caught? Or attacking someone?"

He kept staring. Then words tore from his mouth—"*Meet your end, Gatekeeper.*" He fell back to the floor, writhing and convulsing.

"Shit!" I yelled. "Someone help him."

River grabbed Morgan's shoulders to steady him, but Morgan pulled himself free, groaning. "Ow…" He squeezed his eyes shut. "You—it's upstairs…"

"Upstairs? Where?"

He slumped back onto the floor. "It's like… a library."

"The library," said River, backing away. "There's a window up there the enemy might use to escape."

I ran after him, ignoring the others' shouts. I'd been too preoccupied with Morgan to notice we'd drawn a crowd. But I didn't dare stop. If the creature knew Morgan had noticed it, it'd disappear, or worse, attack someone else.

"Where's the library?" I asked River.

"First door ahead," he said over his shoulder. I hadn't a hope of keeping up with a half-faerie, but I kept moving, switching my spirit sight on the instant we reached the top of the stairs. Greyness overlaid everything, and within it…

"Sluagh," I muttered. "I think. Some form of shapeshifter. Definitely fae."

"No doubt." River kept up the pace, heading down unfamiliar corridors. I gripped my iron knife and spirit sensor, which went off with a loud beep. *Bit late for that.*

A large room lined with bookshelves greeted us, and within, a shimmering in the air indicated a faerie glamour. A powerful one. I narrowed my eyes, tapping into the book's power, and threw iron filings at the shimmering light.

The light split open, growing into the form of a giant shaggy beast. My hands glowed white, and the beast cringed away.

"How did you pretend to be human?" I snarled at it. "Who are you working for?"

"I can answer that," said a soft voice, and a figure stepped out from behind the shelf. He was tall, with pointed ears and silver hair, and cold blue light flooded his hands. "That ability of yours is somewhat inconvenient, Gatekeeper."

Winter magic streamed from his hands, icy cold, aimed at River.

10

I jumped in the way of the faerie's attack, but collided with the sluagh's huge dog-like body. Teeth clamped down on my arm, and the iron slid from my grip. *Ow.*

My sight flickered and greyness folded in. Three bright lights shone within the spirit world— River, grappling with the other half-faerie, and a horrible clawed thing trapped within the light. So that's what a sluagh looked like without its shapeshifter form. Grotesque, trapped between life and death. I blinked away the greyness, hitting the spirit sensor with my left hand. A white mass exploded from its end, striking the sluagh. It recoiled, screeching, but didn't disappear. *Concentrated salt isn't enough, huh.* I grabbed my knife instead, white-hot bolts of pain making my eyes water. My right arm hung limply at my side. *Not good.*

I stabbed, but my hand sailed right through it. Bloody creature had turned transparent again. Swearing, I slipped out of my body, and the pain faded away. Both my hands worked just fine as a ghost. The beast yowled in surprise as I dived at it and dug my fingers into its fur, but its spirit remained stubbornly attached to its body.

I let go, floating out of reach. As it registered that my body was undefended, the beast's attention slipped, and I crashed back into my body, lunging forwards. This time, my knife sank into its skull. The beast sank to its front, turning transparent, evaporating into wisps of smoke. The knife came free in my hand, and a fresh wave of pain shook my right arm.

Close by, River had managed to pin down the other faerie, both of them bleeding. As I watched, River slammed the heel of his palm into the faerie's temple. His eyes rolled back in his skull and he collapsed. Gripping him with one hand, River hauled him to his feet. Blood dripped down his arm and face. "Bastard," he said through clenched teeth. His face paled at the sight of my bleeding arm. "Shit. Hang on."

"Can't do much else." I staggered to my feet, swaying a little. "Tell me sluagh bites aren't as lethal as hellhound ones."

"It bit you?" He tightened his grip on the faerie. "Can you walk?"

"Yeah. Ow." My whole arm flared up with pain. "Got any healing spells handy?"

"Not on me, no. I should have brought my sword."

At that moment, Lady Montgomery rushed into the room. "What in damnation is going on?"

"We caught the trespasser," River said, indicating the half-faerie. "Ilsa is injured. This guy needs to be locked up and interrogated."

"I'll take care of that," she said coldly. "You take Ilsa to the infirmary. How did you know he was here?"

"My brother picked up on him. Psychically." I swayed, and River caught my non-injured arm. "Can I witness the interrogation?"

"Not until that arm's taken care of," River said, steering me away. Tension was palpable in his whole body, but it wasn't until we were downstairs that he put an arm properly around me for balance. "You shouldn't have gone up against that thing alone."

"I could say the same to you. Where's your talisman, anyway?"

"Stored upstairs," he answered. "I don't carry the blade here, unless I'm patrolling."

"I thought you had to carry it everywhere."

"Not in this realm," he said. "Most Sidhe never leave theirs behind, but they don't see an unsheathed weapon as a threat the way humans would if I carried it everywhere here. There's too much iron to glamour the blade all the time, and this building is supposed to be safe."

"I'm just surprised you can leave it behind. Talismans contain the essence of your magic… right?"

"In effect, yes. If anyone tried to steal it, things would end unpleasantly for them. Touching a talisman with the intent to claim it issues a challenge, and invites the talisman to test you. If you lose, you die."

That snapped me back to alertness. "Wait—are you saying that if I hadn't been judged worthy, the book would have *killed* me?"

"I suspect not, because it's not a usual talisman. It's in your family. I doubt they'd have wanted their descendants to meet an untimely death."

"Holly wanted it," I said. "She didn't try to take it… nobody has. Maybe that's why. They know it'll destroy them."

"Perhaps." We reached an open door, where Lloyd and several others sat in what appeared to be a waiting room.

"Hey, Ilsa." Lloyd waved at me. "Jas is recovering, but they got to her just in time… what happened to your arm?"

"Got bitten by a faerie creature." I sank into an empty chair, wincing as pain jarred my injured arm. I bloody hoped it wasn't venomous, because my family's shield only worked on magic.

River crossed the room and knocked sharply on a door at the back. "Ilsa needs medical attention immediately."

"Looks like you need it yourself," said Lloyd.

"It's just a scratch," River said. His cloak was torn and his hands bloody, but he had healing magic, like some half-Sidhe did.

"Suppose he has faerie superpowers," Lloyd said. "Like that thief. He knocked Jas down before I could even blink."

A nurse handed River a witch spell and he walked over to me. "Sluagh bites aren't deadly, so you'll be fine once you use the spell."

I turned the witch charm over in my hands. Like Agnes's charms, it was shaped like a bracelet, but made out of beads. I slid the bracelet onto my limp wrist and turned it once. Sensation came back to my wounded arm, and I sighed in relief. Another perk to working with the necromancers: they must have access to a local coven's supplies of handmade witch charms. Having a witch housemate who sometimes accidentally turned people green was no substitute for the real thing, especially tricky and expensive healing spells.

River examined the wound through my torn sleeve. "Do you feel all right now?"

I nodded, getting to my feet. Normally I'd be completely okay with his fingers running over my arm, but not with several layers of cloak in the way and a dozen curious onlookers. "Do you need a healing spell? He cut you."

"Minor wounds. He was carrying a knife, but I disarmed him."

"Good. I need to find Morgan."

I walked out of the room, River just behind me. "Your brother wasn't hurt," he said.

"No..." But the way he'd collapsed when he'd heard me,

through the spirit realm, made me uneasy. I didn't have psychic abilities. So could he sense anyone at any time? He'd tracked the faerie intruder… "What'll happen to that faerie?"

"He'll be interrogated, and if necessary, executed. It depends if he wakes up after I hit him. I'm not used to holding back."

"Ah. Well, if he dies, you can talk to him as a spirit, right?"

"In theory." He paused. "I'm glad you're okay."

"Me, too, believe me. I've had enough time as a ghost to know I don't want to make it permanent anytime soon." I looked at my newly healed arm and realised I was still holding the spirit sensor. I slipped it into my pocket. After all, I might need it later.

"I'm going to get my talisman," he said, climbing the nearest staircase. "I won't make the mistake of leaving it behind again."

He led the way to a locker room I hadn't seen before, down the corridor from more training rooms and what looked like a full gymnasium.

"Nice," I said. "They really pulled out all the stops in this place."

"I wasn't joking about giving you swordplay lessons," River said. "You're accomplished enough at using your necromantic power aggressively, but it wouldn't hurt to know how to counter enemies like that faerie."

I shrugged. "Regular swords can't hurt faerie ghosts like your talisman can."

River pulled the talisman itself out of a locker, running his fingertips along the hilt. I recognised the unconscious motion from the way my own talisman demanded attention, but all my mind could conjure were images of those strong hands on my bare skin. *Okay, that's enough, Ilsa.*

"Are you ever going to tell me how you got it?" I asked.

"It was a gift," River said. "What's your aversion to

fighting with swords? You're competent enough with knives."

"Have you seen me?" I waved my newly healed arm. "I'm not exactly a faerie, let's put it that way."

He frowned. "Neither are most of the people in this building. Faeries aren't born with the ability to fight with blades, either. I learnt here."

Hmm. I'd be a fool to turn down any opportunity to spend more time with River. "I'll consider it."

"I'm told that I'm a good teacher." River sheathed the blade, and slipped off his necromancer coat. Underneath, his arm was streaked with blood, but no wounds remained. His black T-shirt and jeans were human-style and shouldn't have looked as good on him as they did, but that was faeries for you. He saw me looking and grinned. "See something you like?"

"You really want me to answer that? I don't think you need another ego boost, Mr 'nobody can execute people like I can'."

He put the sword down and stepped closer to me, close enough for the scent of his magic to overpower the lingering smell of blood and iron from the fight. A curl of golden hair fell into his eye and I suppressed the urge to brush it out of the way.

River leaned in closer, and I forgot to breathe. His mouth came down on mine, soft and warm. My lips parted underneath his, inviting him in. I'd been right—this was a million times better as a living person, not a ghost. I wouldn't be able to feel his warm body close to mine, or smell the earthy scent of his magic. Desire sparked in my core as the kiss deepened, his hands resting on my waist. My own hands moved to his bare arms, feeling the corded strength beneath the skin. He exhaled and stepped back.

"Sorry," he said. "I'm the one who said to play it safe. I shouldn't have done that."

"Do you regret it?" I knew from the heat in his eyes that he didn't, and he didn't back away when I pressed my lips to his again. I shivered as his fingers brushed the back of my neck, slipping under my hair, steadying my mouth against his as I deepened the kiss, brazenly. I'd had enough of holding back. We'd both come within a whisper of death's touch, and I wouldn't let the opportunity slip away.

He groaned softly against my mouth. "Ilsa."

There was a buzzing noise.

He let go of me, both of us flushed and breathless, and pulled out his phone. "Interrogation's on. We need to go."

"Dammit."

We were definitely breaking the rules now, and I hardly cared. If I'd ever doubted he wanted me as much as I wanted him, seeing his faerie-bright eyes glowing with heat cured that notion.

"Later," he said, retrieving another black coat from the locker and slipping it on, strapping the sheathed blade to his waist. "If you keep looking at me like that, I'm not going to be able to concentrate on the interrogation."

"Serve you right for taking forever to get round to the point."

He smiled. "You mean staying in Faerie? If I'd known you missed me that much, I'd have brought you a present. Maybe those cursed faerie ballads, since you like books so much…"

"Don't you even think about it."

His grin turned wicked. "I'll have to think of something else."

Oh boy. I was in deep.

"So I take it the way to your heart isn't through private swordplay lessons?"

I'd take private lessons in almost anything else. "I wouldn't object to another coffee date."

"Tomorrow." He brushed his lips over mine. "Perhaps somewhere further from the guild. We can't sneak off together while we're here. There are rumours… since it was just the two of us who fought the intruder."

"They might think we're behind it. Honestly, I was kind of expecting that after what happened at the summit. Since the enemy apparently hasn't changed their strategy, I'll probably have a murder charge on my head next."

"Not if I have anything to do with it," he said firmly, leaning forward to brush his lips against mine again. "We'll finish this later."

"I'll hold you to that." I walked after him downstairs, the warmth of his embrace fading as we drew closer to the cold testing rooms. A number of cloaked necromancers had gathered there, and drew back as River and I walked through.

The faerie sat within a circle of candles, hands and feet cuffed, gaze slightly unfocused. He wasn't bleeding anymore. Maybe he had healing abilities. Healing magic was more common in Seelie faeries, but the magic he'd used had been unmistakably Winter. Still, whatever skills he had, nobody could leave a spirit circle. From my brief check of the spirit world, it wasn't just his hands that were bound, but his very soul.

"What's your real name?" River asked. The other necromancers moved to make room. Seven of them were gathered in the room, including Lady Montgomery.

"What's it to you?" said the faerie. He glared at Lady Montgomery, then screamed as though in horrible pain, his body convulsing on the spot. *Whoa. What's she doing to him?*

"Were you trained as a necromancer?" asked Lady Montgomery. "Records show you were only a member of the guild for a few weeks. If anyone trained you, I need to know who it is."

He groaned and shifted back into a sitting position, his body shaking. "No."

"Liar." Lady Montgomery stepped in close and he fell back, his head hitting the stone floor as his body shook with spasms.

"I—" he coughed, lifting his head from the stone floor. "I wasn't—not here."

"Were you trained in Faerie?" I asked, wishing I could question him alone.

He shook his head. *I didn't think so...* but either that faerie beast had already been here, or he'd brought it from the Vale himself. But if he already had the skills, why would he need the guild? Unless... he was working for someone else who'd sent him in as a spy. He was a half-faerie, and could lie even under duress.

Lady Montgomery said, "What was your purpose in joining the guild?"

"Information."

"Be more specific," she said sharply.

"Information on..." He choked on the words.

"He's under a faerie vow," I said suddenly, recognising the desperate terror on his face as his mind fought the bounds of the person who'd cursed him to keep their secrets to the point of death. "If he can't tell you the mission, the person employing him ensured it. Nothing can break a faerie vow."

"Except death," River said quietly. "Do you want me to?"

Lady Montgomery gave him a sideways look. "I'll handle it."

She produced a dagger and stabbed him in the chest. The faerie screamed, his body falling back—and his ghost came *out* of his body. There was a resounding *snap* through the spirit world, and the faint glow around his body died entirely.

Holy shit. Watching someone die as a necromancer was a hell of a trip. His body fell limply to the floor while his ghost floated above.

"Now you're dead, you're no longer bound to tell the truth," River said. "I'm surprised your master didn't think of that one."

"He did." The faerie smirked. "You're all fools. The fetch signals your demise, and she'll lay waste to this pathetic little organisation."

"You're still trapped," Lady Montgomery pointed out. "Who exactly is 'she'?"

He smiled, and evaporated into mist.

There was a long silence, in which everyone watched to see if he reappeared.

"He's gone," Lady Montgomery said, in a cold voice. "It seems he had one last trick up his sleeve."

"I should have known," said River. "The person he worked for plainly knows necromancy as well as they do faerie magic."

"He said 'she'," I said. "And—the fetch. Who is the fetch?"

"That should be, *what* is the fetch," River said grimly. "And it's bad news. According to faerie legend, the fetch is an omen of death… and they can only be heard by people whose own death is coming."

"Nonsense," said Lady Montgomery. "We deal in death here. Omens are meaningless to us."

"Then what was he trying to steal?" I asked.

"Case files," said Lady Montgomery. "From past clients."

"People the guild has helped," River explained. "People hire us to do all sorts of things. Which cases did he steal?"

"He was unsuccessful," Lady Montgomery said. "I'll deal

with the rest myself. You can leave. Ilsa, you should find your brother."

I nodded, but I couldn't get the image of the faerie's spirit being torn from his body out of my head. He'd been startled, but he truly didn't fear death at all. He'd been prepared for it.

"Maybe 'she' is Holly," I muttered to River as we left. "Using an intermediary, like those two other necromancers. I can't believe he duped us like that."

"Nor me." His mouth tightened. "We've lost our lead."

"What kind of case files might the thief have tried to steal?" I asked. "More to the point, why?"

"If I had to guess, it's because the enemy wanted to know how a particular case was handled so they can replicate it," said River. "Some of them involved dark magic. Others involved summonings, banishings, bindings... it might have been any of them."

"Damn," I said. "Are you worried about this... fetch? Seems a bad time to be ignoring faerie legends, especially ones involving omens of death."

"There's no guarantee he told the truth," River said. "The fetch is a rarity, and besides, she's right—we spend half our time in Death, technically speaking." His hand briefly touched mine. "I'll see you later, Ilsa."

What a day. I hadn't even got Morgan up to speed on current developments, but he'd tracked that ghost psychically without any training at all. His powers were off the charts, and he *did* have more experience than he'd let on. Heaven knew what else the rest of us had overlooked while we'd been living together.

One thing was certain—if the enemy found out what he'd done, he'd be a target, too. No disputing it this time.

The fetch signals your demise, and she'll lay waste to this pathetic little organisation.

11

I walked down the corridor, doubled back, realised I was lost, and walked in circles for a while until I found myself beside the infirmary again. Lloyd and Jas sat in the waiting room, and the former waved at me.

"I'm glad you're okay," I said to Jas, walking into the room. Most of the other chairs were vacant.

"Yeah. I got lucky. I just have to wait for some test results to make sure what he stabbed me with wasn't magical, and then I'm clear." She didn't sound thrilled at the idea. "He's dead, right? I heard he killed himself in the interrogation."

"Lady Montgomery killed him, but he was apparently prepared. He hopped through the gate before we could get him to tell us who he was working for. Where's Morgan, anyway?"

"I thought you knew he left," said Lloyd. "What do you mean, hopped through the gate? The faerie *wanted* to go to the afterlife?"

"Apparently. Morgan did *what?*"

"He got bored waiting for you to come out of interrogation and went home."

"Oh, for god's sake." I sighed. "He's going to get himself killed. You two—keep an eye out for trouble, okay? I'll be back."

I ran down the corridor, my head spinning. Why had Morgan taken off now? Maybe he'd thought the faerie was after him. Okay, so the attack had been unfortunate, but the iron in the building made it the safest place for him to be until we figured out our next move. Outside, he was entirely vulnerable.

I reached out with my spirit sight, catching sight of him two streets from the guild, and broke into a run. Necromancers stared as I bolted through the entrance hall, not slowing until I reached the street's corner.

"Morgan!" I shouted. "Get back here."

"Stop treating me like a kid."

"Maybe try acting like a rational person rather than storming around like angry spirits aren't looking to mount a psychic assault on you?"

He whirled around. "I suppose you know all about that, don't you? You don't tell me things and then get pissed off when I won't play by your rules."

"I said I was sorry I didn't tell you I'm a necromancer. I literally joined the guild two days ago, and to be perfectly honest, I didn't trust you. Was the testing really that bad, or are you leaving because of the faerie attack?"

"They said *you* killed them."

"Yeah, I did. One of them. Why?"

He looked me over. "You're still not telling me everything. The Ilsa I grew up with wouldn't kill a fly, and sure as hell didn't have necromantic magic. How do I know *you're* not spinning a glamour?"

"Because only the real me could piss you off this much. If you want me to tell you things, you could try not stealing, begging for money off your little sister, and disappearing for over eight years and making Mum and Hazel cry."

He blinked. "What—I made them cry?"

I shook my head. "Forget I said anything."

His attention sharpened. "You're serious. I didn't think they'd care I was gone."

"That's the problem. You don't *think* about the consequences of the stunts you pull. You're getting on my last nerve, if it wasn't obvious, and if you put your mind to it, you might actually be able to help the guild."

"And what exactly would they do for me?"

"Keep you alive," I said. "I wish I could do that, but I can't see what's following you and neither can you. But you said you couldn't hear the voice anymore when you were inside the guild headquarters, right?"

He shook his head. "No. What were you thinking of doing? Like an exorcism?"

"Possibly," I said. "I know literally nothing about psychic sensitives. I can't track what I can't see, unless you can give me a description of the person whose thoughts you can hear. You saw where that faerie was, didn't you?"

"Yeah. You're saying I was right?"

I rolled my eyes. "That's what I'm getting at. The reason River and I caught the guy is because you tracked the trespasser before he killed anyone else. It's a useful power. So can you do the same for the one who's been giving you grief for the last few days?"

His mouth hung open a little. "Uh. Yeah. She's standing right there."

I hit him in the arm. "Seriously."

"Okay, okay. Since I'm apparently *useful.*" He shook his head, and then stood and stared into space. "I think the guild might have scared it off."

"I hope that's true, but considering... I don't know if

going back to the house is a good idea. Won't you consider letting the guild help you?"

"I didn't get the impression they wanted me to stick around."

"They just got attacked. People nearly died, and now they have a dead prisoner to handle. I think they've had quite enough—" I broke off as he fell to his knees. "Morgan—what is it?" I looked around, spirit sight on, but didn't pick up on anyone aside from a few humans down the road. "Someone's speaking to you, right? Where are they? Can you tell me?"

He hit out and overbalanced, falling painfully to the pavement. "Whoa!" I grabbed his shoulders, trying to avoid his flailing arms. "Morgan, we're going back to the guild, okay?"

"You're not going anywhere, Gatekeeper," he hissed, in a voice that definitely wasn't his own.

"Who the hell are you? Get out of my brother's head." My spirit sight remained switched on, but only Morgan's spirit was present. He wasn't possessed. What the hell was the intruder doing—using him as a mouthpiece?

I grabbed his arms to hold him down, but he kept flailing, horrible laughter gargling from his throat. "Get *out!*" I snapped, feeling the book stir in my pocket. *Oh, now you want to get involved.* "Too much of a coward to face me in person?"

My brother lunged at me, knocking me off my feet. I kicked out, gripping the book, and drew on its power instinctively. Cold energy rushed to my palms and sent him reeling backwards.

I got to my feet. "Sorry about that. I—"

"Gatekeeper," he whispered, still in that creepy voice. "Thank you for your assistance."

Two undead walked out in front of me, glowing with wraithlike power.

Shit. The book had broadcasted our location.

I positioned myself in front of Morgan, hoping he didn't

attack me from behind again, and drew on the book's power. White light spun from my palms, slamming into the undead. They staggered, falling back, and I took the opportunity to throw salt down in front of us. The undead wouldn't be able to cross it, and I'd take them down before they got within an inch of Morgan.

The forms of the two wraiths hovered, black as pitch against the fog of the spirit realm. If they were full-powered, we were in a public location, and the guild was still recovering from the last attack. I didn't have time to call backup.

Better hope the book was on its best behaviour.

My hands glowed white, and I sent the charged burst of power at the wraiths. One of them was torn free of the undead body with a ripping noise, but the second vanished into the grey mist. Oh hell.

I spun around in time for it to grab Morgan from behind. He screamed as its cold hands latched onto his soul, and terror shone from his eyes. The bastard possessing him had withdrawn, leaving only Morgan behind.

"Let him go," I warned, my own hands glowing with power. "*Now.*"

I detached from my body and slammed into the wraith. It let go of Morgan, hissing in surprise, and I gripped its shimmering hands in mine. The image of the gates came to mind —wide, uncontrollable—but my brother's spirit was right there, and if I opened the gate, he might get sucked into it, too.

The wraith wrenched free from my grip and a cold blast of icy air hit me from the front. The first wraith advanced, back in the undead's body. Cold clammy hands pawed at me over the salt boundary. I kicked the undead's leg which gave way beneath it, and threw more salt, but the wraith continued, undeterred. The two of them had me caged in.

I gritted my teeth. Tapping into the spirit world again, I

pushed at the wraiths with all the power I could conjure, binding words flowing from my tongue. They recoiled, but didn't fade, or disappear beyond the gates. With no candles, the book would have to do. I took in a breath, and Morgan rose to his feet.

The wraith behind me fell back, a horrible keening noise tearing from its throat—if it had one. The second wraith stopped inches from hitting me, also screaming. *What the hell?*

I drew on the book's power again, white light exploding from both palms. This time, the wraiths disappeared in a flash of light. Morgan yelled again, dropping to his knees, clutching his head.

"Morgan!" Whoa. Whatever had been influencing him couldn't have attacked the wraiths. Somehow Morgan himself had. Could I get him to the guild from here? Unlikely. I grabbed my phone and dashed off a message to River, which I really should have done from the start, and crouched down beside Morgan. His gaze was unfocused, his hands hanging limply at his sides. "Morgan. Talk to me."

"Gate—keeper."

"Stop hurting him, you piece of shit." I grabbed Morgan's arms and tried to haul him to his feet, but he was surprisingly strong considering how scrawny he was. When he hit me in the face for the fourth time, I let go. Tapping into the spirit realm, I yelled at the glowing spot where my brother's soul was attached to his body—"Let go of him, you dickhead."

"How the hell are you talking to me like that?" he said.

"Wait, you know?" I squinted, and the greyness receded a little. Morgan stared at me—at my spirit, not my body below. And he wasn't flailing and screaming like his living body. "Can't you get back into your body and stop it doing that?"

"No. The noise won't stop. How are you here?"

"Necromancer trick. Morgan, I need you to calm down while I get you to the guild. That means getting your body under control. What's the spirit doing to you?"

"Screaming. All the time. I can even hear it here."

"Where did you learn to disconnect from your body?" I asked. "You're—you do realise only necromancers can do this, right?"

"I thought everyone could." He looked around at the grey smoke. "It's quiet here."

"It won't be where you're going. Really sorry about this." I grabbed his arms, and with the book's power, *pushed* him into his body. He yelled aloud, and the sound reverberated off the streets. Once I was sure it'd worked, I flew down into my own body again. He stood awkwardly, hand on his forehead. "Ow. I don't think I can shut it out for long."

"Then we'd better run. Race you to the guild, okay?" I said, like we were kids again.

"You have a fucking weird life. And you'd better tell me the truth this time."

"I will." I started walking in the direction of the guild, checking he was right behind me. I'd need to ask someone to move the undead from the road, but not until Morgan was safe. *Nobody attacks my family and gets away with it.*

Around the corner from the guild, River approached us from the opposite direction. "Ilsa!" he called, moving swiftly towards us. "Are you both okay?"

"I think so, but we need to get into the guild, asap. Whatever's haunting him really didn't like that we stopped them."

"Stopped who?" asked River.

"Wraiths," I said. "Two of them attacked us. Morgan… he used some sort of psychic ability to paralyse them so I could banish them."

He looked at Morgan. "Are you sure? How did you do it?"

Morgan shook his head, wincing. "I don't know. I was

trying to shut that *thing* out of my head, and I think I crashed into their minds, psychically, by accident."

"They just stopped," I said. "But it sounds like you used some sort of psychic attack on them."

"And you banished them," said Morgan. "You said you'd tell me the truth."

I glanced at River. "When we're alone, yes, but we need to get that spirit out of your head first. I've been told how to perform an exorcism…"

"Usually it only works if the person doing the possessing is right nearby," River said. "This spirit might be miles away, and it's not directly possessing him. We can't extract and trap something that's not present."

"But it can't get at him here," I said. "It also knows what I am."

River's mouth tightened. "Are you certain?"

I nodded. "Yeah. I used the book, when it was attacking Morgan, and it picked up on our location that way. But it couldn't attack me. I think it must be miles from here, using him as a proxy. I guess the defences on the guild must keep it out, whatever it is."

River opened the oak doors to the guild ahead of us. Morgan staggered into the lobby and leaned on the wall, groaning. "Ow."

"It's not still in your head, is it?" I asked, closing the door firmly behind me.

"No, but it's angry. What in hell is it?"

"I may have an idea," River said. "I looked into the possibility of what the intruder said being true, and—apparently, the fetch isn't only a death omen. They're minor fae, and there's evidence that some of them have latent psychic abilities."

A death omen. "Are you sure?"

River reached into his pocket and handed me a small

book. I flipped it open onto the bookmarked page, and the word *fetch* loomed out at me.

"An omen of death… and they can only be heard by people whose own death is coming," I read. "Well, that's not true, considering it sure wanted *me* to hear it as well… They will often encourage people to take their own lives to fulfil their own prophecies. Target those with spirit sensitivity. Rare creatures believed to originate in the faerie realms." I looked up at him. "Shit. Guess the iron in this place keeps it out. But why target him?"

"What the hell is a fetch?" said Morgan.

"It appears when you're going to die, apparently." Chills raced up my arms. "Which apparently doesn't mean much to necromancers." I looked back at the page, but there was no other information.

"I can't see it," he said. "It can't see me, either. You mean to say there's no cure?"

"I have an idea," said River. "You're not allergic to iron, right?"

"Obviously not. I'm not a faerie."

"Iron works as protection against faerie magic," River said. "The fetch's abilities fall into that category. So if you wear an iron charm, in theory, the voices should stop."

"Oh," I said. "I really should have thought of that."

"Right." River nodded. "We don't have witch spells of that type here, but they should be relatively easy to get hold of. For now, hold onto anything made of iron…"

"Those weapons?" asked Morgan.

"No," I said. "You'll probably end up injuring yourself. Here." I passed him my container of iron filings. "Keep hold of it. Is there anything else I need to do here?"

River shook his head. "The necromancers are running interrogations to see if anyone else was working with the intruder. The three of us are already cleared, don't worry."

"And—Morgan. Is it best if he stays here? We need to take that fetch out of the picture."

Morgan folded his arms. "Yeah, might be a bit difficult when nobody can see the damn thing. Don't I get a say in this?"

"You can come back to my house, but only if the iron is definitely working," I said.

"I'll speak to Lady Montgomery later," River said. "She's running the interrogations. Technically, I'm supposed to be helping her."

"Ah. Sorry I dragged you away."

"Don't be. Will you be okay finding a witch spell? We don't have any spare iron charms here, otherwise I'd loan you one."

Of course he wouldn't own any himself, being part faerie.

"Our housemate does custom spells," I said. "Or we'll go to the market. Should I come back later? Because that creature knows where the guild is…"

"A lot of enemies know where the guild is. It's a little difficult to ignore." He looked at Morgan. "Come back tomorrow. I'll find everything I can on fetches. Read the rest of that handbook, if you haven't already."

Morgan began to walk away as though he hadn't spoken.

"I'll watch him," I said. "See you later."

Morgan grunted. "What a total knob."

"Morgan," I said warningly. "River's been to a lot of trouble for our sakes."

Morgan gripped the iron container tightly. "Guess I'll ask Corwin. He runs a witch stall at the market."

I hope he's right. This was a temporary solution, I knew. But I wouldn't risk Morgan's life. He kept shooting me disgruntled looks all the way home whenever I not-so-subtly checked he wasn't possessed again. *You can hardly blame me for being jumpy.* My whole body ached from where he'd hit me and knocked me into the road, and when it began to rain heavily, blood dripped into my eyes from a cut underneath my hairline. I rubbed half-heartedly at it with my sleeve, wondering if the necromancers' coats weren't intended to hide bloodstains after all.

I tensed when the house came into view, seeing someone on the doorstep again. But I didn't need to tap into the spirit world to see the universe hadn't finished trampling on either of us for today.

Hazel stood there waiting for us, arms folded, fury in her eyes.

12

Hazel gave my brother a blistering stare. "So it's true. You're back."

"Oh," said Morgan. "Hi."

"Hey, Morgan," said Hazel, icily. "So nice of you to call and check up on me. Really appreciate it."

"Ah." Morgan shifted from one foot to the other. "Didn't know you were coming."

"That'd be because the phone number I have under your name is a few years out of date. When I tried calling it, I got a witch called MacDougal."

"Ah. Yeah. The witches stole my phone."

"The witches stole your phone," Hazel repeated. Anger brewed in the air, so heated that I expected the rainwater dripping from her hair to evaporate on the spot.

"I'm going to ask Corwin for a spell," I told them. "Meanwhile, you two can stand out in the rain and yell at one another, or come into the warmth and keep your tempers under control. I'm starving and bruised and entirely too many people have tried to kill me today."

"Bring me up to speed," said Hazel, shooting Morgan a look. "I'll behave if he does."

"Then try not to blow up the house." I unlocked the door. "I'm serious. This place isn't quite as sturdy as home. If you smash the furniture, it'll stay broken, and I'll have to deal with disgruntled housemates and angry rental companies. So please try not to damage anything."

I walked inside. A moment later, the others trailed after me, their glares searing the back of my neck. They needed a good screaming match to get it out of their systems, but that was on them, not me. I took off my necromancer coat and threw it over the back of the nearest chair in the kitchen, where Corwin had left spells strewn everywhere. I guessed he was working at the market today. I went to the corner where he kept his chalk circle supplies and found an iron charm.

"I brought food from the house, by the way," said Hazel.

"You did?" I looked back at her. "Good, because I don't have enough for three people."

"Thought not. Also, if you're as bad a cook as I remember, I don't want you poisoning us."

"Hey," I protested, handing the iron charm to Morgan. "Hope this doesn't turn you green, because it's all I've got."

Hazel put the bags down on the table, completely blanking Morgan. Good strategy, because I wanted my hands on the Lynn house's divine cooking and nothing else. Luckily, the others seemed to agree, and Hazel seemed more interested in Corwin's magical props.

"Watch the spells. They sometimes have unintended side effects," I warned her around a mouthful of pastry.

"Let me guess, Morgan touched them," Hazel said.

"Got it in one," I said, then swiftly changed the subject. I brought Hazel up to speed on my necromancer training, including my surprise at Lady Montgomery being River's mother.

"I'll bet Mum knows her," Hazel said. "She knows all the leading supernaturals who fought in the war."

"I didn't know any of this until I came here," I said. "I didn't know the necromancer guild's practically a fortress, or so… organised. Compared to Greaves's place anyway. Have they elected a new leader yet?"

"I think so, but they haven't come visiting. Pretty sure Greaves came back as a ghost and told them himself." She looked at Morgan, her expression guarded. "I take it you know all of this."

"I do now. Took her long enough to tell me."

"I'm not surprised," said Hazel. "I wouldn't go around shouting our secrets to someone who ran off eight years ago."

"She said you cried when I left."

Thanks, Morgan.

Hazel gave me an accusing stare. "Excuse me? If you remember, it was tears of joy that the scrounging bastard was finally out of our lives."

"Guys!" I said, before the situation devolved into a shouting match. "Okay, I wasn't expecting you to show up, Hazel. It's been a Week. With a capital W. People have tried to kill both of us. Several times. Also, Morgan has psychic powers."

That shut both of them up long enough to finish my explanation. When we were finally done, I prepared myself for an onslaught of questions.

Hazel spoke first. "So the two of you are like, honorary necromancers now?" Did she sound a little jealous? No way. It was only right that the pair of us got to have our turn in the spotlight.

"Not until I pass training," I said. "I'm junior level… if I ever get to sit any more exams without being interrupted. And Morgan went to the guild today so we could work out what his powers are. Turns out he's being psychically haunted by something, and the guild is the only place where it stops."

"So it's a faerie ghost?" asked Hazel.

"Fetch," I said. "For whatever reason, it's figured out he's a psychic and keeps tormenting him. And it's linked to whoever's summoning the wraiths, but the guy working for them got caught and died, so we're back to square one."

"Fetches." She swore under her breath. "I'll have to think… they're death omens, kind of like banshees. But instead of screaming when you're about to die, they just… show up."

"None of us actually saw the fetch. It spoke through someone else. Can they do that?"

"No clue," said Hazel. "Psychic stuff definitely isn't my area." Worry laced her tone. Despite her and Morgan's outward hostility, Hazel's main reason for embracing her role as the Summer Gatekeeper's heir was because she'd wanted to keep the rest of us safe. Ghosts and fetches alike were immune to her powers, putting this situation way out of her area.

"You want to stay here overnight?" I asked. "We're running an experiment where Morgan wears an iron spell to keep the fetch out. If it doesn't work, he'll have to stay at the guild. The other night, he ended up sleepwalking on the orders of a murderous ghost and wandered outside."

"Damn." Hazel shook her head. "Sure, I can stay. It's quiet at the house without you there."

"Is Arden around? He flew after me the other day."

"He comes and goes. I don't trust him enough to let him see anything important these days. None of the notes Mum left behind. He's still refusing to tell me where she is. I kind of hoped River would have given you an update."

"Nothing. If there's anything new, he can't say." I exhaled in a sigh. "Not sure I want to explain to her how I ended up joining the necromancers…"

"Let alone me," Morgan put in. "Thanks for telling me Mum's been kidnapped."

"I don't think she's been kidnapped," said Hazel. "She's just held up in Faerie. It happens a lot. You know that. Remember when she left for a month and we turned the garden into a fortress?"

Hazel hadn't brought up that memory since Morgan had gone, but I remembered clearly as though it'd happened yesterday. It'd been just after Hazel's Gatekeeper's power had manifested, and Hazel had used it to create a proper medieval castle in the back garden. It'd scared the crap out of Mum when she'd come back.

"She still left us to handle it alone," said Morgan. "Sounds about right."

"Look, you can take your grievances straight to her," I said. "I'm dealing the best I can. And so is Hazel. She's acting Gatekeeper, and I'm—"

"Some other kind of Gatekeeper."

I shrugged. "It's to do with the gates between the veil and Beyond. The afterlife. Specifically, faerie ghosts."

"And you mentioned a book? Can I see it?"

I hesitated, but I'd chosen to trust him. Pulling the book from my pocket, I held it up. At least it wasn't glowing.

"I wouldn't touch—" But of course he'd already snatched it from my hands, flipping through the pages.

"How much is this worth?"

"Several lives," I said.

"If you steal it," Hazel put in, "Grandma's ghost will appear and smite you."

"It's also cursed," I added. "And only works for the Gate-keeper. Hence the blank pages. Give it here."

I ended up having to tug it from his hands. Morgan's expression was a little glazed, and I hoped it was just the book's magic, not anything more sinister. He'd said the fetch's link to his head was one way… that it couldn't read his mind. And nobody could take the book, especially not a ghost. Still, I'd be sleeping with the damn thing under my pillow tonight.

"Also," I said, "its magic means that we can only discuss it within the family and people who already know. So it won't let you tell another soul. It took ages to figure out how to tell River. It's also been mostly blank until fairly recently, so I'm learning how to get it to tell me what I need to know. I wish it had more info on psychics and fetches, but I think its speciality is dark faeries."

"Fetches *are* dark faeries, though," said Hazel. "If it's been following Morgan, it must have been in this realm a while… I wish we could track it."

"Me too, but he can't hear its thoughts without getting a headache, and it damn near killed me earlier. We'll go to the necromancers in the morning and see if they have any more ideas."

"I thought they knew the Summer Gatekeeper here," said Hazel.

"They know *of* the Gatekeepers," I said. "Not necessarily the details. Lady Montgomery does, but that's because she's been poking around trying to learn as much as possible."

Her brows rose. "She knows about Aunt Candice?"

"She does. That's why she's reserving judgement on whether to trust us or not. But she doesn't know what I am, or about the book."

Nor how I might have drawn the enemy's attention by using its magic. It'd been risky enough to use it at the Winter estate, but the Ley Line went through Edinburgh, too. Maybe our enemy was counting on exactly that. The curse of the Gatekeeper was that I held all these lives in my hands, whether I acknowledged it or not. Not just the lives in this room.

Maybe the fetch hadn't come for Morgan at all.

———

Unsurprisingly, I didn't get much sleep that night. Hazel and Morgan kept bickering all evening, and while my housemates tolerated the arrival of a new Lynn, the peace lasted up until she brought out a bottle of elf wine. Within an hour, Hazel and Morgan were metaphorically off their faces and literally at one another's throats.

As for me, I woke with a raging headache at five in the morning to a bright light in the corner of my eye. I turned over, seeing the book glowing under my pillow. "Stop it," I mumbled. My mouth tasted like I'd washed it out with swamp water, and my head pounded with the drumming insistence of an oncoming hangover. I squeezed my eyes closed against the glare, but the book, if anything, grew brighter. "What?"

The bedroom door rattled, and my throat went dry. *Intruder.* Even my spirit sight was fuzzy, but there was definitely something outside the door that shouldn't be.

Crap. What is it now?

Hazel lay on my floor on the spare mattress I'd borrowed from one of the others, dead to the world. Grabbing a knife and some salt as well as the book, I crept past, opened the door, and paused. Shadows trailed up the staircase. Not regular shadows, but solid-looking ones.

"Hazel!" I hissed. "Get a weapon. Now."

She woke up, mumbling in confusion. I backed up to the

door, trying to see through the shadowy haze. Death faeries… in the house. We had iron wards up. Someone must have turned them off.

I'd given Morgan my iron filings, so I used my knife, which passed straight through the shadows. My hands felt cold, clammy, and the temperature had plummeted overnight. Hazel crept out of the room behind me, her hands glowing with Summer magic along with the circlet on her head.

"Show yourself," I whispered to the shadows. "Go on." My Sight worked fine, so the creature must be trying really hard to hide itself. The shadows lengthened, creeping along the walls.

"Gatekeeper," a voice whispered.

"Which one of us?" Hazel asked. "You picked a fight with the wrong—"

The house trembled as though a heavy blow had struck it from the side. Morgan's shout came from downstairs.

Hazel threw Summer magic into the gloom, lighting the dark, and revealing a creature hanging upside-down from the ceiling by its suction-cup-covered, tentacle-like arms. It resembled a two-armed octopus, flesh-coloured and hideous. Its flat face was made entirely of a huge mouth, toothless and covered in barbs designed to snag its victim and rip their skin clean off. One of the Vale's nicest creatures.

"Your illusion skills are crap," I told it, stalking forwards, dagger in hand. Hazel's Summer magic wouldn't be as effective as usual, but iron worked as well as anything.

The walls rattled again. Shit. This guy was the diversion. And Morgan couldn't defend himself. Certainly not as well as Hazel or I could.

It let go with one arm and swiped, and I stabbed it. The iron cut through its fleshy arm and it wailed, letting go and dropping to the floor. Shadows extended behind it, revealing it wasn't alone, and another creature was behind the illusion. Death stealer. Three of those things had nearly killed Hazel and me a few weeks ago.

The skin-eating faerie lunged at me. If I let any part of my skin touch it, I was dead, so I flung the knife through its head instead. Dark blood splattered the hall, and the death stealer moved forwards into its place. *Damn.* I'd had no choice but to throw the knife, but now I was unarmed.

Shadows lunged at my heels, cold on my bare skin. I jumped backwards, dropping the salt canister but managing to keep hold of the book. Cold power leapt to my hands, drawn from the same darkness that powered this Vale creature. *You'll die before you hurt us.*

Hazel attacked. Her magical assault knocked the creature off the wall, right into the path of my necromantic magic. The beast screeched, burned all over by punishing white light, and exploded into nothingness.

"Nice," she said. "I haven't seen you do that before."

"I got a lot of practise."

A bone-chilling laugh came from below.

"Morgan." I ran for the stairs, taking them two at a time. "Get the hell out of here, faerie."

The wards must be down. One of us would have to go outside to switch them back on, but the attacker's laugh came from the living room. I kicked the door open. Discarded spell residue, ingredients, beer bottles… but nobody living.

"Did they take him?"

"No," growled a voice. Morgan jumped from behind the sofa. "Die, Gatekeeper."

A horrible cackling laugh came from my brother's throat. He was being possessed? I'd thought the fetch couldn't do that, let alone turn him into a faerie.

He lunged with blinding speed, his hand wrapping around Hazel's throat. *What*—no, his *ghost.* His transparent hand latched onto Hazel's neck, lifting her with inhuman strength.

"Morgan!" I held my knife up, left my body in a defensive position, and leapt out, straight at the ghostly figure strangling Hazel. In ghost form it was plain to see it wasn't him. The spirit *looked* like my brother, but when it turned on me, eyes glowing with eerie white light, the smile was a stranger's.

"Gatekeeper," purred the voice. Hazel screamed and flailed, but couldn't fight off a ghost. It was trying to rip her out of her body like a necromancer had once done to me.

"Let her go, you bastard." I grabbed the ghostly assailant's arm, wrenching it loose from Hazel. White light shone from my hands, and I willed the book's power to flow into me. My fist connected with the spirit's nose and it stumbled backwards, its appearance warping. Pointed ears. Smiling face. A... faerie? No. They couldn't die, not here. But half-faeries could.

"You can use glamour as a ghost?" I said in disbelief.

"I'll be able to do more with that book of yours," he said, grinning.

Horror filled my chest. Morgan's hands were on the book, held in my body's limp hands. If the monster possessing him used him to try to claim it—one of us might die.

I dived back into my body in time to wrench the book out of reach. Morgan fell forwards, his expression confused. "What—?"

"Oh good, you're back," said Hazel, her hands aglow. "What in hell is going on? Who attacked me?"

"Half-faerie ghost possessed him," I said. "Can you stop him from touching the book? Same goes for her."

I left them staring at one another in confusion and hopped into Death again. Grey smoke covered my vision, and the half-faerie faced me, his expression laced with fury. "You bitch."

"Sorry I ruined your schemes." I blasted him off his feet with necromantic energy, then grabbed him by the throat. "Tell me who you're working for. What the hell does this fetch want with me and my brother?" Except the book, but that went without saying. Who wouldn't want control over life and death, especially a faerie? Any of them might be behind it.

He flailed, struggling against my grip, and a fresh boost of power sprang to my palm. The half-faerie went limp, his ghostly form evaporating into ashes.

"Ah, shit." I dropped back into my body, looking down at the book. "You couldn't have let him talk before you blew his head off?"

Hazel and Morgan both stared at me.

"What?" I said. Ow. My headache was back. Yet another bonus of being a ghost—no hangovers.

"You're kind of scary, Ilsa," Hazel commented.

Morgan grunted in agreement. "What the hell's going on?"

"You were possessed by a half-faerie ghost," I told him. "Possibly on the fetch's orders. It wanted the book. Which is a faerie talisman, so if you'd tried to claim it, you'd have died a horrible death."

He sank to the floor, pale as a ghost himself. "What...?"

"I didn't know that," said Hazel.

"River told me that's how talismans work. If someone intends to claim it, the talisman... senses it, I guess, and if it doesn't think the person is worthy to wield it... they die. No idea if the same applies to this one, but if anything tries to make you take the book again—" I broke off. Morgan had covered his face with his hands, hunched behind the sofa. Thinking back to some of the irrational stunts he'd pulled as a teenager… maybe he hadn't been as in control of his decisions as I'd thought.

Hazel looked at me helplessly as though completely unsure how to handle the situation. *Join the club.*

"I'm going out to switch the wards back on," I told them. "Someone turned them off—that's how the ghost got in. Also, that iron spell must be a dud. So get a genuine one."

Once I'd switched the wards back on, I sent a message to River. I thought it was too early in the morning for him to be awake, but I got a response right away—*your brother should stay at the guild tonight.*

No kidding. I walked back into the living room to find Morgan hunched on the armchair, while Hazel stood by the boiling kettle, probably making coffee. "Guys, it's looking likely that we'll have to relocate to the guild tonight, unless we find a way to get rid of that fetch."

"It didn't show up in person, did it?" said Hazel. "I couldn't see a thing. Just you two."

"No, but those half-faeries aren't average spirits. They're powerful enough to possess someone, and still retain all their magic beyond death. That's not something even most necromancers are equipped to handle."

"But we are," Hazel said. "If they can use magic, we're immune."

"We don't know who they're working for," I reminded her. "This fetch is the orchestrator, but hell if I know what the endgame is. It knows me… knows the Gatekeepers."

Why did the Gatekeeper part of me recognise the fetch, on some weird instinctual level? It sure as hell seemed to think it knew *me*. But I definitely hadn't seen it before, either in the spirit world or outside it.

"Another one of Great-Aunt Enid's nemeses?" Hazel said, pouring coffee. "Sounds like she had a fair few."

"Or she inherited them from the last Gatekeeper," I said.

"I'm writing all this down, you know, so the next Gatekeeper isn't taken by surprise."

"Good idea." She hesitantly approached Morgan, carrying the tray of coffee cups. "Hey. Morgan. Earth to Morgan. Want me to get you some painkillers?"

He grunted. She sighed and laid the coffee cup on the table next to him, then came and joined me on the sofa. "Elf wine hangovers are a bitch. Bet that's why your housemates are still passed out."

"Glad they are," I said. "I told them to expect weirdness from living with me, but faerie ghosts are a step too far."

"No kidding." She eyed Morgan. "The question is—which of us were they targeting?"

13

River met us outside the guild. Hazel had refused to stay behind, saying she wanted to confirm our story if we were questioned. From the way she watched Morgan's back on the walk to the guild, I'd guess she'd taken the attack personally.

"You weren't followed, were you?" His hood was pulled up against the rain, his expression wary.

"If we were, Hazel would have glared it to death," Morgan commented.

I elbowed him in the ribs. "Didn't we talk about not being a dick?"

"I don't see how this guy can help us," Morgan said, eyeing River. "It was a half-faerie who attacked us."

"As a ghost?" River asked, letting the insult slide. With Morgan, that was probably the best move if we actually wanted to get anywhere.

"Yeah, a ghost," I said. "With his magic intact. I'd guess the fetch, or someone else, talked Morgan into switching off the wards on the house. Two Vale monsters got in, too."

Corwin and Torrance had come out of their rooms while

I'd been cleaning up the mess, which had led to an awkward conversation. While Corwin seemed fine with Morgan staying there, Torrance hadn't looked too happy, though I'd kept the details vague so as not to freak them out. I didn't think ghosts would target my non-necromancer housemates, but keeping Morgan away seemed a smart move.

River frowned. "The fetch—I did look it up in more detail, and it seems their own abilities are fairly minor. It can only target psychic sensitives, and seems mostly unable to do any harm. That's likely why it attacked you using an intermediary."

"And it didn't know where I am," I added. "But now it does. It knows where the house is, too. I'm trying to think of a solution which doesn't involve using the others as bait, or luring it somewhere else."

"So it's a coward," Hazel said.

"And clever," I said. "It's been attacking Morgan from a distance for days now. So it might be anywhere."

"Not for long," said Morgan. "I don't mind being bait. I just want it gone."

"The easiest way is to lure it back to the house," I said. "It's that or move out, but the house has a target painted on it and innocent people might get hurt."

"Lure it there… and then what?" said Hazel.

"Trap it, for a start," I said. "Get the beast in a summoning circle, surrounded by candles. If it's not a ghost, it can be killed—permanently. I can do it, with or without the book. The house is empty now. We'll have one shot."

The others looked at me. Morgan nodded slowly. "Okay. We'll do it."

The guild was a downright ghost town. Apparently everyone had been interrogated to within an inch of their lives, then told they didn't have to show up today unless they were on the rota for patrolling or taking on cases from the public. That included Jas and Lloyd, who I found standing in a corner, not looking any worse for their narrow escape yesterday.

"Hey," I said. "Glad to see you're alive."

"Likewise." Lloyd looked at Hazel. "I didn't know you had a sister."

Hazel blinked, looking startled. "Er… yeah. That's me. I'm Hazel."

"And you're not a necromancer?" asked Lloyd. "What do you do?"

Hazel's expression said *seriously? Nobody knows who I am?* "Er, I'm Gatekeeper. That means I deal with matters connected to the Summer Court and its relationship with the mortal realm."

"Like River?" asked Jas.

"Not exactly. I'm human."

"Wow," she said. "Didn't know there were humans who went anywhere near Faerie."

"Lady Montgomery must have," said Lloyd. "If she got knocked up by a Sidhe—" He broke off. "Er, don't say that in front of either of them."

"That goes for you too," I hissed to Morgan, who looked intrigued at those words. "We aren't on the rota today, by the way," I added. "A ghost attacked us last night so we're gonna booby trap the house and lure it out."

"Really?" said Jas. "That must be why Lady Montgomery told me to give you this." She handed Morgan a solid grey bracelet. "Iron."

Morgan looked at it in confusion. "She's giving it to me?"

"Looks that way," I said. "Better than a spell. Go, on, take it."

Apparently his close encounter with the book had momentarily switched off his kleptomaniac tendencies. The iron band clipped into place on his arm, and his expression instantly cleared. "That's strong. I could knock a faerie out with this." He swung his arm, and nearly hit Hazel.

"Watch it," she said. "Maybe this isn't a good idea."

"Well, good luck," said Lloyd. "We should go arm ourselves if we're on patrol in half an hour."

"See you later," Jas said. She must have volunteered to patrol, because surely even Lady Montgomery wouldn't have forced her to after her near-death experience yesterday.

River walked up to us. "We have permission to borrow props, but Lady Montgomery expressed concern about you using yourselves as bait."

"You mean, me," Morgan said. "I'm the one who has a direct link to the fetch."

"That's why it's dangerous for you," I told him. "You can't go inside the house while the trap's active. It might send one of its friends to possess you again, or worse."

"I think you're both forgetting that I'm the only one who's ever sensed the damn thing," said Morgan. "You said I was *useful.* Now I can prove it. You know what I did against those creatures before, the psychic attack? I can try using it next time I hear the voice, to draw it in. Then one of you puts iron on me before it gets in my head again. It gets mad, runs right into our trap."

"It's not a bad idea," said Hazel.

"Except for the part where you willingly open yourself to a psychic assault from a fae monster who wants all of us dead?" I said.

"Well. There's that."

"One of us has to take the risk," said Hazel. "I know you're in self-sacrificing mode, Ilsa, but you're powerful. Too much so to use as bait. As for me, I'm not a necromancer. I have nothing to offer. This fetch is already attached to Morgan. It won't be able to resist. I don't like the idea, believe me, but it's probably going to try to attack him again. So we'll kill the bastard before it can."

I turned to Morgan. "Are you absolutely certain? Because if this decision is in the same category as 'let's steal and sell Mum's antique family heirlooms, I'm sure she'll never notice', then it's more than your neck on the line. It might use you to attack other people."

"Jesus, I get it, okay? I'll gladly jump in as bait if it gets that fucking thing to stop wailing in my head."

"If you're sure," I said. "Morgan, you wear the iron until you get to the house. Hazel… want to set the candles up? I'm not a hundred percent sure it doesn't sense the book, and if it does, our cover is blown."

"I'll set the candles up," River said. "If it can sense your thoughts, Morgan, you might not want to think about us following you."

"Good idea," I said. "Think about whatever irrelevant crap you like, just not that. Got it?"

He nodded. "Sure, I can think of nothing. I'm good at that."

Hazel snorted. "He's not wrong. Good luck, you two."

River took the lead, while Morgan followed behind. I looked at Hazel. "Go with River. I'll stay behind. If it can sense me, I won't take chances."

"Okay." She took in a steadying breath. "Let us know if there's a problem."

"Will do." I waited, already regretting letting them take off alone. I counted down thirty seconds, then followed.

The book hummed in my pocket, but thankfully decided to keep the glowing to a minimum. I didn't know how much of the world outside it picked up on—hell, for all I knew, it had psychic tendencies of its own—but it knew the fetch was searching for it, or at least for me. I waited, walking slowly as I dared, and reached the house after the door had closed. A light clicked on in the window—Morgan's signal. He'd take off the iron cuff when I was hidden. River and Hazel would have moved out of sight, but they'd be nearby, ready to move in and help if necessary.

I ducked behind the wall of the alley beside the house. I couldn't see the candles, so River must have hidden them well. Taking in a breath, I focused on counting seconds. *One. Two. Three.*

Morgan's strangled yell cut through the air, sharp and painful. I winced, hoping he was in control of the situation, not the fetch. Screaming at a monster until it attacked from sheer annoyance was a risky strategy. Reaching into the spirit world, I detected humans, supernaturals, even a few faeries… and Hazel and River, just down the street, waiting for the signal. But no sign of any monsters.

Maybe it was hidden from the spirit world. Like the wraiths. I let the greyness slip away and focused on the house again. My legs cramped from crouching. The screaming died down but didn't disappear entirely. A crashing noise sounded, and then a cry of alarm.

The tone was unmistakable this time. I leapt the wall and ran into the garden, kicking the door inward. In the living room, Morgan lay on the floor—and a monster stood over him. Six or seven feet tall, huge shaggy body like an over-sized dog—and gleaming fangs dripping green drool onto the floor.

Hellhound.

"Shit," I whispered, drawing my knife. Unlike sluaghs or other fae beasts, hellhound bites were potent and even we weren't immune. It didn't look like Morgan had been bitten, but the hellhound's drool had eaten holes in the carpet like acid and I didn't have a weapon capable of dealing a deadly blow without risking our lives.

I grabbed my iron filings first, throwing them at the

monster. The beast's attention left Morgan and its dark eyes locked on me. Primal fear shot through my core, and it leapt at me. I threw myself aside over the sofa, which collapsed under the monster's weight. Its jaws closed a hair's breadth from my face, and I rolled off the collapsing sofa and stabbed it in the leg. Blood spilled onto the carpet, but though iron wounded it, I'd need to get close to its deadly teeth and stab it in the eye or brain to deal a fatal blow.

The hellhound's slavering teeth snapped again, inches from my leg. Then my brother appeared, slamming a chair on top of its head. It shook off the blow, turning on him. Morgan hit the beast again, screaming the whole time. *Ow. That's loud.* My head felt like it was splitting open, and the hellhound flailed a leg clumsily, falling sideways. The noise was hurting it.

I took my chance and sank my knife into its leg, hoping to hit an artery. Could half-dead dog-monsters bleed out? Who even knew. My head pounded with the racket, a thousand times worse than a hangover, but the hellhound growled in pain, too. I stabbed it again, this time in the neck.

Morgan stopped screaming, and the beast twisted, knocking me flying into the coffee table. Pain shot up my spine, mingling with the echoing agony of the psychic scream, and I gasped for breath. As for Morgan—his shadow moved, splitting in two. The second shadow, less substantial, shrank to the size of a small dog, solidifying. Smiling teeth entirely too fae-like, eyes gleaming like coals…

"Hello, Gatekeeper," purred the beast.

The fetch. That little creature was the thing which had been tormenting my brother for a week?

"Get fucked." I pushed to a sitting position, the hellhound's blood soaking into the carpet and glowing with blue faerie magic.

The hellhound spasmed, falling still. I'd killed it after all.

The book's magic filled my veins, strengthening my resolve, and I climbed to my feet, not taking my eyes off the fetch.

"You," I said. "Stay the hell away from my family."

"Gatekeeper," growled the beast. "You're less than I expected."

"Sorry to disappoint you. I'd like to stay and chat about how much of a shit you are for attacking my family, and ask how you summoned that monster, but I kind of don't care." White light exploded from my palms, crashing into the beast. It grinned at me, its body growing to the size of a hellhound. *Okay... that's a little more impressive.*

I raised my knife, and a hand grabbed my arm, driving the knife towards my own leg. I fought against the hands grabbing at me—grey, insubstantial ones, belonging to a pointy-eared figure floating on a level with my face. Of course the fetch hadn't come alone.

"Coward," I snarled, yanking my arm free. *Bloody faerie ghosts.*

Its solid hands lashed out with blinding faerie speed, and latched around my neck to choke the breath from my lungs. I stepped back, willing my spirit to fall out of my body, and twisted to face the half-faerie ghost at my back.

"What're they paying you to take yourselves into an early grave?"

The half-faerie's hands glowed blue, and it *shoved* me. Unprepared for the blast of cold air, I floated backwards. Coldness fogged the windows in the real world, ice spreading across the floor and ceiling. Winter power, enough to outlast death.

I ignored the magic and grabbed the half-faerie's arm. The image of the gate appeared in my mind's eye, encompassing the house—its siren song calling to everyone within the area. If I opened it, the fetch would ensure my brother went through the gate, too, never to be seen again.

"Goddamn you," I growled, dropping the book's power and punching him in the face. Magic blasted me, bounced off my shield and hit the wall instead. Icicles sprang up where it hit… and the hellhound rose to its feet again.

The fetch reanimated the hellhound? I jumped back into my body in time to shove Morgan out the way of the beast's wavering steps. The fetch leapt, but I kicked it hard. The creature hit the iced-over wall, laughing in a high-pitched voice. Morgan sobbed in pain, hands clutching his head.

"Get the hell away from him."

I grabbed my salt canister, threw it at the hellhound's undead body, and jumped into death once again. I looked around, focusing, looking for Morgan… there he was. Morgan's spirit remained still, as his body fought against the fetch.

"Morgan!" I shouted. "Look at me. You can't stop the fetch from possessing your body, but you can attack him here, as a spirit. You've been doing this for years, right? Just pretend this is the real you. He can't harm you as a ghost."

Morgan turned to face me. In the waking world, his screams quietened. Of course that meant the fetch was possessing him for real—but his mind wouldn't break here in Death.

"You sure?" he said.

"Absolutely. As a necromancer, you're stronger than they are by default. That's why they're using cheap tricks against us. They're cowards. I'm gonna go back down there and put the iron on you, and then we can sneak up on the little bastard from behind. Ignore everything the half-faerie does —you're stronger than it is. Got it?"

He nodded, bewilderment flashing across his face, and I closed my eyes and dropped back into my body. I'd barely moved an inch, but Morgan staggered to his feet, eyes glowing, the fetch's presence struggling for control.

"Need a weapon?" I grabbed Morgan's hand and closed it around the iron knife's hilt.

As the fetch recoiled from his mind, a strangled noise came from its physical body. It writhed and flailed, rolling onto its back. I kicked it, viciously, and Morgan himself plunged the knife into the fetch's neck. It gave a gargling screech. The fetch's body stilled, then disintegrated into smoke.

Morgan stood holding the knife, an expression of stunned disbelief on his face.

"Morgan, I said pin it down, not possess it."

"You're welcome," he said. His eyes rolled back in his skull and he fell over backwards.

I gasped, dropping to the floor beside him. "Morgan?" I felt for a pulse and sagged with relief. "Dammit. Where's that faerie ghost?" I switched on my spirit sight, but the ghost had disappeared. Already the ice on the windows was melting, but the house needed a major clean-up. The bodies of both the hellhound and the fetch had left bloody streaks everywhere, the sofa was a wreck, and melting ice dripped down the walls.

The door slammed open and running footsteps came from the hallway. Hazel and River ran into the room, both covered in blood. "What the—" Hazel stared at Morgan and the bloody knife clenched in his hand. "Morgan?"

"He just did something risky and stupid and I'm gonna yell at him when he wakes up, but—"

River strode to the hellhound and his blade flashed, decapitating it.

"It was already dead, twice over," I explained.

"Just taking precautions," said River. He was breathing heavily, but the blue-tinged blood all over his coat wasn't his.

"Two of those bastards ambushed us outside," said Hazel. "Should have figured the enemy would have backup waiting."

I nodded, lifting Morgan's limp arm. He still had a pulse, but now the adrenaline had begun to wear off, worry crept in. "This is my fault. The fetch was driving him literally out of his mind, so I told him to fight it as a ghost. He interpreted that as *possessing* the fetch himself, and I think it screwed him up."

"He's breathing," River said, crouching down beside him. "If it's anything like when an untrained magic user overdoes it, it won't kill him."

"Good." I sank to the floor, my body trembling. "I just—he was in Death, and I know he's apparently been hopping back and forth between there and here for Sidhe knows how many years, but he's not trained."

"It's not your fault, Ilsa," said Hazel. "He *would* interpret what you said in the riskiest, most ridiculous way. He does that."

"I don't think he's ever come close to this before," I said. "I didn't even know someone who isn't technically dead could possess someone, let alone use their psychic powers at the same time."

"It's not common," River said. "The necromancers don't like to broadcast their riskiest techniques, but in this situation... I think he should move permanently to the guild. If we tell them the full story, he'll fall into the category of a rogue by the very nature of what he did."

"Worse than what I did?" I asked.

"Not worse than controlling the gate, but that's not possible at all, as far as most people are concerned. Is the fetch definitely dead?"

"I think it's gone," I said, shivering. "Bloody creature. I wish I'd seen if I got rid of it for real. How did it get into the circle?"

"It used your brother to turn this circle into a place of dark magic," River said. "The candles came on by themselves.

Morgan must possess enough necromantic talent to be able to switch on candles when used as a mouthpiece. I should have seen this coming."

"Dark magic?" asked Hazel. "I take it you don't mean faerie magic… but hellhounds *are* faeries."

"Not the usual type," River said. "Any type of magic requiring a blood sacrifice or which falls outside the bounds of conventional necromancy is labelled as 'dark magic'. I wish there was a more specific label."

"How about 'grey magic'?" I asked. "Summoning from the Vale? That's what it was… right?"

He nodded. "Apparently so. It *is* possible, because the Vale and the spirit realm are so closely linked. If you know what you're doing, you can summon someone… or something… from the Vale directly here. Usually a hellhound. They're particularly receptive to necromantic traps. I think they live directly on the spirit lines between realms somewhere, but that's just a theory."

"Holy crap," said Hazel. "You can—a *human* can summon monsters from the Vale? And the fetch used our brother to do it?"

"He won't suffer any lasting damage," said River. "Not if he's used necromancy before. There's always a risk element involved."

"But…" Hazel trailed off. "Look at the state of this place. What are we supposed to do with the hellhound?"

"Not a problem." River raised a hand and the hellhound erupted into white flames. Quickly, they devoured its body until there was nothing left.

I raised an eyebrow at him. "When do I get to learn to do that?"

"In advanced training," River said. "I'd advise you not to mention this to the guild. Not until I figure out what type of magic was used. They're likely to pin the blame on your brother, and using dark magic carries an automatic jail sentence. The good news is that Lady Montgomery will be pleased that your plan worked, and it will work in our favour to tell her that your brother killed the creature in person."

"Guess so," I said. "Er—Hazel. Did you bring any spells which can fix broken furniture?" I indicated the collapsed sofa. "Or get hellhound blood out of the carpets? Everyone in this house will have to foot the bill."

"Actually, in situations like this, I can pull strings with the necromancers," River said. "Also, most houses have undead damage covered by their insurance. I'll ask someone to write in a note."

"First piece of good news I've had all day," I said.

Morgan sat up, groaning. "I feel like crap. What happened?"

"You were attacked by the fetch," I said. "In fact, you killed it."

Morgan looked between us with an expression of disbelief on his face. "I killed it? Me?"

"You're holding the knife."

He looked down at the bloody instrument in his hand, then at me. "Oh. Awesome."

I just hoped it was gone for real—and that nobody else would get the idea of summoning monsters directly from the Vale itself.

14

Another day, another necromancy test. I shut down the circle with a wave of my hand, still feeling the ghost's clammy hands on my skin. I'd probably never get used to the sensation of being touched by the dead.

"You pass," said the examiner. "I've never seen anyone do a binding that quickly, Ilsa."

"Thank you."

The easiest way to take compliments on my necromantic talents was to imagine they were addressing the book, not me. I imagined the book basking in all the attention and hid a smile.

It'd been relatively quiet at the guild since the fetch had perished. Lady Montgomery marched around snapping at anyone who moved out of line or who didn't stick to the guild's rigid city patrol schedule, while the other senior necromancers had taken to spending long hours consulting their predecessors. I hadn't been invited to any more summits, but considering everyone had ignored me at the last one, I had little to say to the guild. Being invisible suited me just fine, and a few weeks of peace were exactly what I'd needed.

Now I'd passed this test, I was one step closer to being River's colleague rather than his apprentice. My heart skipped when I saw him waiting for me outside the testing room. He must have come back early from patrolling to meet me.

"Hey," I said, closing the door behind me. "I passed."

"Of course you did." He paused, not speaking again until we were out of sight of the room, in the otherwise deserted corridor. "There's a problem. I overheard Lady Montgomery talking about your next test, and it's going to be held in front of the council. You're not allowed to take anything into the room. No props. They'd pick up on the book for sure."

"Ah—crap." Could I even use my powers without it? *I must be able to.* "Can you use magic without your sword?"

"Of course I can. I just thought I'd warn you."

"Warning accepted." Considering Lady Montgomery had him running around at all hours patrolling, killing undead, and taking care of wraiths before they ambushed other unsuspecting necromancers, I appreciated how much effort River put into my training. He even managed to fit in a few sword lessons, and had been patient with my many failed attempts to swing a blade around. I was more than content to stick with knives—and the book. "Does this mean I'll be a full-fledged necromancer soon?"

"Not soon enough for my liking." He pulled me to him and kissed me. I wrapped my hands around the back of his head, and he broke off the kiss. "Your hands are freezing cold."

"Blame the ghosts. How long until we can stop this charade?"

"Aren't you enjoying it?" His bright green eyes gleamed as he looked me up and down, as though he could see right through my necromancer cloak. Heat rose to my cheeks. I didn't need psychic powers to imagine his thought process.

"I'd enjoy it more if I didn't have to think about what Lady Montgomery would say about me corrupting her perfect rule-following son."

"Hmm." He brushed his lips over mine. "If I were better at following the rules, we wouldn't have met in the first place."

"True." He'd taken to leaving presents on my doorstep whenever I was unlucky enough to be chosen for early morning patrols, since I'd opted to remain at the house. I'd said it was so Hazel had somewhere to stay when she came visiting, but I needed to spend at least a fraction of my time in a ghost-free zone. "Thanks for the books, by the way. How'd you find them?"

I'd casually mentioned an old book series I'd never been able to complete, and he'd somehow tracked down every single title.

He grinned. "That's for me to know."

"Spoilsport." Frustration aside, I had to admit life was good. Half the time we walked to the guild via Edinburgh's gardens or the witches' café. I'd risk being tailed by piskies if it meant sneaking another hour with River. The fae didn't seem to bother me as much as they used to. Maybe it was the fact that I wore necromancer uniform all the time so they couldn't see I was a Lynn.

River leaned closer to me. "After you pass, Ilsa, I'll do whatever you want me to."

I grinned. "Anything? You sure?"

"God, get a room," said Morgan, appearing from behind with his arms folded. "Stop groping my sister."

"He isn't," I said. *I wish.* "What is it?"

Morgan shrugged. "I was gonna congratulate you on passing the test. Passed mine too, obviously."

"Did they need an extra room for your ego?" I rolled my

eyes, but part of me was kind of proud of him for not screwing anything up so far. It seemed a low bar, but Morgan had taken to his new position at the guild with more patience than I'd expected. Okay, he'd also made inadvisable comments to almost everyone by now, and his relentless bragging about slaying the fetch was starting to get tiresome to most people. Including me.

"I stole some candles," he said. "Borrowed, I mean. For the test. Since I kinda broke the spares."

"Well done," I said. "How'd you manage that?"

"Set them up in the middle of the road, forgetting people actually use it. Massive truck came along and well…"

I sighed. "Good luck explaining that to Lady Montgomery."

"I wouldn't mention it," River put in. "So you're junior level now?"

"Yeah. Still have some catching up to do. What's next for you, Ilsa?"

"I have to go through a test without the book that has all my powers contained inside it," I said.

"Ah. Guess you're kind of screwed?"

"Not necessarily," I said. "I can use magic without it. I'll test whether I can leave the book somewhere else before I go through with the exam."

"It's worth giving it a go," River said. "Since you're both free."

"What do you want me to do?" asked Morgan warily. He hadn't mentioned the book to me since he'd nearly stolen it under the fetch's influence.

"I'll take the book," River offered. "You help Ilsa. Use one of these rooms."

"C'mon." I beckoned Morgan after me into one of the empty test rooms. "The book won't actually attack you if you touch it, you know. You're not still hearing voices, are you?"

He shook his head. "I haven't taken the iron off since that monster nearly killed us."

"Good." That explained why he looked so much more alert, and like he'd actually got a decent night's sleep for the first time since the fetch had started stalking him. "You have the candles, right?"

He nodded, laying them out on the floor of the empty classroom. "Yeah, I'm supposed to return them upstairs. They don't trust me with props yet."

"Hmm." The book's absence was like a rattling in my skull, perhaps not unlike the presence of the voices which had hounded Morgan. "Let me try lighting the candles."

I snapped my fingers, and the lights came on. *Good.* The spirit realm remained at my fingertips even now. The amount of iron here must keep outsiders away, because I never saw any spirits randomly floating around like I did outside. Bonus to being in the guild: I'd learnt several ways to deter them from following me by now, and to only draw attention of the ones I wanted to speak to.

I extended my awareness to cover the guild. River was in the corridor outside, and I felt the book pulsing from that direction. *Hope nobody else can sense it.* I doubted it—they'd have got suspicious by now. I moved beyond the guild's boundaries, suddenly assailed by a hundred impressions at once. Outside the guild, spirits wreathed the city in grey light. So many living, some dead, and…

There was a long, horrible scream, reverberating through the endless smoke.

With a snapping sensation, I was wrenched back into my body, trembling with the aftershocks. "What the hell was that?"

"What?" Morgan looked puzzled.

I sank to the floor, breathing heavily as though I'd run a mile. "I heard screaming. Outside the guild."

"You went outside the guild?"

"Just to see if I could." I sucked in a breath, willing my racing heart to slow down. The scream had been loud, but unfamiliar... and the way it'd struck me was horribly similar to Morgan's psychic shout.

The door opened, and Lady Montgomery came in. "What are you two doing in here?" she asked. "You're not yet authorised to use those props unsupervised. Where's River?"

"He just went outside for a moment," I said, aware that the glowing candles and Morgan's presence didn't make me look the picture of innocence. "He'll be back in a second."

Sure enough, River appeared at the door. "Ilsa and I were practising... is something wrong?"

"Undead," she said. "All over. We're organising patrols. You take these two, since one of them is your responsibility."

"Of course." He dipped his head. "We'll stop at the weapons room on the way."

She swept from the room. River looked over his shoulder then passed me the book. I nearly sighed in relief when the tapping on my skull ceased. "At least we know it works."

But there were undead attacking outside. Was it connected with what I'd heard?

"I'm coming, too," Morgan said.

"Are you sure?" I asked. "I didn't know you were on the rota."

"A child could get rid of an undead," Morgan said in a self-important voice, having apparently forgotten nearly being killed by one a few weeks ago. "Easy."

River gave him a brief look. "If there are wraiths involved, it's another matter entirely. It doesn't sound like there are, but this might be a trap."

"That, or someone trying to sneak into the guild again," I said.

"There'll still be people here," he said. "We'll get more weapons. Bring those candles with you."

Morgan picked them up, and we headed upstairs to the weapons room. Naturally, Morgan made right for the iron swords.

"Put that down," I told him. "It'll only slow you if you don't know how to use it."

"What makes you think I don't?"

"Because I've seen you every day since you signed up," I told him. "And you refused to join us for sword practise."

"Only because I get enough of you two drooling over one another anyway."

"No swords. Take a knife, but make sure you don't accidentally cut your hand on it. Otherwise, salt, iron filings—"

"Yes, mother," he said. "Next you'll be telling me that undead are the ones with real bodies and ghosts aren't."

I ignored the jibe. "You didn't know any of this before joining the guild. Also, don't take off that iron band. The fetch might have a friend."

Armed and ready, the three of us walked out of the guild, heading towards the sound of raised voices across the rooftops. Veering into the high street, I spotted three undead lumbering past, terrified humans fleeing into the nearest shop.

Morgan whipped out the exterminator and hit the button. A jet of pure white slammed into the first undead, and his head exploded into a thousand grisly pieces. Morgan crowed and fist-pumped the air.

At least until the undead staggered to its feet again, head missing, body still functioning.

"Idiot," I said. "You just wasted your best weapon."

Worse, the undead wasn't going down that easily. River swung his blade, cutting its legs off at the knee. I threw salt at the second undead, its grey flesh peeling from its bones.

River sliced effortlessly through the third undead, leaving it in pieces, while Morgan stomped on the remains with a grin on his face.

"That'll teach them," Morgan said. "And yeah, I know they're not conscious, Ilsa. Wonder who sent them."

"We've got more company," River remarked.

The rotting smell of undead blew on the breeze, and I fought the urge to gag. These undead moved quicker than the others, and from the smell, they'd been dead a few days at most. Long enough to rot, but not long enough for the flesh to fall from their bones. Vacant-eyed, three of them advanced on us, hands outstretched and grasping.

I readied my salt shaker, aiming at the nearest zombie's face. Salt ate through its flesh, but I hadn't thrown enough to bring it down. Its legs kept moving, far faster than I expected. My foot connected with its knee, expecting it to give way, but it didn't. Instead, its hand latched onto my arm, dragging me forwards. And its other hand clutched a knife.

Whoa. Undead shouldn't be this strong, let alone armed. The knife sliced my sleeve but missed the skin beneath, and I kicked its leg, hard. Its grip didn't break, and the knife sliced again. I threw the salt at its knife hand, which dissolved around the weapon. Grabbing its clammy hand in mine, I gripped hard, wrenching at it, but it was like trying to shift solid stone. Definitely not a normal undead. They didn't feel pain, but they shouldn't retain their living strength.

The undead seized me with its free hand and threw me into the wall.

Pain exploded in the back of my skull. I groaned, coughing on the stench of dead flesh. The undead's left hand was gone, rotted away, but its freakish strength was undiminished. Its boot came down on my hand and I barely dodged in time. I glimpsed River cutting and slicing at a second, also wielding a knife. Iron. He'd be in even more trouble than I was if he got cut.

Blood trickled down my forehead where my head had struck the wall. I briefly let the spirit world seep into my vision, but no wraith controlled the undead's movements. Its overpowering strength had come from somewhere else.

I raised my hand and threw salt into the undead's face. His flesh melted away but the bones remained. The wall rattled when I ducked under his remaining fist and it bounced off the brick instead. His wrist gleamed with a bracelet—a spell. A witch charm? Was that what powered him?

Behind the undead, Morgan swore, hitting the exterminator. "Bloody thing is broken."

"No, it has one shot inside it," I said. "Told you not to waste it."

The undead punched the wall aside me again, and while it moved slow enough to dodge, its fists gouged holes in the brick.

I called the book's magic, my hands glowing white, and *pushed*. The undead's feet left the ground, slamming it onto its back.

"Get those wristbands!" I shouted at the others, lunging at the undead. I tackled it in the chest, grabbing its right hand, and wrenched off the gleaming band. At once, the undead's punches turned feeble, and when I threw the last of the salt onto it, it stopped struggling.

Morgan wasn't so lucky. His hand was wedged in an undead's chest, while its fists beat at him. An identical band gleamed on its wrist. I jumped in and pulled the witch spell off, and the undead went still.

Morgan tugged his hand out of its half rotten chest and kicked it. The manoeuvre would probably have hurt him more than the enemy if his opponent hadn't been dead. As it was, the undead fell in a heap.

"Fuck." He looked at his hand, which was covered in rotting bits of flesh, and attempted to wipe it on his cloak.

"Lovely," I said. "That's why you don't punch zombies. Especially when they can punch back."

River, who stood surrounded by dismembered undead, swore softly. "Those spells are strength enhancers," he said. "I can't tell if they were put on them while they were alive, or afterwards. They haven't been dead long."

"I figured," I said. "There's a witch involved in this? Or is someone selling spells to rogue necromancers now?" The street was empty, giving no signs of where they'd come from, and of course you couldn't use a tracking spell on a zombie even if we'd had one to hand. "Damn. If they're all like that, there's no way everyone's prepared."

"Exactly." River grimaced. "You're out of weapons, Morgan. Go back to the guild. If there are more undead wearing those spells, they need to be removed immediately."

"I'm not going back," Morgan protested. "I can kill zombies. You saw."

"Morgan, you blew out your exterminator," I said. "Also, we need to take these spells to someone who might know what they are."

"Corwin," he said.

"Wait, you're still in contact?" I hadn't spoken to him a lot, but I'd assumed Morgan had been too out of it to remember his time at my house. Not to mention his new position at the necromancer guild.

"Yeah, we're going to the pub tonight, but he'll be working at the market if you wanna talk to him." Morgan looked disappointed that he wouldn't get to kill more zombies. I'd almost preferred it when he was sleepwalking around on the orders of a ghost, but not quite.

As River turned to walk back to the guild, I spotted another group of necromancers heading our way. My brother walked in their direction.

"More undead to fight?" Morgan asked hopefully.

"Someone's dead," said one of the necromancers. "Killed by necromancy."

I looked at Morgan. *No way.* That scream I'd heard…

"Lady Montgomery wants everyone back at the guild —immediately."

I turned around, my mind whirling. *It can't be true.*

"What's up, Ilsa?" asked Morgan.

"When I heard screaming earlier, did you hear anything at all?" I asked.

He frowned. "No. But I'm wearing iron, aren't I?"

Had I heard it because the person who'd died had been a necromancer? It'd sounded human, for certain. I'd thought Morgan's gift was rare, and psychics were rarely aware of their own talents. That scream had rang across the spirit world, laced with a horrific familiarity.

It'd sounded like a psychic sensitive. Which meant the fetch was still at large.

15

Lady Montgomery waited at the guild, asking each returning group of necromancers for their reports on the mission. Everyone reported encountering undead, but only one group had faced ones with freakish strength.

"Witch spells," I said, drawing her attention to me. "That's why they were so strong. Someone put strength-enhancing spells on the undead."

"And how do you know that?"

I held up the spells in answer. "All three zombies we faced were wearing them. River recognised them as strength enhancers, but we'll need to check with a witch to see where they came from. I've never seen them before."

"Spells shouldn't work on the dead," she said.

"They haven't been dead long," I said. "The undead were overpowered as hell. They could easily crush a human without trying. Someone gave them those enhancers— someone living."

"We have several witch members who can check for a spell signature," Lady Montgomery said. Her gaze went to

154

Morgan. "I should also inform you that another psychic sensitive was just murdered."

"Another one, or the same one?" Morgan said.

She arched a brow. "The same one?"

Shooting Morgan a warning look, I said, "We heard someone died before we came back here. Guess the news reached us before you."

"Nobody knew it was a psychic sensitive until two minutes ago."

"We didn't know," I said. "It was a guess." I hadn't known Morgan had come to the same conclusion as me, either. Maybe he was sharper than I'd given him credit for.

"Based on what, exactly?"

"I heard screaming," Morgan said. "Sounded like when that thing was in my head. I'd taken off the iron."

Thank you, Morgan, I thought, genuinely grateful that he'd picked up on the precarious nature of our situation. If he hadn't been wearing the iron band, he might well have heard the screaming, too.

Her brow furrowed. "It was still too far away for you to have been able to hear. Even taking your psychic abilities into account. As for you, Ilsa, I wasn't aware you were a psychic sensitive."

"I'm not, but I can go further than the guild with my spirit sight."

Big mistake.

"That's impossible," she said, her hands clenching. "Ilsa, I'm afraid I'm going to have to ask you to step into isolation until the necromancers return with news of the specifics about the murder. You'll also have to undergo drug tests."

"*Drug* tests?" I gaped at her. "For what?"

"Magical enhancements. Please come with me. Morgan, you too."

"He's fine. I'm the one who tracked the screaming—"

"Both of you," she said, in a low, dangerous voice. Apparently River didn't get his *don't mess with me* tone from his faerie side after all. "Now."

Drugs? Seriously? They had nothing on me. Except the book, but even that wasn't illegal. As for Morgan, he'd been on his best behaviour. Too bad innocence meant nothing to someone who saw the world as black and white as Lady Montgomery did.

She led us to a dark staircase. I hadn't seen the lower parts of the guild yet—River had said they were off limits to most necromancers. But I knew before I saw the barred rooms that there really was a jail here. I reached out with my spirit sight and didn't sense anyone else nearby. There was no point in putting up a fight when we'd done nothing wrong, so I walked in silence. Morgan and I were directed into cages side by side, and Lady Montgomery locked both doors.

"Don't look so alarmed," she said. "I'll be back in half an hour at most, or I'll send someone to test you."

She left. We looked at one another.

"This your first experience in jail?" asked Morgan.

"Yes. I take it it's not yours."

He shook his head. "Nothing serious or anything. Mostly disorderly behaviour... shoplifting..."

"You're not helping, Morgan."

"Sorry."

I looked at him. An actual apology? Whatever was the world coming to?

Footsteps echoed outside. "That was fast," I said.

River walked into view. He still carried his sword, his clothes torn and bloody, and had a bright bruise over his left eye.

"I'm sorry." River stepped up to the door. "I have to guard

you. I'll make sure she lets you out as soon as the others return. You shouldn't be punished for committing no crimes."

"I'm seriously confused here," I said. "Why would she think I was on drugs?"

"There have been incidents in the necromancers' history where drugs to enhance necromantic abilities have had unintended violent side effects."

"Pot doesn't work," Morgan helpfully put in. "It makes you a really chilled out ghost. Doesn't give you a power boost."

"Thanks for that," I said. "I haven't been smoking anything. And I couldn't have killed the person who died. Lady Montgomery must know I was nowhere near them."

"Right," said River. He looked paler than usual, the bright bruise standing out on his face.

"She sent you to guard us when you're injured?" I asked.

"I volunteered. I have healing magic, anyway, though it's slowed down here."

Oh. Every cell in here was made out of iron. This prison would be a horrible place to be imprisoned as a faerie. I bloody hoped he wouldn't end up taking the fall for the latest screw-up. At least Morgan seemed genuinely contrite.

"So we're not murder suspects?" Morgan asked.

"No," said River. "Once you've been through testing, you'll walk away free. But the victim was definitely a psychic sensitive."

"So might the fetch still be alive?" If I'd known… but it'd been so damn hard to track the creature in the first place, I'd never have had a clue it was back.

"I don't get it," said Morgan. "I stabbed it to death. It died."

"Who knows how death faeries work," I said. "Can they survive being killed? Or attack people as a ghost?"

"I wish I knew," River said. "There's so little information available on the subject… but it's possible that fetches might be like banshees, which are reborn after they die."

"Damn," I said. "I thought—" *faeries aren't immortal anymore.* But were death faeries an exception? I hadn't even told River what Ivy Lane had told me yet—that the Sidhe's source of immortality had disappeared. After all, it was a bombshell which might shatter the Courts, and River would be obligated to reveal that information on pain of death if questioned by one of the Sidhe. I wouldn't be responsible for starting a war. At the very least, it'd put Hazel's life at risk, as Summer Gatekeeper, not to mention Mum's.

I couldn't do anything about that now. My priority had to be proving my innocence, and there was still the question of who'd been behind the spells that gave the undead super strength. The events in this realm were doubtless tied to Faerie in more than one way, but seeing the connection from this angle was as futile as using faerie magic in an iron cell.

River glanced over his shoulder. "She's here now. You might want to give me the book."

An hour of vigorous questioning later and I left the questioning room, having been thoroughly prodded by no fewer than three examiners into demonstrating the extent of my abilities, and standing in a circle of candles while they scrutinised me from every angle.

"Are we done?" I asked.

"Yes, you're clear," said the examiner.

I left the testing room to find Morgan and River waiting outside. The former had his arms folded and a disinterested expression on his face, while River looked at me, relief evident on his features "You're good?"

"Yep," I said. "I'm assuming whoever put those witch charms on the undead is long gone."

"We had several people check, but they couldn't get a handle on the signature," River said. "It's not a standard market spell, though the actual spell type is fairly common. We have people looking at their contacts for potential matches."

"And the murder?" I asked.

"We're waiting for an update, but there were traces in the spirit world that suggest it wasn't a normal murder. The killer wasn't found at the scene, however. It seems the victim died of fright."

"Damn." I looked at Morgan. "You really didn't hear anything? You didn't have to take the fall."

"I couldn't let them lock my sister up alone," he said, running a hand through his hair. He'd finally cut it so it looked less like a mop, and what with his newly shaven face and necromancer coat, he looked almost respectable. But it was his tone that surprised me the most. *Who are you and what have you done with Morgan?* Not that I was complaining.

"Well. Thanks," I said awkwardly. "So—Corwin is at the market, right? You think he'll know about those spells?"

"Maybe," said Morgan. "He has all this weird knowledge. Are we free to leave now?"

"Yes, you are," River said. "If you want to. Details on the murder haven't come in yet, and as for those witch charms..."

"We have a friend we can question. One of my house-mates," I said. "Let me know if I'm needed back here. I get that murder investigations aren't my area, but if it's targeting psychic sensitives again..." I looked at Morgan.

He shrugged. "I have iron. It's fine. The examiner said I'm a highly advanced psychic. I can handle the little shit if it comes back."

"Most people have iron," I pointed out. "It sure as hell isn't foolproof. Look what happened even inside the guild."

Apparently being called an advanced psychic had inflated his ego more than killing undead had. Morgan swaggered out of the guild, grinning at the novices filing in, and marched off down the road. I walked slower, pulling my hood up against the rain.

"Good lord," I muttered as Morgan still didn't slow down. "Are you really that excited about killing a bunch of zombies, or is it about meeting up with your witch buddy? You could have told me you were dating."

Morgan walked headlong into a lamp post. "How the hell did you know?"

"I don't need psychic abilities to be able to see the obvious, Morgan."

"Ow." He stepped away from the lamp post. "You haven't told Mum I'm gay, have you?"

"Why do you think Mum would care?"

"I'm the firstborn Lynn," Morgan said, blood dripping from his nose. "Mum thought I'd be Gatekeeper, or at least one of my kids would be the future heir. It pissed her off when I told her I don't want children, and I think she still thinks I'll change my mind."

"I'm fairly sure she's more annoyed that you vanished off the face of the earth for eight years," I said. "Also, Hazel or I could offer up our kids as bait when it comes down to it. God, I almost went five minutes without thinking about how screwed up our family is."

Morgan looked thoughtful. "If you and River had children, how would that work with the curse? I always wondered why they put in that rule about not dating faeries…"

"Don't finish that thought," I said warningly. "That's a *long* way off, if ever."

Morgan laughed. "So much for seeing the obvious."

"Your nose is bleeding. Your powers of foresight could use some work."

He flipped me off.

Like many cities, Edinburgh's supernatural population ran a weekly market, this one on a street parallel to the high street which had once been hidden before the faeries' arrival had killed the spells keeping it hidden. We ducked down an alley between tall, old buildings, and came out onto a cobbled road covered in stalls. All manner of supernaturals came here to buy and sell, from witches hawking rare charms from across the country to faeries selling enchanted weapons and other items supposedly from within Faerie itself. I had my doubts that most of them were genuine.

I spotted Corwin behind a display of beautification charms and other trinkets. He smiled at Morgan. "Want one?"

"No, he doesn't," I said, before Morgan could speak. "We're here to ask about a particular type of spell." I pulled the bracelet from my pocket and held it up. "Know where this came from? It's a strength enhancer, but not one of the mass produced type."

He squinted. "Must be a custom job. Not my style."

"I may be able to help you with that," said a croaky voice from behind me. I jumped, then turned around to see an old woman with braided silver-grey hair, wearing a heavy traveller's cloak, peering at the spell in my hand.

"Er… hello, Agnes," I said. "What are you doing here?" I'd thought she hadn't left Foxwood in years.

"I follow where the rumours go."

Corwin raised an eyebrow. "Can I help you with something?"

"Hmm." She cast a critical eye over the spells. "Maybe go

easy on the nettles. It'll reduce the risk of the spell backfiring."

"Er… thanks. I think." He stepped back, as though Agnes's presence intimidated him. It wouldn't be the first time. She scared most people back in Foxwood. But I'd never thought I'd run into her here.

"Best go somewhere quieter," she said, weaving through the market. The crowd parted around her, without even looking at her. Those who did lay their eyes on her wore awed or scared expressions.

"Cool trick," Morgan commented. "Where have I seen you before?"

"You know Agnes," I said. "From Foxwood? She's more or less her own coven, along with her husband."

"Oh. The weird ones?"

I cringed, prepared for her to retaliate, but she gave him a good-natured smile. "You've changed since I last saw you, Morgan."

"Probably." At least he sounded wary. I was beginning to worry that the little that remained of his common sense had evaporated along with his psychic link with the fetch.

"You travelled hundreds of miles to get here. How?" Unlike Hazel, she didn't have access to the paths of the Ley Line.

"I have my ways," said Agnes. "It sounds like you're deep in trouble again."

"That's one way of putting it. You said you recognised this…" I passed her the spell.

"Thought you were a mage, not a witch," said Morgan.

"Why not both?" She turned to me. "This is a strength enhancer. I would assume you didn't acquire it from the market."

"Nope," I said. "I found them on a bunch of undead who

attacked a few hours ago. They were way too strong. Might have been put on while they were alive, might not. But apparently they aren't mass market spells, so they came from a specialist. Do you know who?"

She shook her head. "I can't pretend to know every witch, much less here. It's been years since I last came. I will tell you that something drew me here. The same thing that alerted you and your brother."

I blinked, confused. "Alerted? You mean, the book?"

"She knows?" said Morgan.

"Quiet," I hissed. "Yes, she knew Grandma. Our whole family. But I've been careful with the book."

"Not that," she said. "The presence of a beast more ancient than most, and more dangerous."

Morgan swore. "The fetch?"

"What—" Now I got it. "You're a psychic sensitive?" I'd once heard her mage ability involved mind powers in some way, but she'd never elaborated on the subject.

"Not in the same way he is," Agnes said. "I'm no necromancer. But the realms of magic are more closely linked than many would believe."

"How do you know *I'm* a psychic sensitive?" Morgan asked. "Did you read *my* mind?"

"No, but I know the signs," Agnes said. "I used to deal in memories, before I decided to specialise in unique charms instead. There's more money in memory spells, but also more consequences."

"What, you mean erasing memories?" I asked. "You can do that?"

"Yes. But most people who request that I erase their memories regret that decision, and I can't perform a spell on anyone without permission. However, my psychic talent is such that I can pick up on signals like that creature's scream."

"Miles away?"

"Distance is relative in the veil."

From the context, I wasn't sure whether she meant *veil* or *Vale.* "It killed someone," I said. "But—it's supposed to be dead."

"I killed it," said Morgan. "I thought it was a weak faerie creature, an omen of death."

"Not weak as far as psychics are concerned," she said. "As for its type... like banshees, fetches are reborn into a new body when they die. It's part of their magic."

My heart sank. *I was afraid of that.*

"Seriously?" Morgan stopped walking, the colour draining from his face.

"Absolutely. It's as strong as it was when it was alive before."

"It nearly killed Morgan," I said. "But he locked it out with an iron spell. So I guess it went after a new victim. How do you permanently kill something like that?"

"I think you know the answer to that."

I did know. Use the book. Open the gate wide, and put the city at risk in the process. I couldn't test *that* in the training room. Using it on the Ley Line had been risky, but the instability had worked in my favour. This city straddled the Line, too, but contained countless innocent lives.

The fetch just claimed one. How many more will it take?

If it was hiding in the Vale, maybe I could lure it outside the city. Get Arden to open Paths along the Ley Line from the house until I found somewhere I could safely open the gate without repercussions... if there *was* such a place. And who was controlling the creature? It couldn't be working alone.

Morgan and I looked at one another. "You can do it?" he asked.

"Possibly," I admitted. "But I don't know... the undead

attacks, the thief in the guild… this isn't a one-person operation. Someone is ordering this fetch around, either in the Vale or here, and I doubt the gate will swallow *them* up on command."

Also… a small detail I'd overlooked. The Grey Vale might be linked with Death, but faeries who died there *couldn't* move on. So was the gate of Death accessible there at all? Or could I only banish the fetch when it was in *this* realm? I couldn't see a way to manufacture a trap without asking someone to offer themselves as bait. Meaning: Morgan… or Agnes.

Her gaze met mine. "I would volunteer to hunt this creature myself, but no faerie would dare to attack me, psychically or otherwise. I hoped that my presence here might discourage it from attacking at all, but it will only target minds it can easily overcome. Mine is unbreakable." She said this so matter-of-factly, I couldn't even see it as egotistical. She really was that powerful.

Morgan shuffled from one foot to the other. "I beat it once. Does that mean it'll come back, if I take the iron off?"

"Probably," I admitted. "You're not invulnerable, you know."

"No," he muttered. "Is there nothing you can do to help us?" he asked Agnes.

"I can give you this." She passed me a handful of spells. "That's a redo on your disguise spell… I can tell yours is close to running out. Two shadow spells and a tracker. It may be that the people investigating the murder already used one, but I'm sure you can find a use for it." She turned to Morgan and passed him some spells, too.

"Wait—these are mine?" he asked, looking down at the spells in confusion. "What do I do with them?"

"Not waste them, for a start," I said. "That's a shadow spell and a disguise charm, right?"

"Disguise? What for?" asked Morgan.

"I'm sure something will come up," said Agnes.

"Thank you," I said. "How much do I owe you for this?"

"What you've done already is more than enough repayment." She paused. "Be careful. Both of you."

And she melted back into the crowd and disappeared.

16

I woke early the following morning to a pounding headache and the sound of Hazel and Morgan arguing in the hall downstairs. I groaned and ran a hand over my forehead. I'd had only one drink last night before crashing from exhaustion, so hell if I knew what I'd done to deserve a hangover. My whole body ached, but that was nothing new these days, thanks to the necromancers' relentless patrol schedule. I must have been exhausted to sleep through Hazel's arrival, let alone half her argument with Morgan. He wasn't even supposed to be living here anymore, but Corwin had invited him here after they'd watched the match at the pub, and he must have stayed over.

I grabbed a hoody, shoved it on over my pyjamas, and went downstairs to confront them. And I'd thought we'd been getting along so well. Morgan and Hazel hadn't argued at all since our narrow brush with death, though admittedly she'd only visited us a handful of times, being busy with her duties as Gatekeeper.

"What's the problem this time?" I asked.

"He's being a prick," Hazel answered.

I didn't need to ask for the details. The two of them could turn an innocuous discussion about baby kittens into a screaming argument.

"Well, try to keep the noise down. Morgan and I are off to the guild later. I'd invite you to come, but everyone's a little on edge.

"No worries," Hazel said. "I thought I'd go looking for Agnes. I can't believe she gave you free spells and not me."

"I can't believe Ilsa stole mine," said Morgan, his voice slurred. Ah. He wasn't hungover—he was still drunk.

"You'd have wasted them on something trivial if I hadn't." I rolled my eyes. "Don't deny it. Have you heard from the guild?"

"Nope," he said. "I should be on the rota now I've passed their test."

"So you do want to work at the guild?" Hazel asked. "Even though they threw the two of you into cells yesterday?" I'd texted her the latest, which must be why she'd shown up.

"It wasn't a big deal," said Morgan, leaning on the door frame. "They thought my superpowers meant I was on some kind of necromancer drugs."

Hazel sighed. "And you said the fetch is back. Didn't you say you were attacked at the guild, too?"

"Only because we caught the guy stealing. They've tripled security since." My feet were blistered from so many hours patrolling.

Hazel's lips pursed. "What was he trying to steal?"

"Information on clients the necromancers had worked for. You know, the names of people they performed exorcisms for, or…"

"Psychics?"

"Maybe, but they wouldn't show up as clients unless they called the guild specifically."

It wasn't like the faerie had stolen highly classified information on how to use dark magic, and the fetch plainly knew how to do that already. It'd used Morgan as a puppet... I needed to consult the book. Which I'd left upstairs. "Give me a second," I said, and walked back into the house. I ran upstairs and pulled some clothes on, then retrieved the book from under my pillow.

The book's cover had gone blank, the symbol no longer there. I turned the book over, my heart sinking, and then opened it. No words appeared on the pages, not even the basic introduction. It'd been wiped clean, and no longer glowed at all.

"Er... hey." I shook it. "Wake up."

No response. Not so much as a splash of ink on the page.

"C'mon. Don't die on me now."

Had I done anything with the book yesterday? I didn't think so. Aside from testing to see if my powers worked without it. Maybe it'd been insulted that I'd even considered it.

"I'm sorry I neglected you," I whispered, feeling for the familiar rush of cold energy that connected me with the spirit realm.

Nothing.

"Ilsa!" Hazel called from downstairs. "I'm going to the market, okay? Catch you two later."

"Be careful!" I called back, giving the book another shake. *Maybe I need to find Agnes again.* But the murder...

I tried to switch on my spirit sight, sighing in relief when a familiar greyness took over my vision. But there was no accompanying rush of power, and no ghosts.

I ran downstairs to Morgan. "The book's switched off. It's not working."

"What? Your spirit book?" He blinked. "You sure?"

I held it out to him. "It's blank. Even the cover."

"Shit." He hesitated, then ran his hand over the cover, opening it to show blank pages. "Maybe it needs recharging."

"It's a book, not a battery."

My phone buzzed with a message. I put the book away and found a text from River. *Another victim. I talked Lady Montgomery into letting you and your brother come and check the murder site.*

My heart sank. "Someone else died."

"Another psychic?" His voice sounded clearer, less slurred.

"I'd guess so. River wants us to go and meet him." Lady Montgomery had said we could go to help investigate the murder? After yesterday, I'd have expected her to pin the blame on us instead.

"But the fetch isn't there," said Morgan.

"No, but I have a custom-made tracker," I said. "If they don't already have one, I can try to figure out what happened."

"Or I can take off the iron."

"You might die. Don't joke about that, Morgan."

"I'm not joking." He buried his hands in his pockets. "I'm... okay, I'm not sober, but I'm not kidding around. I stabbed the fetch, so now it's probably pissed as hell and murdering every other psychic it can get its claws in."

"Don't forget I helped draw it out," I said. "You'd think it'd be angry with all of us. We should go and meet River."

River waited outside the guild... with Lady Montgomery herself. So that's how he'd managed to persuade her to let us help. I'd have to tell him about the book later, but I didn't need the talisman to solve this crime. Unless the fetch showed up.

"Hey," I said. "Whereabouts is this murder site? Was it definitely a psychic?"

"Yes," said Lady Montgomery. "It's this way."

She took off in the direction of the bridge. River followed, with Morgan and I close behind. *Another death.* Morgan might feel responsible, but guilt churned inside me all the same.

"I have a tracking spell," I said. "Just in case nobody else does."

"I've got a shadow spell," put in Morgan, hardly slurring his words. "In case you wanna blend into shadows."

Lady Montgomery didn't react to his comment. Apparently picking up on the precarious nature of the trust she'd placed in us, Morgan held his tongue the rest of the way there. She halted at the end of a row of terraced houses.

"The victim apparently stabbed himself to death," said Lady Montgomery. "But he was psychic, and had shown no other signs of instability until now."

I didn't hear any screaming this time. And unless Morgan had ignored it in his drunken state, he hadn't either. I hadn't been tuned into the spirit realm while I'd been sleeping, but what if the book's lack of magic had stopped me from being able to sense the fetch at all? The timing couldn't be worse. Two people were dead in less than twenty-four hours.

"All of you, be careful not to contaminate the crime scene," she added. "The body has been moved. We're here with the permission of the human police."

"Wait, so you've already had people comb the place?" I asked.

"I thought you two could apply your unique talents," she said. "The tracking spells we used confirmed what we already know."

Hmm. If the fetch was at large, it was long gone by now. But I followed her and River into the house all the same.

Bloody handprints smeared the living room wall. The imprint of where the body must have been lay in a red smudge in the middle of the carpet, though the murder weapon had gone. Still, I pulled out my tracking spell, checking into the spirit realm first. Greyness smothered the room, with no ghosts beneath.

"Can you contact his spirit?" I asked.

"That's River's job. Can either of you two sense anything?"

Morgan made a choked noise and ran outside. I heard him throwing up in a bush.

"No," I said. "I can't see anything. Not in the spirit world, either. But I can use the tracker." Agnes's spells were always more powerful than regular ones, but tracking spells tended to be pretty limited. They played out the last scene to have occurred in a particular place, but like a poor quality black and white video with no sound. It wasn't possible to get an accurate reading from a witch spell, especially as they couldn't be used on ghosts or undead, let alone the fetch. But I had to start somewhere. I crouched down and placed the spell in front of the bloody smear, then hit the button on the side.

My vision tunnelled, a sense of claustrophobia closing in as everyone in the room disappeared, leaving only a black-and-white image of the living room, the carpet now blood-free. I jumped when someone walked in front of me, a male stranger, blurred around the edges. He fell to the floor, mouth open in a scream, flailing madly in a way horrifyingly reminiscent of Morgan when the fetch had been attacking him. But the fetch didn't appear. The stranger ran in circles, tripping over nothing, and I was glad I couldn't hear him screaming.

He ran from view and returned with a knife. His mouth

moved, forming words. Clear words. It almost looked like he was saying… *Gatekeeper.*

The knife plunged into his chest, and the real world crashed over the vision in full colour. I damn near joined Morgan in vomiting outside. Taking in several deep breaths, I braced my hands on my knees. A flash of light drew my attention to the corner, where River and Lady Montgomery had set up a summoning circle.

"I summon you, Stuart Raymond," River said. Must be the victim's name.

The air fogged within the circle. I used my spirit sight, rotated on the spot, but no ghosts appeared. Nothing.

"He must be through the gates by now," said River.

Morgan ran back into the house. "I can't hear anything," he announced. "In case you were wondering."

"I expected not," said Lady Montgomery. "The victim's ghost is not within reach. What did you see in the tracking spell, Ilsa?"

"He stabbed himself. Like you said. Nothing more."

Except that word. *Gatekeeper.* The murderer had wanted me to see it—expected me to. Which meant the killer was targeting psychics to guilt-trip both of us for not finishing the bastard off the first time around.

"Did he know he was a psychic?" I asked her, pushing the guilt as far away as possible. Blaming myself for the actions of a monster would help nobody.

"Yes, but like the first victim, he wasn't an active practitioner. There isn't really a place in the supernatural community for people with those gifts. Witch covens would be their natural fit, but they distrust anyone who can read minds with good reason."

"I'm not a witch," said Morgan.

"No, but you can also connect with the spirit realm, and project yourself in there," Lady Montgomery said. "And both you and your sister have demonstrated you can track down any spirit. Did you hear this one?"

I shook my head. "Guess I slept through it." But I'd woken with the book switched off, changed. I couldn't have done something to the book while I was asleep, could I? Or Morgan? No way. If nothing else, I'd have heard him. Right?

"I can try tracking it," Morgan said.

"Not here," I said. "At the guild. It's playing a game. With me, or with us. Which means as soon as you remove the iron…"

"Yeah, no thanks," he said, his face pale. "But—do you know who it'll target next? I might be able to track the other psychics, but I'd have to take this thing off. I can lure it into a trap."

Lady Montgomery looked from one of us to another. "It's not a bad idea."

My heart sank. "I—don't know about this. It seems too obvious a trap. The fetch must have figured we'd try luring it out again, like we did last time."

"That doesn't mean it won't work again," Lady Montgomery said. "River, collect the candles. We're going to the site of our summit."

The house *was* quite close to the site of the necromancers' graveyard, but it struck me as a risky move. "Are you sure?" I asked.

"I rather think I'm not the one at risk here," said Lady Montgomery.

———

The cemetery looked no less creepy during the day. I'd once found the presence of the dead relaxing, soothing even, but now every shadow carried a hint of menace that no light would erase. Even the necromancer candles which remained there from the summit, arranged in a perfect circle I could never hope to achieve. I looked around uneasily, while Morgan strode into the circle's centre.

"The candles will stabilise you if you enter the spirit realm," Lady Morgan explained. "This is how *normal* necromancers disconnect from their bodies."

Huh. Maybe she did have a sense of humour after all. Graveyard humour. Too bad I really wasn't in the mood, especially with Morgan dead set on risking his life again. I understood why—hell, in his place, I'd have made the same decision. Didn't mean I had to like it.

"Take it off." He held out his wrist.

"Are you sure you want to do this?" I asked.

He nodded, still looking pale. "Go on."

I pulled the iron band free. Morgan froze, in the circle's centre. "Damn, that's cold. Okay, you guys are there…"

I took a step closer to River. "Cover for me," I murmured, and plunged into Death.

Grey smoke. White lights. Morgan was easy to spot, turning expertly on the spot with more grace than he displayed when he was sober, let alone now.

Morgan turned on me, eyes wide in alarm. "It knows what you did. It tricked us—dammit, where's that iron?"

I swore. "What—is it here?"

He stiffened, eyes blanking out, and gave a low chuckle that sounded nothing like him. "If you don't want to be next, Gatekeeper, I suggest you listen to me."

Shit. That voice wasn't the fetch's. It was lower pitched, and if it came from a human, I'd guess the speaker was female.

"Get out of my brother's head."

He laughed again. "Feel free to take me out… you won't win this in the end, Gatekeeper… we have everything we need already."

"No."

I pulled myself out of Death and back into my body, gripping the coldness of the iron band in my hand. I lunged and grabbed Morgan's arm and shoved the band back onto it. He flailed and tripped over, knocking candles everywhere.

Catching my balance against a headstone, I straightened upright. "Morgan, are you okay?"

"Yeah. I think." He shook his head, his face white as a sheet. "That wasn't the fetch. I didn't feel it in my head like last time."

"Someone was using you as a puppet," I told him. "But who?"

"Your voice was distinctly female," River said. "And human. I think. Not fae."

"Shit." I looked for Lady Montgomery and saw she was outside the gates, speaking on the phone. "What's she doing?"

"Another call came in," said River. "I expect we'll be called to report in a minute."

"Forget reporting," I said. "The person possessing him knows who we are, and they said *I already have everything I need.* And—the book went blank this morning. I woke up and it was switched off." I glanced at Lady Montgomery to make sure she wasn't listening, but she was still on the phone.

"Switched off?" echoed River, his brow furrowing in confusion.

"Totally blank. Even the cover. I woke up and it was like this. And it happened at the same time as the murder, I think."

River's eyes widened. "Are you sure?"

"Yeah. God knows why. I don't know what can drain a *talisman.*"

"Nothing can," he said. "Unless you used up all its power yourself, but you'd still be able to sense it."

"It's been on the verge of burnout since I opened the

gate," I said. "I have to ask someone who knows. Aside from Agnes, that's just Grandma. Or—hell, Greaves will do. Someone *must* know why the bloody book switched off. Most people can't touch it."

"Most people?" echoed Morgan. "Who can?"

"River, Agnes… I'd count old Greaves, but he's a ghost, he can't technically touch anything. Possibly Everett, Agnes's husband. That's it, aside from our family."

"Where's your sister?" asked River.

Morgan and I looked at one another. "She went into town," he said. "To find Agnes, I think. Why?"

"Just a thought. Call her. We're going to need help."

"Mind cluing me in?" I pulled out my phone and found the battery dead. "I swear I plugged this in… Morgan, can I borrow your phone?"

He dug his hand in his pocket. "Can't. It's gone."

I swore. "How?"

"Dunno. I don't remember a ton about last night…"

"Like borrowing my book, for instance?"

"No, of course not," he said. "What do you take me for?"

"Not the most reliable person when inebriated, for one thing," I snapped, fear coursing through me. "I don't have my old phone here… it's at the house."

"Never mind the phone," said Morgan. "What about the psychics? How're we meant to know who's gonna be next? Can Agnes help?"

"I think Agnes implied that she can't sense psychics like you can, because she's not one. So she can't track people, and she's not a likely target." But Hazel might be. "River, can I borrow your phone? Wish I knew her number…"

"I do," said Morgan, to my astonishment. "She never changed it. Always the same one, since we were kids. She said it was just in case I wanted to call."

I blinked. "Seriously?"

I'd never asked. I'd wondered how they resolved their differences, and considering how they'd been bickering, I'd assumed they still hated one another. As much as you could hate family, anyway. *Please let her be okay.* If the enemy had targeted Hazel... but of the three of us, she had the most powerful magic.

Morgan dialled Hazel's number on River's phone, and we waited in tense silence. "Not answering," he muttered. "I'll message her. *Oi. Ilsa thinks you're dead. Stop nattering with Agnes and answer the damn phone.*"

I put the book away. "Of the three of us, she's the only one who's not trained as a necromancer, but she can also turn anyone into a tree with minimal effort. I don't see why anyone would pick her as a weak link." But maybe that was why they'd chosen her, since all our attention was on making sure nobody possessed Morgan again.

Lady Montgomery approached us, her expression grim.

"Two of my people are dead," she said. "We're going back to the guild. All of you. That's an order."

17

Lady Montgomery didn't stop when we reached the necromancers' place. She marched through the doors, and River, Morgan and I followed close behind. The crowd parted around her, recognising the danger signs as surely as we did. The atmosphere was more subdued than I'd ever seen it.

Morgan broke the silence by asking her, "Who died? How?"

"They were ambushed in the spirit realm."

My mouth dropped open. "Oh shit. In here?"

"Yes. Apparently a spirit was responsible." Her tone was icy cold.

"You're not taking us to jail again?" said Morgan.

"No," she said. "I want the two of you to use your abilities to hunt the attackers down."

For the second time, my jaw dropped. "You really want us to help?"

The book wasn't working. Could I project as far without it? Morgan could, but he'd have to take off the iron—and the enemy had slipped through the guild's defences once already.

"Sure," Morgan said. "Let me try."

"If we both have to do it at the same time, someone needs to have iron on standby," I said. "I can't put it back on him if this goes wrong while we're both in Death."

"River, inform two senior necromancers that Ilsa and Morgan require supervision," said Lady Montgomery. "I'm going to set up a spirit barrier around our headquarters, and once you're done, all spiritual activity within this building will cease."

Whoa. An actual spirit barrier? I hadn't seen one since Holly had used a barrier around her territory to keep the Winter Gatekeeper contained. In the end, it'd required so much power that she'd accidentally killed someone.

"I'll bring them." River looked at me, worry clear in his gaze. He was probably thinking of the book and the Winter Gatekeeper, too. Like I needed more pressure.

"Why's she suddenly letting us use our powers now?" asked Morgan.

"She always intended to," River said. "Once she's removed the possibility that the two of you were a threat."

"About bloody time," said Morgan.

The annoying part was the two necromancers I didn't know, who followed us to the room, giving both of us suspicious looks. The room River picked out was twice the size of the others, containing several sets of candles arranged in circles of twelve.

"You'll have to go into separate circles," said River to Morgan and me. "And the iron—one of the other necromancers will have to be prepared to put it on Morgan if he's attacked again."

The two necromancers exchanged glances. Apparently they'd heard enough about our abilities to be wary of both of us. But River couldn't touch the iron himself, so we'd have to put our trust in a stranger.

Morgan shrugged and walked into a circle, holding his arm out for me to remove the iron. I did so, passing it to one of the necromancers, and got into the neighbouring circle myself.

"If he starts screaming or anything, put that iron back on him immediately," I told them.

River gave me a nod of reassurance, and then the smoke of the circle moved in, greyness blanking out the world. Everything went fuzzy. No sign of anyone else.

"Morgan," I whispered. "You here?"

"Yeah." He came into focus, hovering in the air. He had more experience of this than I did, without a prop. Everything was too blurred for me to figure out where the guild's limits were. "What're we meant to be doing, interrogating every ghost that comes our way?"

"I think the killer was probably half-faerie," I said. "Like the spirit who attacked us." Instinctively I called the last half-faerie attacker's face to mind, reaching out, but my abilities felt muted. I focused harder. I should at least be able to sense Morgan, but I wouldn't if he wasn't standing right next to me.

I shook my head. "It still isn't working. I can't project. I don't think you should be exposed like this either."

"I can't see the killer," Morgan said. "Necromancers… plenty of those. They have people scouring the whole building. Why send us in, too?"

"To search *outside* the building," I said. "But I can't. This is a waste of time. Wait, what about Hazel?" I should at least be able to find my sister. I closed my eyes, pushed outwards with my mind, and hit a barrier so solid, my head throbbed. "Ow. I hit something."

"Where?"

I waved a hand around. "I don't know. My focus is totally shot."

"Cause of the book?"

"Maybe. I can't focus like I used to. I'm not so sure I can fight, either. But I tried to find Hazel and something *hit* me."

"What—psychically?"

"I don't think so. But I'm not one."

"Lemme try." He closed his eyes, his ghostly body flickering at the edges. Then he yelled and fell backwards, writhing on the spot.

"Morgan!" I grabbed his arm, and my hand passed right through it. *Focus... the book...* My grip tightened. "Come on. Snap out of it."

He groaned. "I can't. It's coming—*now.*"

I snapped into my body, shouting, "Iron—get the iron."

But the necromancers had gone, and the iron band lay discarded on the floor. Cursing, I dived out of the circle, but River got there first, picking the iron up in a gloved hand. He grimaced, threw it to me, and I grabbed Morgan's arm. As I snapped the iron into place, his body jerked, then his eyes flew open.

"Where in hell are those necromancers?" I gasped.

"There was another attack," River said, removing the glove. "I apologise—I should have been quicker with the iron."

"It's not your fault." I took in a steadying breath.

"You'd better not have any psychic sensitives in here," Morgan said. "Holy fuck. It's projecting at everyone nearby. I think it's gonna kill someone."

My stomach turned over. "We have to stop it. Can you do what you did last time?"

He shook his head. "It's stronger—much stronger. It'd have killed me if I hadn't been here."

I tasted bile in my throat. "Stronger. How can it be stronger? Are the deaths... is it feeding on them, somehow?" Some dark fae gained power from pain and death, and the fetch was definitely a Winter fae, even if it'd come from the Vale. All death faeries were. "Just how many psychic sensitives are there in the city?"

"Not many," River said. "Couldn't you find anything specific?"

"Hazel." I swallowed. "I tried to find her, and that's when we hit some kind of invisible barrier. I couldn't reach her."

"She's not a psychic sensitive," Morgan said. "They shouldn't have reason to go after her. It's weird that she showed up here today in the first place."

"Not really," I said. "She thought you were being attacked, remember?"

"Not that. She let herself into the house. I kinda thought you let her in, though things were fuzzy…"

But she doesn't have a key.

"She can't be affected, right?" I asked River. "I mean, I know she's a relation. She has necromancer ancestry, like us. You don't think…" Morgan and I looked at one another.

"The motherfucker," Morgan said quietly. "It got her, and now it's going after the other psychics."

"It can't." I shook my head. "There's no way—Hazel is stronger than either of us."

"Not against the dead," Morgan muttered. "She… I know she was acting weird, but I felt kind of out of it this morning, to be honest."

"Pretty sure that had nothing to do with Hazel."

"That's just it. I… when I left the house, it stopped. I only had two drinks, I shouldn't have been that hungover. It's like the house… I dunno. Like I ran into a spell."

"Hazel seemed fine to me." But why couldn't I sense her? And what in hell had happened to the book?

"It shouldn't have known Hazel was there," said Morgan. "It shouldn't have known where to find the psychics either. I possessed it. It's really not that powerful."

"No," River said. "The fetch sensed you because you were projecting for miles. But it can't track psychics if they don't draw attention to themselves."

"Just how does it know who they are in the first place?" I asked. "That document—did that faerie show anyone? Is there another traitor?"

River shook his head. "No. If the information *was* in that document, nobody saw it aside from the thief, and he passed beyond the gate."

"Which gate?" I asked, remembering how he'd evaporated into grey smoke.

He frowned. "What?"

"We've been played," I said. "The fetch is in the Vale. What if the ghosts are, too? That shit with the gate might have been a ploy. He might have handed the information over to someone else before he went through."

"He couldn't have done. He was unconscious, and then dead."

"Not before he got caught," said Morgan. "I've talked to a lot of people since I joined up here, and I can't think of any other way the info got out. There's no record of psychics. But it's killed at least three of them in the last day, since it came back."

"But—even if it's true that the thief managed to pass on the information before he died, what does that have to do with Hazel?" I said.

"Nothing," Morgan said. "Except for her being Gatekeeper, and you..."

"If it wants me, it can come and face me itself. That's precisely what I wanted the bastard to do in the first place."

I have everything I need, the fetch had said. Technically, the Summer Gatekeeper's heir was important enough on her own. But she should have been able to stop him. And since when was she vulnerable to the fetch's psychic influence?

No… it must have captured her in some other way. Because it wanted me. And it wanted the book.

The book, which had shut down, leaving me entirely vulnerable.

I squeezed my eyes closed, then opened them again. "Do you think she's still in this realm?"

"If she hadn't been, I wouldn't have been able to trace her at all," said Morgan. "I can check again, but it sensed me coming."

"What are you doing?" demanded the other necromancer, running back into the room. "You're supposed to be helping track the attackers."

"Thanks for running off," Morgan snapped.

The necromancer ignored him and turned to me. "Lady Montgomery wants to see you in her office, Ms Lynn."

I shook my head. "The fetch has our sister. I'm almost certain of it. But it's put up some kind of barrier in the spirit realm so we can't track it. We have to find her."

"That was an order." He seized me by the arm. "You've bent our rules enough, the pair of you. You brought this attack on us."

River moved towards him, but the necromancer snapped his fingers. Candles lights glowed, and River stopped as though he'd collided with an invisible force. The necromancer hauled me from the room, and it took everything I had not to punch him in the face. If Lady Montgomery wasn't understanding—that was it. Logically, I'd stand more of a chance of tracking Hazel and the fetch with the necromancers at my back. But getting her to understand would take time I couldn't afford to lose.

Lady Montgomery stood waiting for me behind her desk in her office.

"So," she said. "The Vale."

My heart skipped a beat. "Which one?"

"I overheard enough to know you've been playing us."

She'd eavesdropped on us in Death? Should have known she'd try something like that. But—had I mentioned the book? I couldn't think clearly. Hazel was missing. And without the book working, I wasn't sure I could fight my way past the leader of the necromancers.

"Look, don't take this personally, but I don't have time for accusations," I said. "The fetch is holding my sister hostage right now, and I can't track her. When Morgan tried to use his psychic abilities to reach her, he ran into the fetch again, and it nearly broke into HQ."

"Precisely why I can't allow you to stay here and put my people in danger. You broke your agreement to serve our cause when you lied."

A cold sensation spread through my chest. "I had no choice but to lie. My magic—it's kind of like a faerie vow."

Her mouth thinned and anger flared in her expression. I'd picked the wrong wording.

"I see. Faerie necromancy... like those criminals."

I shook my head. "No. It's not a crime. My family used the magic I have to defend this realm against the Grey Vale—the part of faerie which overlaps with the spirit realm. The enemy is there, and they have Hazel. Please. I'll go through more interrogations, jail, whatever, but not until I'm sure Hazel's alive."

The door crashed open as Morgan staggered into the office behind me, having apparently broken free of the other necromancer's hold.

"What she said." He nodded at me. "We're not leaving Hazel to die."

"And how do I know you're not lying to me?" she asked in a soft, deadly voice. "You both have, on numerous occasions. Not only are neither of you necromancers, you're the targets of the threats to our guild."

"We're not lying now," I said. "And if I could have told you the truth—look, this isn't about what I want. It's about the safety of everyone in this city, in the world even, and we're sitting on a ticking bomb." I might not know the fetch's goal, but mass murder using faerie magic on the Ley Line would have one hell of a knock-on effect.

"You're both forbidden from entering here again for the foreseeable future. Your brother sent out a psychic beacon to our enemies, while you told lies that endangered our people and put lives at risk, and River enabled that."

"River had nothing to do with it. Please, let me find my sister."

"Not until you tell me the truth. River, come in. I know you're outside."

He walked in. His face was pale and his eyes, when they met mine, shone with remorse mixed with a hint of fear. For me, or the guild? He was bound to them before me, possibly before the Seelie Court, even.

"Son, when you were summoned to Faerie, we parted on the understanding that you would never let your obligations to the Court outweigh the promises you made to serve our guild."

"And I did not," said River. "The Court has nothing to do with my helping Ilsa. The decision was mine."

I shook my head. "He can't speak of it either. It's a curse, on my family. And it's why the fetch wants me. I thought it wanted my brother at first, but it's me who's the target. I'm—"

"Gatekeeper, you said. For which Court?"

My mouth fell open. She thought I meant *I* was like Hazel.

"I'm… part necromancer. That's not a lie."

"Blood isn't everything," she said. "You're clearly not

committed to our cause. And if you refuse to tell me what we face—"

"It's the fetch, and a bunch of half-faeries," said Morgan. "I don't know who's pulling the strings. They're beyond Death. In the Vale. The fetch can cross realms, I guess. Thought only Sidhe could do it."

Her mouth tightened. "Sidhe. I see how it is. You two, leave the premises immediately. I'll be having another word with my son."

River. "He got dragged into this by accident," I said warningly. "He's from Summer, not the Vale—he's working *against* the Vale."

The necromancer bruiser grabbed my arm again, dragging me to the door, and another grabbed Morgan. There was no point in fighting. I couldn't rescue Hazel from a jail cell, but River—*dammit.* Maybe Lady Montgomery would jail even her son if she thought he was a threat to the guild, but rescuing my sister had to come first.

Outside the guild, necromancers assembled, laying out candles in lines. *They're setting up a spirit barrier.* No spirits would be able to enter the guild, good or bad.

The necromancer let go of me. "I don't need to tell you that if you're seen sneaking into the guild again, you'll both be locked in jail."

"I couldn't give a fuck," I told him.

Morgan didn't say a word until we'd left the guild behind. "Is now a good time to say I stole a bunch of candles?"

I hugged him. He yelped in surprise, tripping on the edge of his coat.

"Thank you," I said. "Seriously. I need to out what's wrong with the book, so—first, we should find Agnes. Hazel was looking for her in the first place, so maybe Agnes saw her before she was taken. It's as good a place to start as any."

18

We ran in the direction of the market. The crowd of supernaturals shopping was an over-whelming presence, and I briefly opened the spirit realm to hone in on our target. But I didn't sense Agnes at all.

"Can you sense her?" I asked Morgan.

He shook his head. "She wasn't actually staying at the market, right? She was just wandering around last time we met."

"Yeah, but… damn. Okay. Let's ask Corwin. He's the only person we know here."

Morgan grunted, digging his hands in his pockets.

"Something happen between you two last night?" I asked.

"That's just it. I don't remember. I guess I passed out in the living room."

"Wouldn't be the first time, would it?" I led the way through the crowd to Corwin's shop.

He leaned over the stall, looking as tired as Morgan did. "Hey," he rasped. "Anything I can get you? Glamour spells are half price."

"Not today," I said. "I was wondering—have you seen my sister? You've met her, or seen her at the house, right?"

"Sure," he said, and my heart skipped. "I saw her here about an hour ago. I think she was heading to the bridge."

Crap. We'd wasted too much time.

"Er, have you seen Agnes today?"

"No. Thought she left."

"Okay. Thanks anyway."

Morgan and I left, swiftly walking through the market. "It's been an hour," I muttered. "We should track her, but after last time…"

Morgan scowled. "I'll track her. If the fetch shows up, you can kill it again."

"Not here." I looked around, at all the innocent people unaware of the potential war about to erupt in the spirit realm. "If you remove the iron, do it in a circle of candles away from the crowds. I don't like that there's an invisible barrier in the way, either. I'd consult the book, but—well."

"Give it here," Morgan said in a low voice. "Let me see the book."

"What?" I surreptitiously removed it from my pocket after checking nobody was close enough to watch. Not that it looked like a powerful magical object with its cover and pages blank.

"I got this weird feeling when I touched it the first time," he explained. "But not now."

"Because it's broken."

"Because this isn't the book. It sure looks the same, but a book isn't hard to fake, is it?"

"Nobody can have stolen it." But I flipped the book over, turning its pages. It was identical. Down to the last blank page. Same aged appearance, same size. And… I should *know* if it wasn't the same.

If I could have sensed it at all…

"I sleep with it under my pillow, Morgan."

"Do you remember last night?"

I shook my head. "No. I crashed early, then woke up when you and Hazel were arguing in the hall."

"Because she was already in the house. Without a key." His mouth turned down at the corners. "I swear someone used a spell on me last night. I was being careful. And if the iron came off—"

"I thought you were sure it didn't."

"I'm not. It's all fuzzy. That's the point. I think someone bewitched us." He glanced over his shoulder.

"What—?"

"I don't think it was his fault. The fetch marked our house, didn't it? It might have found some other way to influence him. But there was definitely some sort of spell over the house."

I shoved the book back in my pocket. "I didn't sense anything. I felt off, but that's probably because of the book. If it was gone, I'd know."

All I felt was emptiness, a nagging sensation in the back of my head. I'd put it down to the effects of recent events, but maybe... I looked back towards the market.

"You seriously think Corwin was under someone else's control?" I asked. "He's not a psychic."

"No, but maybe Hazel... hell if I know. I dunno if he'll come out and tell us the truth if he's the enemy."

"All right," I said. "I still have the shadow spell Agnes gave me. Two of them. And a disguise charm." We had to make a plan of action, and if Corwin was the only potential link, then he'd better hope he was innocent. I pulled out the spells Agnes had given me, separating one tangled bracelet from another. "Morgan, you take the shadow. Get behind that witch's stall, have a look around. I have a spare one if necessary. I'm gonna get answers." I handed him the other spell. "Don't screw up."

"I won't. I—I'm sorry." He sounded like he meant it, too. "I really fucked this one up."

"It wasn't your fault. That thing would have got to us no matter what. If not through you, then Hazel or me, or even River."

He's probably in jail now. Because of me. I thought of all that iron and tasted bile in my throat. How could I help both River and Hazel at once?

"Also, watch out," I added. "You'll be invisible, but not like a ghost. People can still walk into you, and you'll only be unseen in direct shadow. Got it?"

Morgan nodded, taking the spell from me. The last I saw of him was his shocked expression as I snapped on the disguise charm. "Am I Agnes?" I asked.

"Yeah. Damn, she's scary."

"Too right I am. Get in the shadows, look for clues. Got it?"

"Sure."

I marched into the market. People ran to either side to get out of my way, a marked contrast to walking around as Ilsa even while wearing my necromancer coat. At least half the local supernaturals knew Agnes, apparently. I strode right up to Corwin and bared my teeth.

"Agnes." He swallowed, his gaze darting about. "I thought you'd gone."

"You thought wrong." I loomed over the stall. "Not doing anything illegal, are you?"

"I—no. Please don't hurt me."

Guilty conscience, huh.

"I don't need to hurt you to remove your memories, boy," I said softly. "Your master won't like that, would he?"

He paled so rapidly, I thought he'd pass out on the spot. "No. I'll tell you everything."

I stepped in close. "I'm listening. What did he tell you to do?"

"He? She told me—she ordered me to put a spell on the house that would drug the Lynns. It wasn't hard, honestly. The girl, Hazel, was already on her way to visit."

She. The person running the show was female. A Sidhe? Surely not…

"Tell me. Now."

"The worst part was taking the book," he said quickly. "Because it's cursed. Nobody can touch it. Took weeks to figure out how to do it. In the end we drugged the sister and got her to pick it up. Then we took her."

No. Not Hazel. She must be alive somewhere, in this realm. Otherwise, there would be no Summer Gatekeeper.

"How did you get past her family's magic?" I growled in Agnes's voice.

"That was almost as tough as the book. I'm glad I wasn't involved with that part." He shuddered. "They used my spells, because witch charms still affect her when faerie magic doesn't. They're taking their brother next, I think. I offered to bring him in, but that creepy little fae monster wants revenge on him for stabbing it the first time."

The fetch. Holy shit. If they planned to go after Morgan, either the guild was their target, or the house.

Lady Montgomery was already working on the guild's defences, and if they planned to attack directly through the spirit world, there wasn't a damn thing I could do without the book. But if Hazel was in Death—or the Vale—the book must either be with her, or with the person who'd stolen it. Either way, this guy was useless. His part in this was over.

He screamed suddenly, blood spurting from his neck.

"Too bad they already got me," my brother rasped from behind him. "And it's a pity you can't see ghosts, tough guy."

"Bloody hell," whimpered Corwin. "You stabbed me."

"Should have done that the moment I saw you," he growled. "The thing is, I'm too angry to move on, and I'm the most powerful necromancer in Death. I'm gonna haunt you to the end of your days." Morgan had apparently been hoarding weapons. I bloody hoped he had a plan, short of terrorising the guy.

"I've told her everything I have," Corwin sobbed.

"Not me," said Morgan. "Where the hell is Hazel?"

"I don't know. I swear—"

"Where's that fucking fetch?"

"I told you, I don't know. They needed me for my spells, nothing more."

"The strength enhancers? How many others?"

"A few. They're hard to make, the ingredients are rare."

"You gave them to the perpetrator in person?" I asked. "Who did you sell them to?"

I'd worked out enough to know the person behind this was either dead, or a fae creature not part of the waking world. That's why they had half-faeries acting on their behalf.

"Couple of half-bloods."

"Names?" I snapped.

"I dunno." He yelped, presumably as Morgan jabbed him from behind. "Okay. Um. One was called Rye Granger and the other… Lily Thorn."

Might be aliases, but it's a start.

"Thank you for your assistance," I growled. "If it turns out you've supplied me with false information, I'll have to pay another visit. Good luck dealing with your ghost, Corwin."

"How do you know my name?" he whimpered. "Don't steal my memories. Please. God, go away." He moaned, sinking behind the stall. I marched off, hoping Morgan got the message and followed me.

We had the names. With a name, you could summon its owner. We didn't have a lot of options, but we weren't out of the fight yet.

19

I switched off the disguise charm once I reached the bridge over the disused railway, which was covered in shattered glass and overgrown with plants from the battle of the invasion. I'd heard underneath the bridge was a haven for dark fae, but tourists seemed content to cross it in cars or on foot as though the world had never changed at all. Life went on, even as we waged an invisible war. I repeated the faeries' names in my head, and waited for Morgan to catch up. He wasn't experienced in using shadow spells so I spotted the outline of a person following me, almost hidden under the dull grey sky.

"Morgan, switch the spell off. You might need it later."

"Got a plan?" He appeared at my side, still clutching the knife he'd stabbed Corwin with.

"Yes. For a start, stop waving bloody knives around. I thought you were going to kill him."

He shook his head, pocketing the knife. "Just wanted to scare him. I don't appreciate what he did to screw up my memories."

"Yeah, I see that. I'm going to find a safe place to summon

those half-faeries, if they're dead. I think it has to be the house. The fetch already knows where it is, and it's not like there's anyone at home."

Ten minutes later, we had the candles set up in the living room. I snapped my fingers and the lights came on, filling the room with pale necromantic lights.

Reciting the summoning words, I finished with, "I summon you, Rye Granger and Lily Thorn."

No response came from the circle, though the candles remained glowing.

"They must be alive," Morgan said. "Can't summon the living."

"Dammit." I looked at him. "Normally I'd try to find them in the spirit world, but—"

"I can do it." He stepped into the circle himself, holding his arm out so I could remove the iron band.

"Be careful," I said.

He stood staring into space for a moment. Then his gaze blanked out. The candle lights flickered. I braced myself ready to slam the iron back onto him. Seconds stretched into minutes. Images of what might be happening to Hazel, to River, flashed before my eyes. I clenched my fists on the iron. *We need clues before we go charging off.* As for River, he could handle himself. His mother wouldn't kick *him* out the guild and if she did, he was resourceful enough to survive in Faerie, let alone here. Hazel had to be our priority.

The candles flashed. Then Morgan's spirit appeared floating above his body, his arms locked around the neck of a smaller figure. "Stay put, you little bastard."

I snapped the binding words, and the ghost stilled. I felt a brief flash of triumph that I'd managed to get the spell to work without the book. Then he turned on me.

"Hey," I said to the ghost, who was presumably Rye

Granger. "You're stuck here until you tell us who you handed the witch spells you bought at the market to."

"Who the hell are you?" he asked, staring up at Morgan.

"I'm the angel of death," Morgan told him.

"You're the Gatekeeper," said the faerie, turning on me.

"Who told you that?"

"He did. The one who brought me here." The faerie shuddered. "You can't hurt me here."

"I can hurt you," Morgan added. "Believe me."

The faerie scooted over to the opposite side of the circle, yelping when he touched the candle's burning lights. "I just bought the spells. I'm not strong enough to handle the rest. And it's too late. I'm not allowed back to Faerie." He whimpered as Morgan kicked him, hard. Being a ghost didn't stop him from feeling pain.

"So that's what they promised?" I said. "You gave the spells to someone. Who?"

He shook his head. "I can't—I can't."

"You're bound up in a vow. You know they stop working when you die, right?"

"Not this one," he whispered. "I'm dead. They tore me out of my body, and I can't even move on."

"What?" I said. "Seriously?" Then—he might not even know Hazel had been kidnapped, considering the lack of information the fetch's master's followers seemed to be given.

"Did the fetch do that?"

He nodded. "To cover our tracks. I'm trapped here."

"I can help you," I said. "If you tell us what you know. They took my sister. They locked us out so we can't even reach her in Death. Can you give us a hint about where?"

"There's a graveyard, one nobody else can see unless they have the Sight. It's near Calton Hill. Take those candles. It's all I can tell you."

"Why should we trust you?" demanded Morgan.

Yeah, he might be lying. But it was clear the fetch knew how to make a vow last beyond death, and we likely wouldn't be able to pry any more information out of him. Hazel, if she was stuck in Death, was running out of time.

"I'll banish you. Morgan, come on."

He shot the ghost a look, then he stepped out of the circle and I spoke the banishing words. The ghost vanished, though the gates didn't appear. I'd reverted back to a normal necromancer skill-wise. Which might not be enough to win this.

Morgan hovered outside the circle. It was weird seeing him floating there while his body lay in the circle, inert. "I'm gonna try and find Hazel again."

"You sure?"

He nodded. "I can't figure out *where* she is. But maybe if I hit the barrier hard enough, I can break it open."

"I'll be on standby." I held up the iron.

Morgan stepped into the circle again and disappeared. His body jerked on the floor, then he yelled expletives to the ceiling.

"Ow." He lifted his head. "Bloody thing's tougher than before."

"Did you at least figure out which direction it's in?"

"Way off. Over by the Firth of Forth. Maybe it's in the sea."

"Not helpful," I said. "Time to go visit this grave, I guess."

There were no other options remaining. Worry for Hazel beat in my skull, but if they'd locked her in a spirit barrier, we'd need to find its limits before anything else. The graveyard was in the right direction, which strongly suggested we were running into another trap. But surely the enemy must know that the book had chosen me, claimed me, and wouldn't serve anyone who didn't belong to the Lynn family.

If I got within reach of it, the talisman's power would be mine once again.

The ghost, it turned out, was right about the graveyard. Once we'd taken the fastest route I could find, the spires of an old church came into view. A shimmering around its edges told me that most humans would see nothing more than a ruin when they looked at it. The churchyard was small... and a ghost floated in the centre.

Trap? I'd say so. My spirit sight showed me nobody close by, living or dead. The spirit was younger than I'd thought, and female, with thick curly dark hair.

"I'm not picking up on anything," Morgan said quietly.

I took a deep breath and opened the small iron gate into the churchyard. "Hey," I said to the ghost."

Her gaze snapped to my forehead. "Oh. *You're* different to the usual ones."

She knows what the mark is. "Yeah, I am. I don't want to make threats, but someone I care very much about is being held hostage. So I need to know if you've seen anything unusual. Like the fetch, for instance."

"You came to ask a ghost about death omens?" She sounded highly amused.

"What, you've met it?" I asked. Her clothes were old-fashioned, from what I could tell. How long had she been here? Only necromancers could last for decades beyond death.

"Of course it can. I was its first victim." She laughed. "The fetch first appeared to signal the demise of an old witch over a century ago. The witch was supposedly buried nearby, but her grave was never found. And the fetch, apparently, never left."

"The same fetch?"

"There's only one."

"It's killing people," I said. "You know that? Someone is controlling it."

"I wouldn't know. But if you're marked by the fetch, you're too late. It never leaves its victims alive."

"It's not just targeting us," I said. "It's targeting the entire necromancer guild."

"Pity." Her mouth twisted. "I knew they'd doom themselves eventually. Those who seek to control death always meet an untimely demise."

"You're one of them," I said. "You can't have survived death any other way."

Her eyes flashed, her body momentarily glowing white as anger suffused her expression. "Don't you *dare* compare me to them."

"I don't know what issue you have with the necromancers, and to be honest, I don't care," I told her. "The fetch is holding my sister hostage. Did you ever have siblings?'

"Why does it matter? I have nobody." She sniffed. "And you show up and insult me."

"If you've been hanging around here playing the victim, I'm not surprised. I was told to consult you by someone who worked for the fetch."

Her eyes flashed. "They can't leave me alone, even in death."

"Who killed you?" asked Morgan.

"Why do you care?" She frowned, her gaze dropping to the iron band. "Oh, clever idea. So you're the one who's been marked. The fetch's victims never escape, no matter how hard they try."

"I'm terrified," Morgan said. "I already killed it once. Like I'll kill you, if you don't tell us where my sister is."

"You can't hurt me," the ghost said. "If you truly think the necromancers so noble, ask them about the witch they banished a century ago, the fetch's first victim. The predecessor of the current guild leader was responsible for binding the spirit."

Lady Montgomery? "I know her," I said. "But she doesn't know what's happening now. The fetch... why would it take hostages?"

More to the point, why would it need the book? The talisman might be valuable, but it didn't work without the Gatekeeper present. If they needed me to use it, they'd have kidnapped me, not Hazel. She couldn't use it. Even Morgan couldn't.

"Hostages?" she echoed. "I don't know how the mind of the creature works. And I certainly do not know why it would resurface now."

"You can see the spirit realm, right?" I asked. "Can you— can you tell me whereabouts the boundary is? There's a block, in the spirit realm, but I can't figure out its actual location."

She stared into space for a moment. "There *is* a block." She pointed vaguely over the rooftops. "A powerful one. Whatever lies within is a dark concentration of spiritual energy which if unleashed, will consume the city and everyone inside it."

"What? How do you know that?"

"Because I've felt it before. When the faeries came."

My heart plummeted. *It's the Vale.* Two of us weren't enough to make an army, least of all against *that* place.

"I'm tethered here," she said. "I can't leave. You can thank the necromancers for that one, too. If you want to know the truth, ask them about the witch."

Shit. I didn't want to go back into the guild, but River was held captive there, and his own mother's family had apparently been involved with binding this witch. Maybe there was a link. Heaven knew I had no other clues to work with. Not to mention the guild needed to know there was a Vale army waiting to strike. Jas, Lloyd... there were a lot of innocent people in that building, to say nothing of all the humans, supernatural and non-supernatural alike, outside of it.

We still don't know who is pulling the strings. The ghost? Surely not. She barely registered on my spirit sense, and the fetch was weak, too. Someone much more powerful had set the Vale against us. I doubted the ghost would give me answers, but it begged the question of why the faerie ghost had sent us here.

And if the guild had really been involved with the fetch in the past… presumably they'd managed to stop it once before. Otherwise, there wouldn't be any psychics left in the city at all.

I turned my back on the ghost and left the graveyard, Morgan behind me.

"I don't know anything about murdered witches, but she sure seemed pissed off with the necromancers," I muttered.

"You can't trust her word either," said Morgan.

"Considering we have no other allies, I think we should at least ask the guild. How many ancient ghosts here would know what the fetch is? If the guild's hiding something, or if they have more tips on how to deal with this, we have to check. I have one shadow spell left. I can sneak in and get River out."

"Not without these." He pulled a handful of spells from his pocket. "I swiped them from Corwin. This one's an unlocking charm."

"Damn. Good thinking." I paused. "I'm not sure witch spells will be enough to get us in without being seen."

He grinned. "Good job I took note of the secret entrance to the dungeon, isn't it?"

"What—seriously? Where?"

"It's invisible," he said smugly. "I checked out of my body for a moment while we were in jail and snooped around. But it can be seen by anyone with the spirit sight if you look hard enough."

"You're—"

"A genius."

"More like one of the most bizarre examples of a genius I've ever met, Morgan," I told him.

"But I'm still a genius. That's what's important."

"Quiet. River might be in jail, too, and he'll be under guard. Either way, we're getting him out no matter what."

———

As we neared the guild once again, the first thing I saw were several bright lights glowing before the building's iron-and-brick facade. A row of cloaked figures stood guard outside, lined up behind the candles.

"Damn," Morgan muttered behind me. "The barrier's up. Nobody in there can summon anything at all."

Guess we can't, either. Necromancy wouldn't help us this time.

I switched on my shadow spell, and so did Morgan, who grabbed my arm to drag me into an alley alongside the necromancers' building.

"The hidden entrance is down here somewhere," he muttered behind me.

"I can't see one." The alley was narrow, almost too narrow for a person to fit through. My elbows scraped against the brick, and I stopped, seeing a shimmer that suggested a spell was present close by.

I ran my hand over the wall, and my hand locked to the brick. Pain flashed through my mind. *It's a trap.* I gritted my teeth against the pain as it seared my forehead, not unlike when Lady Montgomery had tested me the first time. "Ow. Stop. I'm an ally—"

I gritted my teeth as pain lanced across my head, my body shivering, grey creeping into my vision. Then—it lifted.

Morgan, who'd reappeared beside me, gasped. "Your head. What's that… mark?"

"Oh no," I whispered. "It recognised me as Gatekeeper, and I think it killed the spell keeping the mark hidden."

"Damn. Okay, we'll have to be quick."

He pressed a hand to the wall and hissed in pain, but the defences apparently recognised him as a non-threat, too. A metal door appeared in the brick, surrounded by shimmering glyphs. I pushed it inwards. Who needed a lock when you had magic to distinguish friend from foe. No enemies could get through that way, which must be why they'd left it unguarded.

A narrow back corridor led down into darkness. Chills broke out on my arms, along with a creeping sensation like walking in an area with a lot of spirits present, such as a graveyard. *I thought the ghosts were locked out.* I swallowed, my throat suddenly dry, my skin prickling.

"People died here," Morgan whispered behind me.

"What…? Oh no." The invasion… the survivors had sheltered underground during the day and a half of hell the faeries had unleashed. And evidently, not everyone had made it out.

Cold. Dark. The smell of iron. Fear poured off the walls, a tangible presence. I expected horrified ghosts to spring into existence, but if they'd existed here, they'd have left by now. But the fear remained, burned into the very walls. I could taste it. My body trembled all over. *What's wrong with you?* I hadn't lived through the invasion close up. I'd been safe and snug in the Lynn house watching the Sidhe from the window… but here, the sheltering humans' terror was so close I could taste it.

"Should have brought a map," I muttered. We must be

underground by this point. And if we didn't hurry, the shadow spells would wear off and getting outside would be pretty much impossible. The creeping sensation lifted as we found ourselves in a corridor similar to the one near the cells.

"Told you so," Morgan said.

"How did you work out the route? There's no map."

"Logic. I remembered where in the building we were in the cells. Undiscovered genius, remember?"

"Only because you dropped out of school." I paused, sensing a human presence. *Please let it be River.* It was bad enough that I'd insulted the necromancer guards. I didn't need to add assault or attempted murder to the list, especially when we needed their help.

I slowed my steps, warily, then breathed out when I recognised the familiar presence, warm and laced with the faint scent of earthy magic. Within a minute, I came to a large cell. River sat on a wooden bench inside it, and looked at me. "I sensed you," he said. "You shouldn't have come back."

"Oh, thank god," I said. "I thought we'd find you in one of those cages."

"Your cell is nicer than ours," Morgan said.

River stood, his gaze leaping to my forehead. "The mark—"

"Your security system exposed it," I said.

"How did you even know about that entrance?"

I nodded to Morgan. "Someone here's been holding out on us. Only thing is, this place is spirit locked and we need to find some important information if we're to catch this monster and free my sister."

"Do you know where she is?"

I shook my head. "She's either in Death or the Vale, but I can't reach her without the book. Which is with the fetch and whoever's running the show, behind that same barrier. I've no clue what they're doing there, but this ghost said it's to do with a witch the necromancers killed a century ago. Someone whose grave hasn't ever been found. Apparently she was the fetch's first victim."

"Thea Allard," said Lady Montgomery.

20

"Lady Montgomery," I said, my heart sinking far below the dungeon. "You know this witch?"

"She was before my time. I gave you the chance to leave."

"You should have known I wouldn't, not while River was imprisoned and the enemy's plotting against you. I'm told the witch is connected to what's happening."

She sucked in a breath. "Ilsa, come with me. Morgan… you, stay down here. I don't need to tell you what the consequences will be if either of you act against the guild. The barrier is set to react if anyone so much as attempts to use hostile magic."

"The door let me in," Morgan said defiantly.

"That's the only reason you're both still breathing." Lady Montgomery led the way upstairs, not sparing so much as a glance for River. My heart twisted. She really had locked him up, and had no apparent regrets. But—she'd also called me by my first name.

When we were in her office, she said, "Who did you speak to?"

"A ghost, one the necromancers killed," I said. "Apparently. It's all guesswork at this point. She seems to really hate you guys, though. And she said you bound the ghost of this witch, and I guess the fetch stuck around afterwards. Something about her grave. Do you know where the grave is?"

"There isn't one," said Lady Montgomery. "If you're talking about who I think you are, she was thrown into the sea, as far as records go. *What* is that mark on your forehead?"

Damn. Guess she doesn't recognise it. "My mark as Gatekeeper." No point in hiding it now. "Not like my sister. Another type of Gatekeeper. I have—or, I *had,* a book which gave me abilities like a necromancer. That's why my powers are so strong. I didn't lie about Morgan and me being related to necromancers, but I didn't have any powers before I found the book. It's linked with—the gates. Of Death."

"And you decided not to tell anyone, even when you knew current events were linked to your position? I take it that's the reason you were targeted here, and people were killed."

Guilt flooded me. "I have no idea about who's attacking the guild," I said. "I wasn't allowed to tell anyone outside my family. The power's bound to the book—when you saw my mark, it lifted the curse, so I can talk to you about it. But the book's gone. They took it. It contains the power that controls the gates of Death. It's the truth."

"You expect me to believe that there's a book with the power over death itself? My family has been necromancers, leaders of this guild, for generations, and none have ever heard of this book."

"Maybe they haven't," I said. "But I'm telling the truth. My family has owned the book for decades, at least, but I can't say I know when it came into existence."

"And you thought you'd get answers here. That was your purpose."

I shook my head. "No. I was trying to avoid the guild until I exposed my powers and got dragged in here. After that, I just wanted to survive. And help my family. Lady Montgomery, my sister's life is in danger. If there's anything you can do to help me, I'll submit to the guild afterwards in any way you like. But as long as they have the book, I can't prove what I am. You're just going to have to trust me." I pointed to the mark on my forehead. "You must know this isn't from Earth. It's from Faerie. There's a conspiracy over in the dark side of Faerie, and that's what the Winter Gatekeeper was mixed up in. The book chose me to stop her, and I succeeded. It sent her through the gates forever."

"I'd be a fool not to believe there's some truth to your words, Ilsa," she said. "But I cannot let you put the guild in danger."

"I'm not. I came here for River, and to find out how to help that ghost so I can track my sister down. If you know who she was… who this witch was, and where she was buried, there's no harm giving me the information. I can't hurt you or the guild the way things are now."

"I suppose not." She paused. "It sets a bad precedent to allow you to walk away free."

"Nobody saw me come in."

"Precisely." She took in a breath. "Thea Allard was killed by the guild for leaving us and using our knowledge to cause damage. She wasn't a witch in the modern sense, she was a necromancer, as far as the records say. As for where she's buried, all accounts say her body was tossed into the sea and was never recovered."

"But she said you bound her spirit… wait. Is the *ghost* the witch? She was definitely a necromancer. Nobody else could have stuck around that long."

"There is no grave," said Lady Montgomery. "And spirits who do not belong to the guild are liars by nature."

"Why trick us? It's not like the enemy doesn't already have the upper hand." I swore under my breath. "Hazel is missing. She's Summer Gatekeeper. Even if you don't believe what I am, she's the one who's supposed to keep the peace between the Summer Court and this realm. If she dies, Summer invades here, or Winter invades Summer, and the knock-on effect causes more faerie invasions. You must know what that would be like. The Sidhe—they took you once, didn't they?"

She gave me a sharp look. "I chose to go with them of my own accord, because I was a fool. I wouldn't make the same mistake again, and I certainly won't allow our safety to be compromised. This book, if it exists, is a repository of necromantic energy, which if in the wrong hands, might have the same effect as another dangerous concentration of energy in one place. Especially here, so close to the Ley Line."

Despite her harsh words, some measure of relief rose at the idea that at least she'd grasped the severity of our dilemma. She knew what she was talking about, at least. "Nobody can use the book but me, Lady Montgomery. I can only assume it's being used as bait, but leaving it in the enemy's hands is risky enough on its own."

Necromantic energy. Like the circle fuelling the Winter Gatekeeper's trap. But none of this added up, nor pointed at the enemy's true location. If the ghost had lied, she'd sent us back to the guild—for what? The book would never unlock for anyone but a Lynn.

Is Holly behind this? Hadn't she learnt her lesson from last time?

"Our resources must be directed towards protecting the city, Ilsa. As for Thea Allard, it's… odd, that you bring her up now. When a powerful necromancer like her dies, their spirit is usually more powerful than most. Death unleashes energy, and one like her would have caused a knock-on effect."

"Energy. Necromantic power." Like the book… and like a psychic sensitive. I looked down at the desk and for the first time, focused on the document lying there. "That's the list the thief tried to steal, isn't it?" I said. "The psychics who got killed were all cases handled by necromancers in the last few years."

"What exactly does that have to do with it?"

"Everything." I swallowed. "When that fetch attacked Morgan… whenever a psychic sensitive dies, it's like a necromancer's death, but worse. The enemy isn't just killing them to get at us, it's gathering energy. The last time I saw a spirit barrier, it was fuelled by necromancers giving their life energy. People died to keep it running."

"And you think the enemy has a spirit barrier of their own?"

"Maybe. There's an invisible forcefield stopping me from getting at Hazel. She's within Death, but I can't find her physical body, either. I'm not sure whether it's the book's doing or not, but it sure feels like a spirit barrier."

My throat closed up. I knew what to do. I also knew that it'd get me kicked out of the guild for good if I went through with it, not to mention arrested. And what I did know was hardly enough to pull my wild idea off without someone winding up hurt.

"If that's the case, I'll contact the other psychic sensitives on this list and invite them to the guild," she said. "It's a temporary solution, and there are more than on record."

"Those are just people who called the guild, right?" I asked. "Why did they ask for the guild's help?"

"All were about encounters with a fae beast of some sort. In the end, there was little we could do for them."

"It's been targeting them for ages." I looked up at the shelf above her head, belatedly remembering that she kept the available books on so-called dark magic here in her office.

There was *one* thing we hadn't tried yet. A boost of energy… and now I knew for sure what I needed to look for, I'd take any chances necessary. Even if it meant implicating myself in the same crimes. As she caught me looking, I let my gaze drop a little to a photo frame balanced on the shelf in front of the books. Lady Montgomery herself was in the picture, with a golden-haired, pointy-eared boy holding her hand. River.

"You're not really going to arrest him, are you?" I asked quietly. "It's none of my business, but he—he's not the villain here."

"I'm aware of that," said Lady Montgomery. "I'm not a monster. What I am is extremely concerned for the future of all supernaturals and non-supernaturals within this city. Knowing the stakes the Gatekeepers generally play with, and that the Sidhe are involved in any capacity, innocents always suffer the consequences."

"Believe me, I know. It's not like I volunteered for this. River didn't either, but I need his help to win this."

"I'm sure your brother has found a way around the locks on the cell by now. I'll call the psychics and ask them to come here, and I'd advise you to leave."

My heart twisted. She was going out of her way to help these people, and I was about to risk the lives of every person in this building.

I'm sorry.

Swiftly, I made my way back downstairs towards the cells. Lady Montgomery was dead right. River and Morgan stood waiting for me.

"You'd think she wanted you to turn into a criminal," I said to Morgan. "How many unlocking spells did you steal?"

"Three. Why?"

"We might need them. But it's bad news. I know why the fetch is killing psychics, and it's not just to get at us. When they die, it's like when a powerful necromancer is killed. The energy surge feeds into any nearby magic. It's how they're powering their own spirit circle."

River swore. "Energy sources… and the book is behind the barrier? Your sister, too?"

I nodded. "Yep. Your mother's going to try to contact the other psychics, but the fetch might get there first."

"So you want me to lure it out again," Morgan said.

"There's another way," I said. "The Vale. That's where it's hidden. It *is* possible to summon something from there, using blood magic, dark magic, whatever they call it."

"No," River said sharply. "Absolutely not. You know what's in the Vale, even if you do know how to do it."

"I do," said Morgan. "I think I remember the words from last time."

"Good," I said. "How else are we meant to track it? It's hiding in the Vale. Maybe with Hazel, if she's not behind this spirit barrier. The only people who can travel there—well, I know I can do it, but not without the book. And if we use Morgan's ability to summon it again—assuming it falls for the same trick twice, it might kill you this time."

River shook his head. "What you're doing—it might make the situation even worse. You *know* the Vale is behind this, and they're likely to attack the guild."

"Exactly," I said. "They're looking for a chance to break through. As long as we don't do it on top of the Ley Line, they won't notice. They're fixated on the guild, and I'd bet they'd never think we'd dare to go directly to them. If it's like actual necromancy, then the same principles apply. It's not like a mass summoning. You can't summon anything stronger than what can be contained in a spirit circle, right? Look, I wasn't planning to do anything without following instructions. That's why I wanted to get hold of the books your mother has hidden somewhere in her office. Then we'll know for sure that using that spell won't cause any more damage."

Morgan frowned. "What, you want us to break into her office? I can do it. You've got into enough trouble."

River shook his head. "She'll catch you."

"Unless someone diverts her attention. It's your choice," I said to River. "The books are here. Either we find out this way or play it by ear and put the city at risk. Go and talk to her. She trusts you."

"What you're asking me to do—"

"Just talk to her," I said. "Do you trust me?"

River looked at me, his expression conflicted. "I trust you. I don't trust the Vale. And you know that creature can't be killed."

"It's not the one behind this," I said. "A small circle with no power contained inside it won't break the Vale. Just because the knowledge is hidden doesn't mean people don't use it anyway. I'm Gatekeeper. That includes the Vale—I guarantee it."

"I'll do it," River said. "But you know what's at risk."

"Yeah, I do. Morgan, do you still have the shadow spell? I'm trusting you not to mess this up."

"I won't."

You know what? I actually believed him. "I'll be waiting here. For both of you. Nobody gets left behind."

I'll get Hazel back. And then I'll make them pay.

21

River and Morgan returned to the dungeon within ten minutes, the latter turning visible again as soon as he saw me.

"I got it," whispered Morgan, showing me an old book with yellowed pages. "I won't look at all of it, I swear, just what we need to know."

"Good," I said. "Let's move."

We left the guild, slipping out the side alley onto the main road. This place had survived the invasion. Surely it could survive this new threat... but the rest of the city was another story entirely.

We have no choice. The enemy has the upper hand, and unless we use the same tactics against them, we'll lose this.

I picked the house as the best spot to do the summoning, and trod the now familiar route back to the row of terraced houses. River followed behind, not speaking, gripping his blade tightly. Breaking the necromancer's law wouldn't get him arrested like it would in Faerie, but the potential consequences might be catastrophic if I messed this up. He was putting an awful lot of faith in me—and in Morgan.

"Morgan," I said, walking into the living room. "Give me the book. I need to look up a basic summoning."

"I know how to do that," said Morgan. "Blood. I got cut on the knife before, that's how they got me last time. One drop of blood, and then say the usual summoning words."

"That's all?" It seemed too easy, but 'dark magic' was just a name. The circle of candles River set up was the same as a regular necromancer summoning circle, and the swirling grey within was no different to the usual. My nerves spiked. "Blood," I said. "Any volunteers?"

"Corwin," said Morgan, pulling the knife from his pocket and throwing it into the circle, which was already swirling with mist, the lights glowing.

I spoke the summoning words, then, *I summon the fetch.*

Grey swirled within the circle. First, like before, it swirled with death energy, the candles burning bright. I swallowed, my hands clenched with nerves. If I misjudged this and summoned, say, a hellhound instead…

A dog-like shape appeared, emitting a furious yowl.

"Nice to see you again," I said. "I bind you." The binding words left my tongue, and the fetch yowled, crashing against the circle's side.

"You—what have you done?" hissed the creature. "You can't kill me."

River's sword skewered him through the middle. He screeched, and Morgan gritted his teeth, but as blood soaked the circle, I shouted the banishing words. The instant he winked out of existence, I snatched the candle away before the blood drew anything else into the circle.

"Not bad for a first attempt at blood magic," said Morgan.

"No more," River snapped, breathing heavily. "It won't stay dead forever."

"Obviously," said Morgan. "But we gave those other

psychics a shot at making it to the guild before it gets to them."

"Exactly." I crouched to pick up the candles, passing them to River. He put them into the rucksack he'd brought, still looking displeased. "Once the psychics are safe, the fetch can't sacrifice them. It's been hours since the last psychic died."

"The enemy will have a backup plan," said River. "What —" He broke off, staring into space. Greyness filtered through, and for a moment, I thought I'd accidentally left some residual necromantic power behind. But I hadn't used my power at all. Grey fog filled the room.

"Uh. Guys?" I said. "Tell me you're still here."

"Someone just did a mass summoning," came River's faint voice from the fog. "Damn. It's shaken up the whole spirit realm."

I caught Morgan's eye through the grey mist. "Did you feel that?"

He shook his head. "I've only ever sensed psychics, and I can't do that with the iron."

"Let's get out of here." I backed towards the door. "River, did you sense where the summoning came from?"

"I can track it." There came a rustling noise, and he pulled out a familiar device. "Spirit sensor."

"Ten percent accurate." Morgan snorted. "You'd have more luck walking blindfolded."

I stopped at the door, relieved that the fog wasn't as thick outside, but a faint grey mist covered everything all the same. The spirit realm... the veil must be thinning, which meant residual energy from whatever had shaken it up would creep into this realm, raising ghosts and undead. Yet the street appeared quiet. Too quiet.

"Let's make for the guild," River said in a low voice. "Before—" He stopped, drawing his blade.

An undead lumbered towards us, bringing a foul stench on the breeze. Behind, a dark mass appeared, the air swirling.

I stilled, swearing under my breath, as the swirling darkness resolved into a human-shaped figure. Icy air slammed into us, ripping branches off trees, rattling the windows in the nearby houses. The ground froze beneath my feet, icicles forming on nearby windows. Winter magic.

I shouted the banishing words, and the wraith fell back, but didn't vanish. Instead, the undead lunged forwards, his hands icing over.

Morgan hit the exterminator. A jet of concentrated salt sent undead and wraith alike flying backwards, exploding into dust.

"Thanks," I gasped.

"Is there anything you *didn't* steal from the guild?" River asked.

"Don't answer that," I told Morgan. "Let's find that ghost. I *knew* she was behind it. Maybe that half-faerie wanted to warn us." Or send us into a trap. It didn't matter at this point.

"This ghost—who is she?" River asked.

"Your mother called her Thea Allard. Guess that was her name when she was alive," I said. "She planned for us to fall victim to the fetch. Let's give her a rude awakening. Or banishing."

"If she could be banished by conventional means, someone would surely have done so already," said River.

"Yeah, I know. But I can't think of another way to find Hazel. If I had the book, I'd have full access to my powers and I'd be able to travel around until I found the hiding place." I shook my head. "I mean, it's some consolation to know that they had to drag half a dozen people into this scheme to get their hands on the book, but I guess even my dead relatives didn't see this one coming. Or whoever created the talisman. This ghost, she duped even the necromancers."

"No, she didn't," River said. "She wanted to bring them down, and she failed. She *can't* destroy them as they are now. Whatever deal she made with the Vale faeries was to further that goal, nothing more."

"You think she did make a deal?" I frowned. "That's what I don't get. She's a ghost. I'm assuming she survived this long because she's basically a necromancer Guardian without the label… but it makes no sense for her to be tethered to the graveyard. Not with the amount of people she has on her side. She must be getting more out of the deal."

"A binding spell must have locked her there," River said. "That's what I'd guess. But it can't be undone by mortal hands, otherwise she'd already have got someone to do it."

I rubbed my forehead. "She makes no sense. Ghosts aren't logical, but she has that many people involved… not to mention the book. If I die, the book would probably pass to Morgan. I mean, he's the logical choice, because Hazel can't be Gatekeeper twice over."

"Maybe the fetch never planned to kill me," Morgan said quietly. "He planned to possess me. And if I'd had your book…"

I stopped dead. "I think you're right. We have to get it back before the fetch rises again. How long do you reckon we have?"

"Anyone's guess," said River. "Considering how messed up the veil is at the moment."

Morgan began to run. "I'll kill the evil bitch," he said over his shoulder.

"Dammit." I started walking after him. "He's determined to make himself into a martyr."

"It seems a shared trait for you Lynns," River remarked from beside me.

"Hey, that's not fair." At least he didn't seem too mad about my use of blood magic. So much for the Sacred Oath of Necromancy. "I can't believe you let your mother lock you up in jail. You knew she planned to sneak you out, right?"

"Of course I did," he said calmly. "It's best for her to give the appearance of keeping the rules."

"While we go and smash them into pieces," I said. "By the way, when this is over, we're going to have words about the adorable baby pictures of you your mother keeps in the office."

"She still has those?" He grinned a little. "I should come back to your house and find yours."

"No way." I smiled back, despite the adrenaline coursing through my veins. If I hung onto that image—of River and I being happy, of my family being reunited, I could fool myself into thinking we'd make it out of this alive.

———

The ghost waited, floating above her grave, as we approached. "I didn't expect to see you back here so soon."

"No, I suppose you didn't. You thought we'd be running around the guild, or locked in their jail… or maybe we'd dive into the sea to follow the rumours of where they hid your body." I shrugged. "You're no threat to me. You're stuck here, aren't you? I assume you must know what I am. I can get you out of here, if you tell me where my sister is being held hostage."

"You know where, Gatekeeper," she said, with a barely restrained laugh.

"It was worth a try," I said, looking at the others. "Get her."

I flew out of my body. So did Morgan. He grabbed one

arm, and I grabbed the other. As a ghost, she was solid, but *cold.* "Let go of me, mortals," she hissed.

"You're not so powerful, are you?" I said.

River strode forwards and stabbed her. She screamed in rage, impaled on his sword, writhing in pain.

"You possess enough magic to stay alive," he said. "What are you?"

What? I looked at her, but I couldn't tell if she was part faerie. River would know, though.

"Were you ever a necromancer?" I asked, gripping her arm. "Or both?"

"That's why they put me to death. They should have done the same to you."

"Too bad things have changed, then," I said. "Guess it got lonely here over all those years, watching the world move on, with only the fetch for company."

"I won't be alone for long, Gatekeeper. You'll be joining me soon enough."

"No chance, Thea," River said. "I know who you really are. You're the original faerie-necromancer, and you've been luring others here so you can bring the Vale monsters to our doorstep."

"So you *have* done your research." She stopped struggling. "The necromancers past were not as cautious as they are now. They always use the candles to contain their rogue spirits because if they don't, things have a tendency to go *very* wrong."

Several half-faerie ghosts appeared in the gloom, as the grey smoke wreathing the air turned transparent. I caught a brief glimpse of a forest path, grey as the smoke, lifeless and cold… and then it was gone.

The Vale.

The spirit broke free of our grip, laughing. River raised his sword, but the half-faeries descended on him, their eyes glowing blue and green. Half-Sidhe... and they still had their magic.

The first half-faerie deflected River's sword with a transparent blade of his own. I flew back into my body, ran forward, and stopped. My legs froze, my arms trapped against my sides, and a bone-deep chill seeped through my every nerve.

That's not faerie magic. It's necromancy. The spirits had *both* types of magic.

Morgan swore, his hands locked to his sides. Paralysing waves pinned me to the spot. River and the half-faerie continued to trade blows, while the ghost looked on.

"You're bored, aren't you?" I said through gritted teeth, relieved I could still speak. "This is all entertainment to you. You're stalling for time because I killed your fetch."

"I planned to take him out of the picture first," she said, indicating River. "As for you, Gatekeeper... there's someone on the other side who wishes to have a word with you."

The other side. "The Vale."

She'd made a deal with the Vale faeries... but for what purpose? Surely not to preserve her life—or what remained of it. She'd effectively gathered an army of faerie-necromancers who had free run of three realms at once...

Magic streamed from their hands, bouncing off my shield. "Is that all you've got?" I shouted, trying to draw them away from River. He'd all but disappeared behind a flood of spirits, and while his blade could cut them, he couldn't kill them. Worse, the grey smoke seeping in suggested that banishing them wouldn't work either.

"Destroy them," said the ghost.

22

Two half-faerie ghosts advanced on Morgan and me, one Summer, one Winter. I couldn't see how Summer magic, which usually revolved around making things grow, might survive death, but if anything, the Winter faerie's magic glowed brighter than most living ones I'd seen, feeding on the necromantic energy present in the graveyard. Blue energy coalesced in a ball, and shot towards River. He glided out of the way, and the energy harmlessly bounced off my shield instead.

"That was pathetic," I shouted. "Go on. You have me tied up helplessly here. Come and get me."

Magic bounced off my shield again, and the energy dissipated into the air. They might have enough power keeping them alive, but they'd fade out eventually. And then they'd be sucked beyond the gate.

Then it'll be my chance.

Book or no book, I was Gatekeeper. When the gate was within reach, I'd make sure the ghost passed on to the hell she belonged in. The same went for her servants. River dealt several blows that would have killed them, had they been living, but they clung on mercilessly to life, or what passed for it in the veil. It seemed a miserable choice.

Morgan swore beside me, sweat standing out on his forehead from fighting against the invisible bonds. "The guy on the left is the one holding us captive," he muttered. "The blue-eyed one. Get your faerie to hit him harder and this bloody spell will break."

The ghostly girl laughed loudly. "You're only stalling for time, all three of you. Meanwhile, your sister rots in the cold and dark."

"I could say the same for you," I said. "What's the matter, is glamour all you have? Don't you have any faerie magic of your own? Or are you too much of a coward to use it?"

Maybe she doesn't have magic. I couldn't tell her eye colour, but they didn't glow green or blue like a half-Sidhe or even the offspring of a lesser Court faerie. She didn't even have the trademark pointed ears under the glamour. So what species was she? A human-appearing one, evidently, but not one with powerful magic.

"You have the nerve to call me a coward, Gatekeeper, when you've been holding back on your own power."

"Please," I said. "You were counting on me using it to trigger one of your plans to break the veil. You had to resort to stealing the book because I wouldn't use it to cooperate with you. I need damn good reason to risk the lives of everyone in the city, and you temper tantrum isn't one of them. I've dealt with humans who were more of a threat than you."

The ghost growled in fury. River, meanwhile, swiped at the nearest half-faerie ghost, sending him staggering through a grave. He'd hit the half-faerie whose magic held me captive, and I twitched a hand, sensation returning to my limbs.

Morgan lunged out of his body at the ghost, but she

laughed as his hands closed around her throat. "I can't be banished, you foolish child."

"I don't see why not," said Morgan. "You're not so special."

The spirit broke free of his grip and spun around the grave, laughing like a child. She *was* one, barely sixteen by the look of her. The necromancers had killed her. Maybe she was justified in hating them for that alone, but that didn't mean she wasn't dangerous as hell. Even without magic. For all her posturing, she hadn't attacked us—though being half-faerie and half-necromancer, she ought to have the powers of at least one of those.

How do you take power off a necromancer? You bind them.

She *was* bound here. By a spell more powerful than she herself was, and one she hadn't managed to get anyone to undo. Maybe that's why she needed the book.

"I'm not letting you stall until the fetch comes back," I shouted at her. "Tell me what you did with my sister."

"I didn't do a thing." She laughed. "The fetch *will* come back. It's undying."

"And what does that make you?" I said. "Seriously, this is going to drive me out of my mind. Half-sluagh? You're almost foul enough, but you look human. Shapeshifter? Or do you really have no magic at all?"

She hissed in anger. "You know nothing about me, Gatekeeper."

"Enlighten me. What do you want with the book? To get your magic back, right?"

"To watch the necromancers burn," she whispered. "They deserve worse for what they did. And you're going to destroy them yourself. It's almost time." She smiled. "You'll die, the same as the last Gatekeeper."

The ghost disappeared.

"What—the fuck?"

Grey fog seeped across the graveyard. The half-faeries

disappeared into the mist, while the world outside was smothered in fog.

"Get back here!" I shouted. "What the hell do you mean, *you* killed the Gatekeeper?"

Silence answered. I stepped back and Morgan appeared at my side. "I vote we get out of this graveyard," he said.

"I would too, but can you sense anyone? River, where are you?"

"Here," he said from several feet in front of me.

"I don't understand." Understatement of the bloody century. "Maybe the fetch is back."

The greyness continued to spread. I grabbed a headstone for balance as cold air blew from somewhere beyond the greyness, sharp and sudden, threatening to rip me free of my body.

The air shimmered over the grey. Then the smoke went transparent, and before us lay... a castle. Shimmering overlaid the world, but the dark shape remained steady, where the church had been moments before. The graves had gone, leaving nothing but damp grass and shadowy edges.

"Holy shit," Morgan breathed. "Where *are* we?"

"The Vale?" I said uncertainly.

"Not the Vale," River said quietly. "This is—*was*—a key point where the spirit lines intersect. A liminal space. The human and faerie realms merge here, I would guess. That castle is no human creation."

Like the Summer estate. But this place couldn't be more different even from Winter. The castle sat beneath a night sky, dotted with stars brighter than any I'd seen, and behind it, shadowy edges suggested trees hidden by fog. But all else faded to the background when a familiar pale light reached me from the castle.

"Oh my god." I pressed a hand to my chest. "The book. It's in there—it's been hidden in a liminal space the whole time."

Not the Grey Vale. No… the Vale wasn't controllable. The fetch must have been operating from here, too. It'd evaded our attention by using the exact same magic our family used to hide the Lynn house. Using a liminal space, a gap between the worlds. The book was inside the castle. Maybe Hazel was, too.

"I'm going in," I muttered. "I can't say it isn't suspicious that nobody's guarding the place, but it's hidden well enough that I suppose they don't need to."

River swore under his breath. "I can't use magic on the castle. It's an illusion—a glamour. A really advanced one."

"This is basically Faerie, right?" said Morgan. "But… linked up to Earth as well." He strode up to the door and shoved it. The door didn't budge. "It's sealed shut. No lock."

"Okay, breaking the door down won't do it," I said. "I wouldn't use magic here. This place has enough power already. Too much. It'll end up spilling over into the city if we're not careful." And where the faeries' magic went, people died. The whole of Edinburgh was covered in endless spirit lines. It'd only take one misplaced surge of energy for the dead to rise once more.

"The ghost isn't here. She can't leave the graveyard," said River. "And the book won't obey her."

"She seemed convinced it would. But even if she kills all of us, it'll go into hibernation. It *needs* there to be a Lynn as Gatekeeper. And I thought she knew that."

"Oh, I know everything about your book," said the ghost, appearing at my side "This is a nice spell, isn't it? One of my half-faeries did it."

"You can't leave your graveyard," I told her.

"We're still *in* the graveyard… technically." She laughed. "It was a powerful curse, the one your ancestor put on me. She took my power, almost all of it, and trapped me in this cursed human form, as punishment for taking her life. It's too bad that you let the book slip through your fingers, Ilsa. This need not have happened. If only you'd handed your brother over while you had the chance. The fetch won't let his victim get away."

"What the—?" Morgan broke off, choking, as two half-faeries grabbed him from behind, locking his arms behind his back. "You should be gone by now."

"Not as long as the gate is locked."

"That's what you did," I said. "You locked the gate. With my book's magic?"

"It had help." She waved a hand. The castle walls went see-through, showing me a wide hall with a high ceiling. And in the middle, Hazel lay in a transparent coffin which stood upright, her hands clasped on her chest, around—the book.

The book glowed bright, yet I felt none of it. I was locked out of my own power. From the glow, it was at full strength. Hazel shone all over with unnatural light, but she hadn't claimed the book. She was in a drugged sleep, unable to fight.

The half-faeries dragged Morgan towards the doors, and I ran forwards. A current of air hit me in the face, knocking me flat on my back. As I surged to my feet, a monstrous dog appeared at my side, its clawed foot slamming into my chest. *Ow.*

The hellhound's foot pinned me down, cutting off my breath.

"Don't struggle," murmured the ghost. "I wonder how I'll kill you. When your brother takes the book and becomes Gatekeeper, taking your life will no longer have adverse side effects. Of course, when *he* dies, the killers will take the curse onto themselves, but that won't be our problem."

My head spun. The weight of the hellhound's foot pressed on me. "You're saying you want to force the book to choose Morgan instead?"

"The book is bound to preserve the Gatekeeper's life. I learnt my lesson from the last time."

"So you want to pass it on to Morgan... so the fetch can kill him, and if the fetch dies and comes back, you all escape the curse. And you'll have the book."

"Right you are." She smiled. "Too bad your ancestors didn't see this one coming."

"You're mad." I struggled. "You have Hazel, who, by the way, is the Gatekeeper's heir to Summer. They'll come here when they know what you've done."

"No, they won't," she said. "According to rumour, the Courts are on the brink of war with one another. The Gate-keepers' jobs will be unnecessary when they're both destroyed. Your sister might even thank me for stopping her from having to deal with the fallout."

A humming noise struck up in my ears. Magic... no, the book, its power glowing brighter than even the castle. That power could destroy even us, the Gatekeepers. Morgan struggled against the half-faeries as they dragged him towards the castle.

River lunged after him, but several half-faerie ghosts shoved him backwards. He spun around, seeing the hell-hound, and stalked towards me, but the faeries reached him first. As his blade flashed, aiming at the hellhound, Winter magic struck his weapon hand. His body froze, ice creeping up his arm, as the blade fell harmlessly to the floor. Three half-faeries swarmed him, holding him down as he struggled, golden hair falling across his face, desperation in his eyes. He shouted my name, as the hellhound's foot came down on my chest, and my vision blurred.

"Take the book, Morgan Lynn," the ghost said. "Or both of your sisters die."

23

Under the hellhound's crushing weight, I shifted, catching Morgan's eye. Panic was etched on his face, and he hardly reacted when the half-faeries jabbed him with their ghostly weapons. They had him surrounded, backed up against the castle doors. In the end, the fetch didn't need to persuade him, not with our lives in danger. He had no choice. If he didn't take the book, the ghost would have Hazel killed. The doors opened, inviting Morgan into the castle. He swore, stepping over the threshold towards Hazel.

"Take it," said the ghost. "Take it, claim it. You've wanted to do it the whole time. Don't deny you have. It's yours as much as your sister's."

"And I take it and let the fetch into my head, right?" said Morgan.

"Naturally," said the ghost. "If you're planning to use iron to stop that from happening, then your sister dies. Stray from the path, and one or both of them will die."

He stopped, with a harsh laugh. "Like I think you're planning to ever let them go," he said. "You're not going to let any of us leave here alive, are you? You won't let the Gatekeeper go wandering off when you have the power you need. I'll be your puppet for however long *my* life lasts, but you know Ilsa could always take the book back from me, at any time. You won't risk that. You'll finish her first. And when Hazel dies, so does peace in Faerie and here. There'll be nothing left to rule over."

"Some would choose nothing over war," said the ghost. "As it is now, nobody can die. They exist in limbo, like us. Like those poor fools left in the Vale."

Limbo. The gate didn't exist here. I swallowed hard, concentrated on the book, and I willed its power to come to me instead—but it didn't respond. The coffin kept it ensnared. No wonder we hadn't been able to find the spirit barrier's boundaries. The coffin *was* the boundary. Nothing could enter it. And nothing could escape until someone picked up the book.

Then I'd have to find another way.

I closed my eyes, and floated from my body, directly in front of the hellhound's face. They weren't very bright, and when it raised a paw in confusion, I lunged back into my body, reaching wildly for River's sword. My hands found the blade but missed the hilt, the sharp edge cutting my hand before the hellhound's clawed foot came down again.

The ghost laughed. "Take the book, Morgan!"

Blood dripped from my cut hand onto the damp grass. "Hey," I said to the hellhound pinning me. "Want to meet a friend?"

"What are you talking about?" said the ghost.

"What I said." I sucked in a painful breath, the hellhound's claws digging into my chest. "Hellhounds, I summon you. Open the Vale."

Her eyes widened. "What—"

Flashes of light speared through the air, and a hellhound materialised, followed by several others.

"They're unattached, you fool," the ghost said. "They won't obey you."

"They will. I'm Gatekeeper. Attack her, and attack those half-faeries!" I shouted at the hellhounds.

The half-faeries, realising they were solid enough to suffer damage, backed away—and River broke free, pelting for the castle door. It'd closed behind Morgan, sealed shut.

As he did so, the hellhound pinning me raised its foot to swipe at its neighbour, and I rolled free, dragging my weary body upright. My hand continued to drip blood, and I caught up with River at the door.

"I can't open it." He'd wedged the blade between the door and the wall, but even his faerie talisman didn't make a dent in it.

"Let me try. Wish I could fetch the book." I grabbed the door and shoved it, pulled at the edges, blasted it with the little necromantic power I could conjure. It was like the damned castle had a forcefield around it. Of course it'd let Morgan through, but that was the plan.

River grabbed one of the half-faerie ghosts by the scruff of his neck. The faerie yelped, struggling, but River dragged him towards us. "Tell me how to get into the castle, you bastard."

"You—can't," choked the faerie.

"If you don't want to be hellhound food, tell me," I said. "How do I get my sister out of that coffin? You should know, hellhounds feed on death energy. Don't think being a ghost means they can't hurt you."

He howled. "Stop! The castle will only let people in who she allows."

Morgan shouted aloud from inside the castle. I spun

around, my heart free-falling. Hazel and the coffin floated into the air, the book clenched in her hands. Glowing white power radiated off its surface, and raw horror pounded through me.

The half-faerie broke free from River's grip, snarling. "Serve him right. He'll die from the very book you risked your friends' lives to protect."

Morgan fell to his knees, clutching his head. Was the fetch back—or was the book hurting him somehow? If he'd tried to claim it... *no. Please, no.*

"I summon you, fetch," I gasped.

It didn't appear. It was still dead. So the book must be affecting Morgan. I hammered the door with my fists, my bleeding hand staining the glass-like surface, to no effect.

The ghost floated overhead, laughing as the hellhounds tore into one another, half-faerie ghosts panicked, and Morgan screamed in pain. She halted beside the castle, letting out another wild laugh, watching the book's power radiate from my sister's unmoving hands and strike the walls of the castle like lightning bolts. I felt none of its power myself. The barrier was too strong. Hazel continued to hover, her eyes unseeing, her forehead glowing. Her Gate-keeper power must be reacting against the book, but being powered by life, like River, she couldn't draw on any magic in this place even if she'd been conscious to use it.

Using more blood magic wouldn't help me. *Think, Ilsa.* I left my body, floating towards the door, but the ghost appeared before me, a manic grin on her face. "Only a Lynn can touch that book, Ilsa," she said. "It's raw, uncontained power. You can feel it, can't you?"

Morgan staggered to his feet and almost immediately fell down again, pushed by the book's raging power. River fended off half-blood ghosts with his sword, but even a talisman couldn't kill the dead. We were losing.

Think, Ilsa. Blood dripped from my hand, and my head

swum, my vision blurring. Blood magic… *dammit.* Ghosts blurred into one, into the grey fog. I swallowed, clenching my uninjured hand. What could I possibly summon to get us out of this situation? The ghost was dead right when she said the necromancers technically *could* use necromancy anywhere, not tethered to a circle. If they were powerful enough, and willing to take the risk of being overpowered by whatever they summoned, or ripped away beyond the veil. But summoning the Vale's monsters wouldn't help us now. Nor old Greaves, or any of the necromancer ghosts who might be around—

"Grandma," I whispered. "I summon you. Grandma—Rebecca Lynn."

For a moment, I thought it wouldn't work. The ghost snarled, blood dripped from my hand, and fog closed in. River and the ghost faced off, and she laughed at his attempts to stab her.

Then the air shimmered, and Grandma's ghost appeared in front of me.

"Ilsa," she said. "What have you done now?"

"Not me. Her." I pointed at the ghost, whose attention remained on River.

"Thea," said Grandma, regarding the ghost with solemn eyes.

"Wait—you've met?" I stared at her.

"I've met most of the residents on this side of the veil by now. What's she done?"

"Locked up Hazel in a castle with the book. The only one who can touch it is Morgan, but if he does, he'll be seen as trying to claim it. It'll kill him, or me. I'd give it up, but Hazel—if anyone goes near her now, she'll die."

"Then I'll remove it," said Grandma.

"What—but you're—"

"The book can be touched by the dead as well as the

living. And I'm guessing the arrangement involves anyone who bears the Lynn name. I'm the only one on this side of the veil who doesn't belong to the land of the living. If I take the book, I won't be able to claim it, and nobody will be harmed."

"Grandma!" I shouted, but she was already floating towards the castle. Thea turned on her with a snarl, but she passed through the door into the hall, past Morgan, whose mouth hung open.

Grandma's hands closed around the book. Power radiated out, bouncing off the walls, and my bones rattled with it. *Hey... I can feel it. Come back, power. You're mine.*

The word *mine* reverberated in my head as she lifted the book out of Hazel's hands. The coffin fell away, and Hazel dropped. I ran forward, shouting her name, but Morgan got there first, catching her in his arms.

The book glowed bright enough to burn my eyelids. I staggered towards the door, reaching out for the book, but a force slammed into me, lifting me off my feet. My back hit the earth and I barely rolled out of the way of a hellhound's claws.

Hazel let out a choked noise. Morgan's hands were locked around her throat. "Then I will take him," growled the fetch's voice. "Too bad—the Gatekeeper dies, and I feast."

The ghost laughed. Hazel gasped, struggling against his grip. I ran towards Grandma's ghost, reaching for the book.

A heavy blow hit me in the back of the head. My vision doubled, warmth trickling down the back of my neck. Pain pulsed from my wounded hand. Grandma shouted my name. The book was within reach, but even that couldn't heal a fatal injury.

No. I can't...

Hazel's body went limp in Morgan's hands, and he turned on me, grinning—

As Grandma slammed the book into my hands.

A familiar power rushed through my veins, but my right hand was too limp to turn the pages, my vision too blurred to read them. I croaked out the banishing words, but even they couldn't banish the ghost. This place was locked out of death.

Leave...

I floated out of my body, still clutching the book. Without the pain distracting me, the right words came to mind, and I waved a hand, the hellhounds vanishing one by one. The ghost hissed in annoyance, but triumph shone from her features at the sight of Hazel lying half dead in Morgan's arms. I floated towards them, shouting, "Hazel—the iron! In his pocket!"

Hazel's eyes opened, and she jumped out of Morgan's arms, drawing a knife. As Morgan grabbed her, she shoved the iron blade into his hands.

The fetch screamed, and I *saw* it float free of Morgan's body, its malevolent dog-like form hovering on a level with me. Hazel shoved the castle doors open and all but dragged a dazed-looking Morgan after her. I backed up, seeing the fetch move behind them. It wasn't dead.

The fetch leapt, its body transforming. Its paws lengthened, its body growing in size, like a hellhound on steroids—and it jumped, straight into River's blade. He sliced downwards, decapitating the beast, and it dissolved into smoke.

"It shouldn't come back this time, not with its spirit trapped in there." He closed the castle door, then ran to my side. "Ilsa..."

"I'm okay," I said, touching the back of my head. Blood. Ow. Not good.

"Hang on." Morgan approached me, digging into his pocket. With one hand, he pulled out a witch spell. "I got a healing charm."

"Good." River took it from him, passing the spell to me. I slid the bracelet-shaped charm onto my wrist and hit the switch, sighing in relief as the pain faded from my neck, back and hand. The rest of my body ached from the abuse, but I wouldn't die today.

And the book is mine again.

I didn't care about the book. I cared about my family. "Hazel. Morgan. Are you two okay? You don't need any healing spells, right?"

"I'm good," said Hazel. "Really confused, but—Morgan, put the iron back on."

"Yeah, yeah." He slid the wristband back into place. "The fetch bastard is dead. And—"

The ghost's scream interrupted him. She beat at the walls of the castle, from the inside, while Grandma's ghost floated near the door, looking incredibly smug.

"You locked her in," I said. "Thank you for saving us."

"It's always a pleasure to help the Gatekeeper," she said. "And my grandchildren. I'm glad to see the three of you together."

"Yeah. We're getting along just fine," Hazel said, and the ghost screamed again.

"Have fun in your castle," I told the raging spirit. "I even left your entertainment." I nodded to the remaining hellhounds. "They feed on death energy, if you didn't already know. That includes you. The curse states that you can't move on… but does it say anything about being devoured by hellhounds?"

She howled, but the doors remained closed. I gripped the book tightly. "Let's get out of here. I think we should warn the necromancers about this place, in case anyone decides to go wandering along the spirit lines."

The book began to glow in my hands, and the castle faded

slightly. With magic in Edinburgh going back to normal, we'd be back home before we knew it.

But Grandma made no move to follow us.

"When we return to the mortal realm, I'll move on," she whispered. "But before I go, I have to tell you, Ilsa—your mother is alive. She's in the Vale, in danger—"

"What? How?"

She shook her head, already fading. The book glowed, the shapes of graves appearing around us. The church towered overhead, below a sky dark with rainclouds.

Grandma waved once, and was gone.

Outside, the smoke was clearing, revealing Edinburgh's stone buildings and spire-like churches. I swallowed hard. "She didn't have to sacrifice herself for our sakes."

"You know she'd have done it anyway," Hazel said quietly.

River rested a hand on my shoulder. I wiped the tears from my eyes. "Let's go."

24

The city was remarkably clean, all things considered. I did spot a few undead lying in the road, dismembered. Before we reached the guild, I paused to look at the others. "Morgan, do you have the book from Lady Montgomery's office?"

"Maybe."

"I should take it," I said to him. "If you get that dark magic into your head, any other psychic might be able to read it from you at any time."

"Not if I'm wearing iron," he said smugly. I hit him in the arm. "Ow! I was joking, Ilsa. Don't worry, I haven't read it all, just the hellhound part."

"Good," I said. "We've broken the law enough times lately. What're the odds of Lady Montgomery throwing the lot of us in jail?"

"She won't," Morgan said. "Not now we're heroes."

"I think that honour goes to Grandma," I said, which sobered us all up instantly. Even knowing she'd stuck around for longer than the average ghost, if Mum was really trapped in the Grey Vale, we could have used her help. My wounds had healed, but tiredness pierced me down to the bone, and the others looked equally exhausted.

Back at the guild, the candles still burned outside, though the smoke had entirely cleared away. The necromancers stared at us, Jas and Lloyd in particular. I couldn't say I blamed them. I wondered if the necromancer I'd cursed at had spread word that I was a dangerous madwoman cut to kill them all.

"Let them pass," Lady Montgomery said to the guards, beckoning us inside. They shuffled aside, questions brewing in their eyes, so intense I could almost hear them like through Morgan's psychic link. What had our battle looked like to them here? Surely they didn't know we'd been to the liminal space… oh. The mark. That's what they were staring at. My Gatekeeper's symbol blazed from my forehead, bright and impossible to miss.

I averted my gaze and followed Lady Montgomery through the oak doors into the lobby. The others filed in behind me. River had kept his blade out, while Hazel's forehead shone equally as bright as mine.

"The ghost is gone," Lady Montgomery said. "Correct?"

"Yeah," I said. "She and the fetch are trapped forever."

"Come and explain," she said, beckoning us to follow her.

Once we were in her office, I launched into my explanation. Amazingly, she didn't interrupt too many times, not even when I talked about the liminal space and the hidden castle.

"So it's still there, just hidden," I finished. "I'd advise you to tell the necromancers not to go near that particular spot to do summonings or anything, but most of her power is gone. She never really had any in the first place."

"Which is why she wanted the book." She held out her hand expectantly. I hesitated, then passed it over. The book hadn't stopped glowing once since I'd got it back. I expected it to reprimand me for losing it by going blank for a month or calling me a clueless amateur again, but for now, being able to hold it again was enough.

"She said she killed the former Gatekeeper," I said. "Did you know?"

"No," said Lady Montgomery. "I didn't. She killed many people, according to our records."

"It's how she lost her power," I said. "The Gatekeeper cursed her, and grounded her in that graveyard, forever. She couldn't move on, and her power was gone. That's why she got half-faeries to help her. But her scheme collapsed around her. Not being able to do anything herself was her undoing, in the end."

"Normally I'd reprimand you for acting behind the guild's back, but there is no doubt that the council would support your actions in this case, Ilsa. And the same goes for you, Morgan and River. I'm going to have to ask for reports for our records—not just for us, but for the future, in case that ghost manages to escape."

"Yeah, my main goal as Gatekeeper is to actually leave the next one some direction," I said. "It's only fair."

"And do your plans involve the guild?" she asked.

I hesitated. I barely had the energy to be afraid she'd lock me up anymore, and besides, Mum's dilemma was paramount.

"Maybe," I said. "I just found out my mother is in Faerie, potentially being held captive. I need to get her back before I begin to make a plan. She's—in the Vale." The words tasted of ash on my tongue. Even knowing the Gatekeeper's power, could she really stand up to the monsters of Faerie's darkest corner?

"And you, Morgan?" she asked.

My brother blinked, looking startled. "I—I wouldn't mind staying at the guild," he said. "Seems the best place to learn how to use my power, right? But I want to help Ilsa find our mother first."

I shot him a grateful look, but I had no intention of dragging the others into the Vale with me, if it was even possible to do so.

River hesitated like he wanted to speak, then stopped and shook his head.

"It's not up to me what you do with your time, Ilsa," said Lady Montgomery. "But as a member of this guild, I at least expect you to follow our rules, as you promised when you joined."

I nodded. "I know, but the book… I don't think the book plays by anyone's rules. I can promise I won't harm anyone or compromise the safety of the city, the guild, or anyone else."

"You speak sense," she said. "If the Gatekeepers have lasted this long without being arrested, I assume they found a way to temper the book's power. Is there a reason it's glowing?"

"Maybe it's happy I found it again. I don't know."

Maybe it wants to show me the rest of its pages. It was about bloody time.

"I'm giving the three of you the rest of the day off, unless you'd like to volunteer to help clean up."

"I should probably check my house is in one piece," I said. "Thanks, by the way. For letting us get on with the job."

"I know better than to stand in the way of a Gatekeeper," said Lady Montgomery. "That said, you will remain under my authority as long as you are a member here. Ilsa, Morgan, you are dismissed. River, stay for a word, please."

Morgan and I left. I hoped River wouldn't be in too much trouble, though from her tone, she wasn't angry with him. Morgan hovered beside the door, then disappeared into shadow.

"What's he doing?" asked Hazel, who'd waited outside for us.

"Returning the book he borrowed, I'd guess," I said in an undertone. "I'll explain later."

"I can't believe she didn't arrest you," said Hazel.

"She already tried that," I said. "Didn't work. Are you okay? The witch said you were drugged..."

"Honestly, I don't remember much before I woke up in that castle," she said. "I—are you sure that creature won't come back?"

"I don't think it's the ghost *or* the fetch we should be worrying about," I murmured. "Mum. The Vale. Aren't you worried?"

"Of course I am." She bit her lip. "But I can't see Mum getting kidnapped. And I'd be able to sense if she was severely harmed." She ran a hand over the mark on her forehead. "Are you going to wear that mark all the time?"

"No." I dug in my pocket for any stray spells. "Spare disguise charm... wish I'd thought to put this on before all the necromancers saw."

"They can see it in Death anyway," Hazel said. "I can't believe you got away with that either."

"You get away with crap all the time," said Morgan, slipping out behind her. "Being Gatekeeper."

"Not here," she said. "I guess you're right, though. You, a necromancer, though? Are you sure?"

Morgan shrugged. "Are you sure *you* want to be Gatekeeper?"

Hazel blinked. "What? I don't have a choice. Neither does Ilsa. That's why I asked. You could go anywhere or do anything."

"Not really. I'm flat broke and I owe a bunch of people money."

"You never mentioned that," I said. "Which reminds me.

Corwin helped the enemy. I guess it's the Mage Lords I should be reporting him to." I looked at River for confirmation as he exited the office behind Morgan. "Or should I have told Lady Montgomery?"

"Nah, he's gone," said Morgan. "Ran off. Guess I scared him."

"You sure?" I asked, as we turned away from Lady Montgomery's office.

"Yeah, he wasn't the mastermind. He knows I'll end him if he came back."

The guild doors opened and we walked out. "Wait, who was it?" asked Hazel.

"The one who hypnotised you into taking the book. Corwin, my housemate."

Hazel nodded. "Oh, that guy. Morgan and he had a thing."

"We did *not*." He looked at me. "Did you tell her?"

"Nope. Didn't need to."

Morgan scowled. "Where are you going, anyway?"

"To check the house is in one piece," I said.

"Oh yeah. Wonder if Corwin left his Xbox behind."

I rolled my eyes. "Didn't you steal enough from his store?"

"Yeah, I got these firework spells—"

"Don't you even think about it," I said. "Anyway. You'll find someone better than that tosspot."

He smiled a little. "Yeah, I guess so."

The book chose that moment to interrupt by glowing bright green. "I think it wants me to read it."

We walked quickly to the house, and I unlocked the door. I threw my necromancer coat aside, my heart lifting a little despite the heavy weight on my chest. We'd made it out alive, none of us had been banished by the guild or thrown in jail— and I knew better than to think Lady Montgomery hadn't noticed how River and I felt about one another, so I could only assume she didn't mind.

But saving Mum had to come first. I opened the book, flicking through the pages. A whole new section had appeared towards the back…

"This is the key to the Vale," I said. "I'm sure it is. Mum's in there, and Grandma said her life's in danger."

"So is yours, if you follow," River said. "The only way to cross to the Vale as a necromancer is to disconnect from your body. You can't do that indefinitely. You'd die."

Morgan gave him a sharp look. "What? You sound like you've done it before."

"He has been there before," I said, lowering the book. "Right, River?"

He wasn't looking at me. My heart beat faster.

"Tell me you didn't know," Hazel said. "Tell me you didn't know where she was this whole time."

"I'm sorry," he said. "I was sworn not to tell on pain of death. Until you figured out—"

"The vow," I said. "You swore a vow to someone there. In the Vale."

The room felt colder, like it'd fallen under another Winter magic spell.

He knew Mum was alive.

He lied to you for weeks.

And he never tried to save her.

"She gave me the orders herself," he said. "She was furious like you wouldn't believe that your life was in danger, and told me that I was to defend you beyond the limits of my vow, if necessary. I'd already been in the Vale and found out about the conspiracy against the Courts, so I knew I had to take on the case."

"So when you said you hadn't heard from her, it was a bare-faced lie?" I said. "I know you aren't bound to tell the truth, but I *trusted* you."

"I'm sorry," he repeated. "She really didn't want me to tell you she was in the Vale."

"Because we'd stage a rescue," Hazel said. "Well, no shit. We're not letting her rot in the Vale. She's the Gatekeeper. What the hell do the Summer Court have to say to that?"

"I didn't know where the client was based when I received the message. By the time I realised I was in the Vale, it was too late to turn back."

"But why can't *she* turn back?" I asked. "Why stay there at all? For that matter, how *did* she end up there?"

"On a quest for the Court, from what I gathered," River said. "She wouldn't tell me the details. But the last I saw, she wasn't a prisoner. She was there by choice."

"We can't leave her there," Hazel said. "Summer needs a Gatekeeper. I can cover for her, but she… *dammit*, she should have told me."

"I don't understand it at all," I said. "Summer should have sent someone of their own, not her."

"The Grey Vale drains the Sidhe's power," said River. "As a human, the Gatekeeper isn't as badly affected."

"But she could *die* there," I said. "Every nightmare from Faerie exists in that realm. Who sent her there?"

"I don't know," River said. "Like I said—I was given the bare minimum of information and then told not to tell you the truth. I can only apologise for it. If it's any consolation, I believe your mother is in every way equipped to survive the Vale. Don't forget less time has passed for her than it has for you."

"Still." I paused, taking in a deep breath to calm myself down. We all knew faerie vows. But I'd trusted him with my life and safety, and Mum… she knew I was Gatekeeper, and had chosen to leave us here alone anyway. Or rather, the Sidhe had. Assuming that, sending Mum into the Vale made a lot of sense. Humans were expendable, after all.

Anger sparked inside me. "Bloody Sidhe," I said. "I'll take it up with the Erlking himself if I have to. Considering what happened to that ghost, they might think twice about threatening me."

"Don't," warned River. "You might be able to go after your mother, but you'd be endangering your own life for no reason. Trust that she knows what she's doing."

"I trust her. The Sidhe are a different story. And that goes double for the people who lie on their behalf."

He paled. "Ilsa…"

I held up a hand. "Give me some space. That's all I ask. Hazel, will Arden take a message into the Court?"

"Sure. I was thinking of sending them a drawing of a giant middle finger."

Morgan snorted. "Yeah, right. Guess I wouldn't survive the Vale, but I wish I could help."

We looked at one another for a moment. Hazel's phone buzzed in the silence and she picked it up. "Hi…" Her voice rose in surprise. "She *what?*"

"What is it?" I asked.

She lowered the phone. "The Winter Gatekeeper's back."

ABOUT THE AUTHOR

Emma is the New York Times and USA Today Bestselling author of the Changeling Chronicles urban fantasy series.

Emma spent her childhood creating imaginary worlds to compensate for a disappointingly average reality, so it was probably inevitable that she ended up writing fantasy novels. When she's not immersed in her own fictional universes, Emma can be found with her head in a book or wandering around the world in search of adventure.

Find out more about Emma's books at
www.emmaladams.com.

www.ingramcontent.com/pod-product-compliance
Lightning Source LLC
Chambersburg PA
CBHW020756190726
48285CB00006B/2054